I0761790

GODS AND HEROES

DAUGHTER OF WAR

GODS AND HEROES BOOK 2: DAUGHTER OF WAR

Hardcover Edition

ISBN: 978-0-6484294-9-4

Brendan is not currently represented by any publishers or literary agents. He can be contacted at:
enquiries@brendanwrightauthor.com

Connect with Brendan:
Instagram: @brendanwrightauthor
Facebook: /brendanwrightauthor
Website: brendanwrightauthor.com

Cover art by Brendan Wright
Map illustrated by Renflowergrapx via Fiverr

This book is dedicated to my mum Christine and step-dad Gary. Your unending support has allowed me to pursue my dreams with confidence, and I can't express how grateful I am to both of you. Thank you so much.

Acknowledgements

I would like to acknowledge once again my brother Damien, who has helped me more than I can say. I also want to thank my mother Christine, and my sister-in-law Emily, for helping out so much with drafts and for just generally enjoying Pandeia. I would also like to thank the Copper Dragon in Greenway, ACT, for being a great place to write and eat, and the owner Isobel for being so supportive of my books. Keep an eye out in the following pages for a shoutout. I'll most likely write this in the acknowledgement section of every single book I ever write, but I also want to thank everyone who buys and reads a copy of this book. A writer is nothing without readers, and the fact that anyone at all wants to read my work is incredible to me. If you read this book, thank you so much for your time.

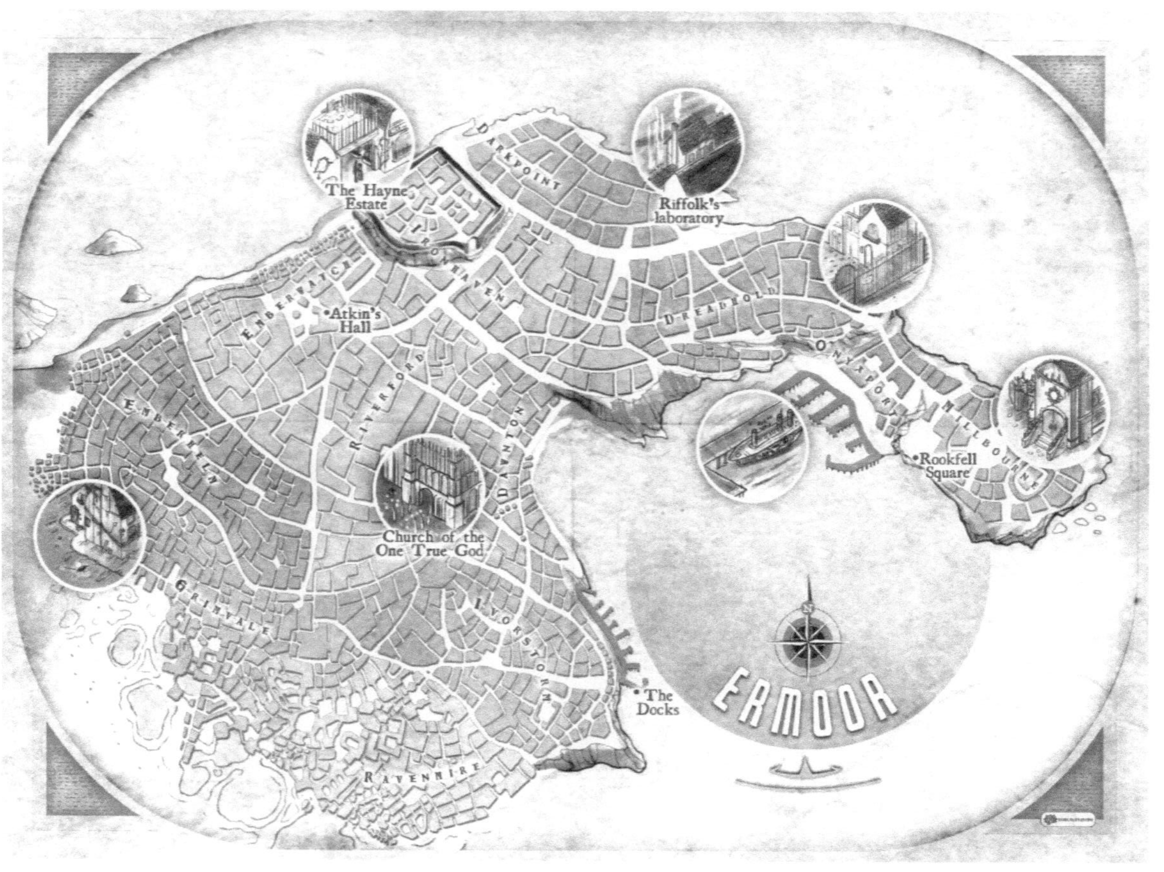
ERMOOR
The Hayne Estate
Darkpoint
Riffolk's laboratory
Ironhaven
Emberwatch
Atkin's Hall
Dreadhold
Onyxport
Millbourne
Rookfell Square
Riverford
Danton
Church of the One True God
Grimvale
Ivorstorm
The Docks
Ravenmire

Prologue

Riffolk Hayne stood on the massive platform in Rookfell Square, looking out at the crowds with a small smile. The man next to him at the dais, Bartholomew Pelham, recited Hayne's already long list of achievements into the amplifier. The amplifier itself was, of course, one of those very achievements. At just seventeen years of age, Hayne was the greatest scientific mind Pandeia had ever seen. Today he was being granted the title of Overseer of Scientific Advancement, a hitherto non-existent role within the Ermoori elite.

When the long list of inventions, formulas and theories attributed to him ceased echoing through the square, the masses roared and clapped. Pelham lifted a heavy, needlessly expensive medallion over Hayne's neck and the cheering grew even louder.

Pelham stepped back behind the dais and leaned into the amplifier.

"With this token of Ermoor, on this fifteenth day of the third month of the year 1762, I hereby name Riffolk Hayne as Overseer of Scientific Advancement; may his brilliant mind usher in a new era of prosperity and enlightenment. For the good of all!"

The crowd launched to their feet as one, and responded in one glorious voice which Riffolk felt reverberate through the solid concrete platform:

"FOR THE GOOD OF ALL!"

Riffolk

Ermoor was a gleaming, beautiful city. Riffolk didn't care for it. It was pure style without function, decoration for its own sake. The only elements of Ermoor that displayed any real function below the shiny, decorative surface were his own inventions. He shuddered to think what this hopeless mass of trinket-loving morons would do without him. He'd built the city into what it was now almost single-handedly. In the almost ten years since he'd been named Overseer, he'd only given Ermoor even more; there were no other scientists who could even remotely compare to him.

His recent move into military technology was bearing fruit already; he held a contract with Ermoor's Navy as the exclusive inventor, developer and engineer for all future products. That, along with his private project, would cement his legacy and ensure the Hayne family remained the most important name in Ermoor's history. Riffolk had already given Ermoor more technological advancement that it knew what to do with, and he had a lot more planned.

Riffolk's laboratory was a study in austere utilitarianism. Stark, white walls and floors and shining metal benches with scientific equipment set up to his exact specifications. Everything was in its place, and there was nothing in the building that didn't have a specific use to him. He had designed it with expansion and growth in mind, but in all the years of its existence he'd only upgraded the equipment a handful of times. The lab itself was usually teeming with assistants doing the busywork he didn't have time for.

Underneath the lab, through a hidden code-locked door, lay another laboratory. No one was allowed in to the second lab, of course, not even his assistants; there were no witnesses to his work. His assistants had seen the blueprints, and had a vague idea of what he was doing, but no one had seen the project in person yet.

His private project stood before him, suspended by wires, hooks and pulleys and contained within a thick wall of glass. It was massive. Bulging organic matter bled into angled mechanical parts; a true monster. Thinking about the scientific advancement he was so close to achieving sped his heart rate and brought waves of electric bumps over his skin. *This will change everything,* he thought.

Mathys

He stood in front of the body, staring at the dark, dried blood on the cobblestones. Murder wasn't common in Ermoor, although it was beginning to become more so lately; this was the fourth in the last two months. Mathys' job, as Commander of Security, was to find out if it was the same murderer, or just a random unconnected spate of violence.

The murders were all based in Grimvale and Ravenmire, two of the three poor districts at the south end of the city. The first happened in Grimvale, the last three in Ravenmire. Normally, Mathys would have left the actual field work to his men and simply overseen the case from Dreadhold; but a friend of his lived in Ravenmire, and the victims were all connected to her.

"Same type of wounds?"

"Yes sir. Same weapon, as far as we can tell."

"No witnesses?"

"No sir, happened in the middle of the night."

Mathys sighed, shaking his head. There was a time when this sort of thing would have never happened. Ermoor had been almost free of crime for fifteen years; or at least free of serious crimes.

"If only the Spectre was still around, eh Sir?"

Mathys smiled and nodded. The Spectre of Ermoor; a mysterious shadow who protected Ermoor from crime and evil. The Twelve Crowns and the military had allowed the Spectre to continue his work purely due to the fact that he couldn't be found or identified. The Spectre had managed to remain a total mystery even to the Twelve; a feat which remained unique to him in all of Ermoor's history.

"If only," he agreed, "but it looks like we'll have to sort this one out on our own."

They had a suspect; the owner of a nearby inn that had been losing business. Rival business owners were a perpetual problem in the lower districts, since they tended to stoop to violence and extortion to gain the upper hand. Now they were stooping even lower; to murder. *If only the Spectre was still around.*

One of his men wrote down everything in a notepad, two more walked up and down the alley scanning for clues, and the man he spoke to, Officer Bernard, called the last of the squad over to begin cleaning the scene. Luckily, they'd gotten there soon after the murder, and the sun hadn't come up yet; they could clean up and leave before the streets began filling with citizens.

"Take the body back to the lab, find out as much as you can."

"Yes sir."

He knew who it was; that was the worst part. He knew, but couldn't prove it. Clarence Massey, owner of the Gilded Goblet, was officially just a suspect. But Mathys knew he was guilty of the murders; he was a thug. The worst kind of man; the kind who beat whoever disagreed with him, the kind who bribed soldiers and stole from families. Mathys knew it was Massey.

The criminal investigation lab at Dreadhold was full of the latest technology designed by Riffolk Hayne, and staffed by scientists taught by Hayne himself. It allowed them to achieve things like determining the time of death, screening for poisons and other traces of foul play, and even recording a person's blood and fingerprints for identification.

Mathys wasn't a scientist, but when one of them came to him the next day stating they had proof of Massey's involvement, he believed them. Finally, it was time to act.

Mathys loved Ermoor at night. As violent and hostile as the poor districts could be, he still loved it. He strolled through the streets, his men close behind, heading straight for the Gilded Goblet. As always happened before combat, his heart was beating erratically, drowning his ears with uneven thumps.

Massey had a group of men in his employ, men as hard and violent as himself; it was going to get messy. He just hoped there weren't too many patrons at this hour, though judging by the Goblet's patronage lately, it was likely to be empty.

They reached the corner of the street and Mathys gestured for his men to stop. If they were seen too early the fight would come to them, and they'd be taken off guard. He knew the streets, and most of his men did too, but it would still require careful execution.

The Gilded Goblet was half a dozen buildings down from where Mathys stood, torchlights flickering from inside the windows. The glow was warm and gentle, utterly unlike the inn from which it came. Looking at his men, Mathys nodded, signalling in several directions. His men knew what to do. Drawing his weapon, and hearing his men do the same, he gave the final signal, and they moved in.

Clarence

He sat at his favourite table, the *reserved* sign nailed to the chipped wood, and puffed at a thick cigar. Smoke curled slowly up through the still air, and a slow sad tune ground out of the piano in the corner. The player was missing a finger, though it was impossible to tell by listening; and though the piano was out of tune, there was an odd comfort in the twanging discord.

Everyone in the room knew who he was, even those who'd never met him before. His three strong-hands, masquerading as friends, sat with him at the table. They were lazily playing cards, none paying much attention to the game. They were waiting for the show to begin.

Clarence Massey was a great man. Everyone who knew him agreed. He'd set up the Gilded Goblet himself when he was seventeen, through a mixture of hard work, dangerous jobs, and genius investments. Business boomed; for a while. He was celebrated by his friends and family in Ravenmire, and workers from Ivorstorm began showing up regularly after the factories shut each day.

The Goblet was the closest inn and tavern to the working district, a fact Clarence had been very aware of when he spent more than his life savings and went into debt to buy the property. Still, he priced his drinks low and his rooms even lower, and customers piled in. For a while.

When things slowed down, Clarence started using other methods to keep money flowing in. He'd spent far too much to let the Goblet die. His family would never see the blood on his hands, and the customers were oblivious. Ravenmire was not the friendliest of places, everyone who lived there knew that; a few beatings here and there were more or less expected.

So he struggled on, and the Gilded Goblet struggled on with him. Even if anyone suspected him of robbing his customers blind and watering the drinks down, no one dared say a thing. If they suspected him of assaulting and murdering those who bad-mouthed his inn, they stayed quiet. The message eventually got out, and was learned very quickly, despite not a word having been spoken; *don't mess with the Gilded Goblet*.

Although he wasn't a hugely wealthy man at the moment, his endeavours had made him a powerful one. His three 'friends' were ready and willing to hurt whoever they had to, kill if they had to, to protect their employer. He had powerful contacts spread throughout all of Ermoor.

In short, Clarence Massey was the kind of man no one had the guts to fight. But he happened to know that a small squad of soldiers was going to hit tonight. Other than Clarence and his strong-hands, there were seven people in the room; the bartender, the piano player, and five well trained shooters. Their guns were hidden, and they acted like customers.

Clarence was ready for whatever wanted to walk through his doors.

Mathys

From a rooftop across the street, Mathys watched his men circle around the building, each taking their place next to windows and doors. He watched intently, knowing his men would wait for his command no matter how long he took to give it. He had to be sure of what they were walking into.

Their armour was dark, matte and as slim as possible. It would be useless on an actual battlefield, but for a stealth approach it was invaluable. He waited, watching, from the rooftop. Clarence Massey sat near the back, but from where Mathys crouched he could see most of the inn's interior, Massey included.

The Gilded Goblet's owner sat at a table with three friends, playing cards. A man sat at the piano, playing something he couldn't hear, and the barman was sleepily wiping down the same section of the bar. They were surrounded by customers. *Dammit,* he thought; he'd wanted to avoid as much potential harm to civilians as possible.

Just before he gave the signal to breach, he stopped, staring at the card game Massey was playing with his friends. It was a game called Twelve Suits, and was a simple but intense game with a reputation for causing arguments and fights among even friends and family. Mathys couldn't see the actual cards being played, but he recognised the layout of the game.

He'd played the odd game himself, and even he was susceptible to red-faced yelling when he played. He'd once yelled at the Lord Commander himself during a game. But Massey and his friends were simply laying cards down in the spaces where they belonged, displaying oddly blank expressions.

Eyes wide, he took a closer look at Massey's friends. Each had a hand resting under the table. Shifting his glance to the customers, he noticed their placement, their posture. Gesturing to his men, he gave the signal that let them know it was an ambush. The plan itself hadn't changed, of course; except now they knew there were no actual civilians inside. No reason to hold back.

Clarence

Waiting was always horrible. Clarence didn't mind battle, he had no problems getting his hands dirty. But situations like the one he found himself in now were like knife blades dragging over his nerves. He wasn't scared, of course; only women and children got scared. He was simply sick of waiting.

He knew they were coming tonight. He knew it. They wouldn't wait much longer. The 'customers' may make them second guess their attack, but he doubted it. They wanted him, and the information he'd received from his contact said they had proof of his involvement in the recent murders plaguing the poor districts.

If that was true, it was all or nothing; they would shoot to kill. For all the useless bureaucracy that bogged down the city, the Ermoori military was famously brutal when it came to removing threats to their city. With proof and justification, they turned to action surprisingly fast. So Clarence had taken precautions. Called in favours. He now had almost as many men in the Goblet as were in one small squad of Ermoori soldiers. He was ready.

As one of his strong-hands threw another card to the table, he thought he caught a glimpse of something out the window. He stared for a few moments, trying to look past the inky black outside. *Damn the torches,* he thought. Light blindness was something he should have remembered. He'd been an innkeeper too long now; his soldier instincts were wearing off.

Still, he felt good about the night. He wasn't scared. A little anxious, maybe, just to get to the fighting, but not scared. The gun he held in his left hand was modified to shoot a single lead shot instead of spraying dozens of ball bearings. More accurate, and far more brutal if it hit.

His favourite table, at the back of the room, was designed for exactly the kind of fight he was expecting. The surface of it looked like any of the other old chipped wooden tables in the room; but it was plated with thick steel underneath, and there were hinges on the two legs facing the door. There was also a sack of extra ammunition bolted to the underside; he was ready.

Mathys

He gave the signal, and jumped from the low roof onto the street as gunfire exploded in the Gilded Goblet, shattering the silence and peppering the dark street with flashes of light. Rolling as he landed, Mathys sprinted into the inn right after his men. *One of ours, four of theirs,* he thought as he rushed for cover; their initial surprise attack had worked perfectly.

He fired at one of the "customers" as the man took aim at one of Mathys' own. The hired muscle went down instantly. *Five of theirs.*

"Get Massey!" he shouted over the gunfire.

Three of his men moved in immediately, and he felt a vibrant stab of pride even through the chaos of battle. One of Massey's friends went down, and Massey ducked behind the table he'd flipped on its side. Mathys shot at the old wood, and a heavy clang echoed through the room, sparks flying from the table.

"Worth a shot," he said as another of the "customers" rushed at him with a knife.

"You messed with the wrong guy, scum!" The thug yelled.

He may have been a good shot, but he hadn't trained enough with a knife; his swings were rushed, his footwork lazy, and he gripped the knife like he'd never held it before. Mathys took the knife off him before he realised what had happened. A second later, the blade was buried in the man's throat to the hilt.

He reloaded behind cover, waiting for the lull in fire. Massey's men were individually well trained, but didn't work as a group; they weren't coordinating their attacks to allow each man to reload while the others fired. *Amateurs.*

As the uneven booms briefly stopped again, he stepped out of cover, scanning the room. One man was almost reloaded, and Mathys shot him down and reloaded with the round he'd palmed in his left hand. He palmed another round and fired again, this time not a kill shot but more than enough to force the target to the ground.

Seven of theirs, he thought with some satisfaction, *and three of ours.* Counting the death toll was a morbid habit he'd picked up on the battlefield, but it helped to plan around the inevitable mess of combat. Including Massey, there were only four men left to fight, against nine of his. Three of them were behind the table, one of them Massey. The last was behind the bar.

"We've got you, Massey," he said, "let's just end this."

Clarence

It was down to him and three of his men. He was a gambling man, and he'd beaten worse odds before. Grabbing a handful of rounds from the bag, he reloaded and shook his head.

"Come and get me, Corby. You ain't my commander any more, I'm not gonna make it easy for you."

A burst of gunfire rattled the room, maybe four or five shots, and he flinched without meaning to. A few seconds later, a thump sounded from behind the bar, then a groan, and then it was down to him and two of his men.

"Fuck," he said, then turned to the men with him, "tell me you got somethin' fun to play with."

One of them, who he thought was named Neville, smiled and fished an explosive from his pocket. Stifling a chuckle, Clarence grabbed it, pulled the pin, and lobbed it over the table.

"You couldn't have told me you had that earlier?"

"Sorry boss. I was busy shootin'."

"Yeah, well next time just give me the damn thing before we -
"

A thunk came from right next to him. He saw the explosive roll a little, and didn't have time to think before it exploded.

Mathys

He saw the explosive sail over the table, and wasn't surprised at all. Pure luck made the grenade fly within a metre of Mathys, and he grabbed it out of the air. They worked on simple fuses, and the designs Riffolk made were impossible to tamper with; he had ten seconds before it exploded.

Counting to six, he lobbed it gently back into the corner of the room. Just as he'd hoped, Massey's armoured table worked both ways; it ended up protecting Mathys and his men from the explosion. The owner of the Gilded Goblet, and his men, were utterly decimated;

there was nothing left of them. Officer Bernard walked up to him, shaken and pale.

"Is it over sir?"

"Yes, son, it's over."

Bernard had never seen actual combat before. Being an Ermoori soldier assigned to city security was one thing; being assigned to Shanaken and the exploratory force was entirely different. There were thousands of soldiers who'd never seen a single battle, fully trained but green as grass.

All of the men looked sick. He saw their hands shaking from across the room.

"Squad, to me."

They gathered around him, staring at him like terrified puppies after a storm.

"Battle is never easy. You stare at death and you force yourself not to run. I want you boys to know that you've done me proud tonight. You stuck together and kept to your training, even when your brothers died next to you."

They lowered their heads almost in unison, some sneaking glances at their fallen brothers and some simply staring at nothing.

"It's over now, and you did your duty. You've protected Ermoor against corruption and violence, and you've kept God's will in order. Now we pray, and then we'll begin cleaning up."

They kneeled, and so did Mathys. He led them in prayer, and when he finally said "for the good of all", their voices responded without shaking.

Mara

Mara Watson sat gracefully on the soft silk covered chair in front of her parents. Her legs were crossed at the calf, knees together, one hand over the other in her lap. Her back was straight. She sat exactly the way a lady should; the way her parents had taught her. She looked up at them now, trying desperately to stop the giddy smile threatening to overtake her face and almost failing. Riffolk Hayne! She couldn't believe the news; she was to be wed to the Overseer of Scientific Advancement himself!

She had been present at the ceremony when Hayne was given the title nine years ago, although she'd only been six years old at the time. She didn't remember much of it, just that he was handsome and young, and that thousands of people had cheered for him. Riffolk Hayne was the single greatest man in Ermoor's history. From a young age, younger than Mara was now, he started inventing new technologies at an unbelievable pace. Ermoor's industrial age was started almost single-handedly by Hayne, and factories sprang up almost overnight to build his creations. In the almost two decades since Hayne's creative mind began working, Ermoor became the most powerful country in all of Pandeia.

Mara's family, though small, were old, respected and well-known among the Overseers and nobility. They were not particularly wealthy, but being joined to the Haynes would change that very quickly. In return, the Hayne family would be joined to a much older family, boosting their social status if not their power. Mara couldn't wait. Riffolk Hayne was by all accounts the most eligible bachelor in Ermoor. He was bafflingly intelligent, incredibly wealthy, and breathtakingly handsome. She couldn't believe her luck.

"The wedding is to be held next year, on the tenth anniversary of Hayne's being named Overseer," her father was saying. Mara had to struggle to focus on the words; her excitement was still too great to think clearly.

"hmm?" she said. Her father's eyes hardened and his mouth set into a grim line, the same expression he wore every time he spoke to her about anything serious. Or any time she disappointed him. She felt a flutter of exasperation at him then, and almost raised her voice.

"Father it's not my fault, I'm just so excited!" Her cheeks flush, she lowered her eyes and regained her composure. The outburst had been decidedly unladylike, and her father's eyes were wide and angry. Silence stretched out, gaining weight and pushing on Mara until she couldn't stand it any longer. Her father stared at her the entire time.

"I apologise, father," she said, her eyes never leaving the richly carpeted floor, "I'll not lose control again." He grunted in response. Mara had no idea if he was satisfied or still angry, and didn't have the courage to look him in the eye. He walked out, his heavy footfalls thumping on the thick carpet. Her mother remained in the room.

"Sweetheart, I understand how excited you are," she said gently, "but a lady must always be quiet and respectful in the presence of her betters. For the good of all."

"Yes, mother," Mara replied in barely more than a whisper, "for the good of all."

Uncle Lewis beamed down at Mara. Her mother's brother was quite close with her, and visited all the time. He always smiled at her, no matter what else was happening. And he was always talking; but Mara enjoyed his endless rants. Today, the topic of Uncle Lewis' conversation was the infamous Spectre of Ermoor.

"Of course," he was stating matter-of-factly, "no one has seen the Spectre for at least fifteen years. But back when he was active, the city guard worked half as hard! He caught criminals, and acted as judge and executioner right there on the street in the dead of night!"

Uncle Lewis' eyes were wide now, and he leaned forward as he kept speaking.

"Some say he worked for the Twelve Crowns. Some say he was their sworn enemy. And some say the Crowns tolerated him, because he was cleaning up the city and because they wouldn't be able to catch him if they wanted to! Ha ha!"

His laugh leapt out of his throat like the bark of a dog, sudden and sharp. It sounded almost like an accident, but Uncle Lewis' laughter was one of the best sounds Mara had ever heard.

"A fascinating subject, truly, if not a little macabre."

He chuckled, and his eyebrows and moustache both waggled like giant caterpillars, making Mara giggle uncontrollably. The Spectre had always scared her, but Uncle Lewis had a way of making even scary topics feel harmless. As always when Uncle Lewis visited, her parents left them to talk on their own, and they sat in the parlour where the teleradio was, listening to music while he regaled her with interesting facts.

It was early afternoon, and soon enough, Mara's mother bustled in, shooing Uncle Lewis away and fussing over Mara to make sure she was ready for the evening church service. Uncle Lewis was the family lawyer, and he was visiting Mara's father to work something out, most likely for the marriage between her and Riffolk Hayne.

He left the room at her mother's insistence, retiring instead to her father's study. After some more fussing over Mara, pulling out her hair and tying it up again, they left the small Watson mansion to go to church. When they got back later that night, Uncle Lewis had already left, and Mara went straight to bed without hearing any more about the Spectre of Ermoor.

Pera

Pera ran through the pitch black tunnel, giggling despite her fear. Exploring was her favourite thing to do; it was exciting and scary at the same time, and she sometimes found amazing things. Her parents hated it, of course, but she never stopped. After all, she wasn't old enough to begin working yet; what else was she supposed to do?

Turning another corner, her hand skimming the rough stone wall, she saw a ball of candle light bobbing up and down in the distance. She stopped, then tiptoed into a corner and crouched down in the dark. Hiding was a fun game. She'd found a particular thrill came from staring right at someone's face as they walked by, oblivious to her presence. Candle light hindered more than it helped, in her opinion.

The small flickering light drew closer, moving up and down with the carrier's hand. Pera stayed as still and silent as the stone wall behind her, not even breathing. As the person walked by her, she caught a glimpse of his face, and recognised one of the workers who was friends with her parents. He didn't hesitate as he walked past her and on down the tunnel.

When he was far enough away, she let out a rush of breath and gulped in air to fill her lungs again. She was getting good at holding her breath, but that had been close. Standing, she continued her run down the tunnel, her excitement overcoming her fear.

She was a curious child. She knew that because her parents said it all the time. But she couldn't help it; she wasn't even doing it on purpose. There were just so many questions to be answered, and not enough people who could answer them. So she made her mind up to find answers herself. It seemed like the only choice, so she didn't understand why her parents were always so angry.

Her latest question was *how fast can I run in the dark?* and so far the answer was *very, very fast.* She'd fallen over a few times, of course, but scrapes on her knees and palms weren't exactly a new thing; exploring was never easy. The tricky thing was finding long tunnels to run down that didn't have too many twists and turns. And avoiding the adults, of course.

None of her friends were as brave as she was. They never joined in when she explored, and they even used to tell the adults on her when she did. One time she pushed Eudos over for telling, and he cried and ran to his mother; but he never told on her again, and neither did the others. Besides, she'd stopped telling them when she went exploring anyway, so they had nothing to tell.

The worst part of exploring was getting lost. It happened a lot for a while, and it still happened sometimes, if she went too far without remembering. But she was starting to learn how to picture things in her head, remembering turns and steps and the feeling of different walls.

She was somewhere new, she knew that; the tunnel she ran down was one she'd never been in. All of Tyra was mapped, and the map was carved on the walls in several places with bumps and patterns labelling the important spots. But Pera was working on her own map, of all the tunnels and rooms that didn't show up in the proper maps. She had her own carving, too, hidden in one of the unmapped rooms. She added to it whenever she could.

The new tunnel was long, just over two hundred steps and still going. Pera was good at counting. She always corrected the other children. It annoyed them, but she didn't care. She learned things faster than the other children.

She reached a place where the tunnel ended, but not in a normal wall; peering closely and exploring with her hands, she realised it was a cave-in. A few of the outer tunnels she explored were caved in, she was used to coming across it. Sometimes, though, there were gaps she could squeeze through... It took a while, but she found one, and scrabbled carefully through to the other side.

It felt different. Warmer, but in a strange and scary way. Her hand trailed the wall, and as she ran she felt it become smoother. She slowed to a tentative walk, fear temporarily overcoming excitement. It kept going, she could feel it in the air; a feeling of emptiness stretched before her. Bending her knees and shifting her weight, she moved silently further on.

Another hundred steps, and the empty feeling in front of her was still there. *How far does it go?* she thought, not quite scared enough to turn back. Eventually, she reached a point where the rough sandy ground beneath her feet turned almost as smooth as the walls. She kept walking, and a low humming grew, coming from everywhere, not just in her ears but vibrating through her body too.

A strange feeling came over her; a sense of something huge, something no one had ever seen before, something unbelievable. She felt as though she was about to discover something truly amazing. Slowly, carefully, she kept walking.

Some way further down, she realised she'd stopped counting her steps; but she still couldn't stop. Finally, she reached a point where the tunnel opened out into a larger room, one that was utterly black. It was so dark beyond where she stood that it made the tunnel look lit up by comparison. It looked like a sheer black wall.

For a few moments, all she did was stand there. She was the bravest person she knew, but she still couldn't bring herself to walk into that complete blackness. A sound crept through the shadow, and she tensed immediately. The tiniest sound, the slightest rasp of fabric touching stone; someone was in the room in front of her.

She was frozen, not wanting to run but terrified of remaining where she was. *What have I done?* she thought as she stood, unable to move, *what am I doing?* The tiny rasping sounds came again, sounding closer now. She could have sworn she saw a shape moving, but it might have been her mind playing tricks in the dark.

Pitch blackness, so complete it was almost physical, covered her eyesight. The movement had to be her imagination; she couldn't have seen anything. But the sound came again, too close now, and she was starting to panic. Somehow, she still couldn't move.

Silence pressed in after that last movement, and Pera tensed, waiting for the sound to appear even closer. Her ears straining for the slightest sound, she stood in a half crouch, ready to run. Just as she began persuading herself she'd imagined the whole thing, something else broke the silence.

"Leave this place, girl."

The voice growled like an animal, grating and stony, and whatever had been holding her in place vanished. She ran.

"He spoke to me, mommy, I swear! It was one of the monsters!"

No one believed her. She was getting in trouble not only for wandering through the tunnels, but for lying too. It wasn't fair.

"Pera, you need to stop making up stories," her mother said, "you didn't see a monster, and they don't talk. And more importantly, you need to stop being so curious. It'll get you killed eventually."

The words shocked her enough to bring tears to her eyes. *She thinks I'm going to get killed, and she doesn't even sound upset!*

"It will not!"

"Okay, calm down little one. It's almost sleep time."

But she didn't calm down. Her mother just didn't understand; she couldn't help being curious. She couldn't control it. Once an idea entered her head, once a question popped up about anything, she simply *had* to know the answer. She needed to learn.

She lay in bed for a while next to her mother, angry with her and grateful for the comfort of her warmth at the same time. After a while, she drifted to sleep, but she didn't know how long. When she woke up, she still hadn't calmed down.

Mara

Ermoor was beautiful. Mara had always thought so. She loved wandering through the neatly paved streets whenever her father agreed to escort her from their family home. The city sparkled and gleamed constantly, thanks to the efficient cleaning machines invented by Riffolk Hayne. Beautiful, colourful lights lined every street and alley, making the city look like it was in the middle of a grand celebration every time the sun set.

"We live in a perfect society," her father often said, echoing the words of the priests at church service, "Ermoor is the height of civilisation. We would live in a perfect world, were it not for the faithless savages living in the rest of Pandeia." Mara couldn't help but agree. Ermoor was beautiful. Everything was clean and new, Anything she wanted was available, her every need catered to.

Hayne's inventions extended to every aspect of Mara's life. Compact, wearable clocks told the time, with a small alarm which could be set by the wearer. Heated blankets kept her warm on winter nights. Horseless carts took her anywhere she needed to go, with her father as escort of course. Cooling boxes kept food fresh for far longer than their old storage cupboards, and a new type of fireless oven cooked their food far more efficiently than the wood-fired ovens they used when she was little. The most amazing invention, to her at least, was the teleradio. People could speak to each other from opposite sides of the city, and it was as though they were sitting right next to each other. Plays full of magic, swords and fire were recorded and broadcast, as well as music, and announcements from the Overseers. It was an incredible piece of technology.

Mara sat in the back of a cart as it glided over the smooth pavement. Her father sat in the seat in front of her, his eyes scanning the printed newspaper in his hands. Ermoor's beauty was utterly lost on him. Not on Mara though; she stared at everything they passed, drinking in the city and its ceaseless wonders. A teleradio sat in the cart itself, blaring the day's announcements until her father switched it off with an annoyed grunt. Her mother sat silently beside him, the perfect lady.

They were going to meet the Hayne family after the morning church service. Mara couldn't wait to meet Riffolk in person. His gentle voice came on the teleradio at least once a day, and she turned the volume up and listened intently every time. He sounded as handsome as he looked; his voice stirred something deep in her belly, an odd tingling, flushed feeling that raised her heartbeat and tightened her lungs.

Meeting him in person was going to be as difficult as it was exciting. She just hoped she could keep her composure and remain ladylike. It was very important for ladies to be poised and dignified at all times, especially in front of suitors and future husbands. *Future husband!* The thought had crept into her mind before the meaning properly formed, but suddenly the words filled her head as though the teleradio in the cart had been switched back on and turned to full volume. *Riffolk Hayne is my future husband!* her mind screamed, *I am his future wife!*

Her friends, Millicent, Abigale and Audrey, still didn't know. It wouldn't be official until after today, when the initial contracts would be signed by Riffolk, his father and her father. Mara didn't know anything about that, as it wasn't a woman's place, but she knew that once the signatures were done she would be able to tell her friends and anyone else who would listen: *Riffolk Hayne is to be my husband!*

She especially couldn't wait to tell Millicent. Millicent was a year older than Mara, and already married to Governor Jothan Salwey. None of her other friends were yet married, and Mara, along with all of their friends, was intensely jealous of the now Governess. Whenever Mara asked her what it was like to be married, she adopted a demure smile and replied "you're too young to understand, but you'll see." It was infuriating, but now Mara was not only to be married, she would be married to the most dashing and wealthy man in all of Ermoor! That would certainly wipe the smile off of Millicent's smug face.

The morning church service was much the same as it always was, not that Mara would ever dare to complain out loud. *Or even quietly,* she thought to herself. After all, God would surely hear her complaints and she would be punished immediately. She sat humbly in the uncomfortable pew next to her parents as the priest talked of the evils of the world.

"... live in trees and eat their own young. They are cruel and savage, and worst of all, they are Godless! If left unchecked, they will bring God's wrath down upon the world, and even the faithful will be punished for their wickedness!"

The priest spoke fervently, passionately. He walked up and down the stage, from side to side, his wide eyes seeking out and locking with every individual in the pews. The words she'd heard a thousand times before. The passion she saw every day. But today, it felt different. She felt uncomfortable, and not just physically; she had grown used to the hard wooden pews. Today, the intensity of the service pushed at her in an acutely unpleasant way. There was always a little fear of course; what sane person wouldn't fear God? Especially with faithless monsters living in their Godless countries dooming Ermoor to an eternal hell.

But today, it felt different. Her heart was beating hard and uneven, her breath ragged, her cheeks flushed. She was sweating, her silk gown sticking to her back and legs and growing cold. She was suddenly terrified of meeting Riffolk Hayne; what if he didn't like her? What if his first reaction to seeing her was disappointment? Disgust? Outrage? Even worse; what if he laughed?

And now she'd ruined her dress! It clung to her, cold and wet, and she felt like everyone was staring at her. Her make-up, the delicate pale powder, dark mascara and pink lipstick, suddenly felt gaudy and cheap, and she was terrified it was running from her sweat.

Mara had fussed over her make-up, hair and dress for hours before they left the house, interrupting her maids to put things the way she wanted. She'd completely undone her hair after they'd spent half an hour on it, and put it up herself. She wiped the bright red lipstick off before they'd finished and selected a much more subtle pink which paired with the blue of her dress. They applied the powder well enough, and the mascara, although she had peered closely at it in the mirror before nodding her approval. Finally, she had stood, turning and staring at herself from every angle, satisfied that Riffolk would be happy with her.

But now? Now she must have looked like a half-drowned rat pulled out of the harbour. Riffolk would think it was a prank, a horribly tasteless joke her father was playing; dress a rat up in silk and make-up and pass it off as Mara Watson, only daughter of Hannibal and Victoria Watson. She started panicking then, and the priest's intense cries of "they must be struck down wherever they are seen! Destroyed! For the good of all!" only served to feed her panic. When the crowd responded "for the good of all!" as they were supposed to, she couldn't add her voice to the rest.

Pera

Orange light flickered against the stone corridors, coming to a cold stop several feet from Pera's face as the darkness took over. Candles only shone so far in Tyra. Light was precious, and simply walking from one place to another wasn't important enough to warrant more than a small candle. She was tired to the bone, just like every time she was done with her work. Now that she'd grown old enough to work, she was perpetually exhausted; there was no time to explore the way she did when she was young. Trudging mindlessly through the tunnels of Tyra didn't help, of course, but she'd be in her bed soon enough.

Shuffling sounds approached her as Eudos, Anios and Lymia went to replace the workers who'd finished their shift. She shook her head; they could be so careless sometimes.

"Better hurry up, you three," she said, her angry voice echoing down the tunnel, "a bunch of us already finished our shifts."

The other two she'd worked with who finished their shifts, Odas and Allas, had turned down a separate corridor. They lived on the other side of the city.

"Oh, shit!" the voice of Anios echoed back, "run, go!"

They bolted past her, the candles in their hands stuttering, almost blowing out. She sped up a little; she didn't want to be anywhere near if they were late. She knew what happened when the wheels stopped turning in Tyra. Everyone did.

Pera lived in Hall 38, on the outer edge of the city. The wide tunnel which served as Tyra's border was adjacent to Hall 38. She shared the living quarters with fifty other workers. A hundred halls the same size as hers were spread around Tyra, some holding up to a hundred workers; Pera was lucky to have what little space and privacy she had.

The bumps and lines on the tunnel wall announcing the entrance to Hall 38 slid under her fingers as she walked, and she turned into the corridor towards her bunk room. Her candle was extinguished; her supply was running low and the candle-makers wouldn't do their rounds for another few sleeps yet. Most Tyrans didn't bother with candles unless they had a real reason; the light was simply too precious.

Pera was different. She was fascinated by fire and by the things she could see when the world around her was illuminated. Everyone else in Tyra seemed content with pushing the wheels, going to sleep, then pushing the wheels again; but Pera wanted *more*. Her parents had told her that when she was young she'd caused a lot of trouble. She had stuck her hand in a fire to see what it felt like; tried to convince the workers to stop turning one of the wheels because she wanted to see what would happen for herself; and when she was a toddler she had eaten pretty much everything she could get her hands on. Her hand was still horribly scarred, and she had been poisoned near death several times until she finally learned to listen to the Foragers when they told her what could and couldn't be eaten.

She hadn't seen the consequences of the wheels stopping then though, not that young. She saw it much later, and was still haunted by the sheer horror of what she'd seen. It was still recent enough that the memory made her heart stop briefly. *Monsters,* she thought as she stepped lightly through the corridor to her bunk room, *that's what they were. Monsters.* She crept into the bunk room, counting the double bunks until she reached the eleventh bunk on the left. She tugged off her clothes, crawled into the bottom bunk, and stumbled into a deep but troubled sleep.

She was nudged awake by a forager, who handed her a bowl full of mushrooms to break her fast. It was a mix today; buttons, flat-tops *and* split-tops. The latest harvest had obviously been good. She envied the foragers. Easier work, plus they grew glowpods and lightleaf, which glowed in the dark; they could work with light and didn't have to worry about running out of candles. Although they did have to deal with the smell; the mushrooms grown by the foragers only grew so well due to the fertiliser. Fertiliser provided by the people of Tyra. Pera tried not to think about it, but there was no way around it; if they wanted to eat, they had to eat mushrooms grown from faeces. The dirt in Tyra simply could not grow anything without proper fertiliser.

After her waking meal, she dressed and checked her belongings by touch as she did every time she woke. Her small supply of candles, a chunk of dried digger meat, a spare set of clothing, her waterskin, and a quarter skin of mushroom spirits. The spirits were distilled from deathcap mushrooms, and then diluted with water until the poison wasn't strong enough to kill. It was dangerous, but one of the only ways a Tyran could take her mind off things. It wasn't made often, however, so Pera barely drank unless she'd had a particularly rough day or a slew of nightmares. It tasted awful, and headaches plagued the drinker once the pleasant effects wore off, but almost all of the adults in Tyra drank it on occasion.

Satisfied all of her belongings were safe and accounted for, she stood and dressed. The life of a Worker was simple, but brutal. They had but one purpose; keep the wheels of life turning. Ten gigantic metal wheels sat sideways in ten equally massive rooms spread evenly around Tyra. Turning them was backbreaking work, but it had to be done, or the *things* appeared. The monsters. Pera walked back down the corridor towards Wheel 6, the closest wheel to Hall 38. She didn't bother with candles. Her stash was too small, and her eyes were always much clearer immediately after sleep. The wheel rooms were usually lit by a few small torches and bunches of glowcaps. As she approached, the low grating sound of the wheel turning floated down the corridor, accompanied by the footfalls of the workers.

It took one hundred workers to keep one wheel turning. The workers swapped constantly to avoid injury, and the wheel rooms were always lined with workers resting against the walls. Once a worker had turned five hundred full rotations of the wheel, they were free to sleep until they were needed again the next waketime.

Pera entered the wheel room, and immediately saw Eudos and Lymia resting nearby. Anios must have still been turning. She waved to them and approached the wheel. An exhausted worker saw her approach, gave a loud sigh, and muttered "your turn" as she slid away.

Ignoring the old joke, Pera took up her position and matched pace with the wheel's turning.

Mara

The church her father took her to every Sunday and Wednesday was in Dawnton, almost an hour's cart ride from the Hayne mansion in Ironhaven. It was the longest hour of Mara's life. She had calmed down significantly, but a sliver of anxiety remained in her stomach like a tiny twisting eel. Her father had pulled her aside immediately after the service and gripped her shoulders roughly.

"I didn't hear you say 'for the good of all'," he'd said flatly. "You will pray tonight that God doesn't punish you too harshly." She nodded silently, her eyes glued to the pretty cobblestoned pathway at the church's entrance. She was already praying.

All the way to Ironhaven, Mara was terrified. Her father hadn't mentioned her appearance, so hopefully her make-up still looked okay. And her sweat was dry now. She prayed as the cart glided softly along the streets, holding her hands together, her head lowered. It was selfish to pray that she looked pretty enough for Riffolk Hayne. But she was also praying that she would please her father and her husband-to-be, and make her family proud, and surely that wasn't selfish?

By the time they reached Ironhaven, Mara was in the midst of another panic attack. Her father got out of the cart and opened the door next to her. He looked at her in the flat, emotionless way he did when he was expecting disappointment.

"You will make a good impression, Mara," he grumbled, "or so help me God, you won't be eating for a week."

She stared at the back of the seat her father had sat in, nodding her head eagerly and trying not to cry. The cart rested at the entrance to the Hayne mansion. It was the most beautiful and elegant building Mara had ever seen. This was the most important moment of her life. All she needed to do was hold her composure and act like the perfect lady for Riffolk; impress him, show him that she would be the perfect wife. All her life she'd been taught how to be a lady. How to be a wife. It pleased God when a woman knew her place; everyone knew that. The priest said so at every service. She was determined to please God, and Riffolk, and her father.

A servant waited at the giant wooden doors, immaculately dressed and standing perfectly straight. He wore a crisp red jacket, perfectly tailored, black trousers with a yellow stripe down the sides, black gloves, and black shoes so polished that Mara could see the cloudy Ermoori sky reflected in them. His eyes were locked at a point directly in front of him until Mara and her father were almost all the way up the stairs to the front doors. Then he cleared his throat and looked down at them with the arrogance normally reserved for nobility.

"Mr Hannibal and Ms Mara Watson, I presume?" he asked. His voice was just as arrogant as his expression, and Mara found herself immediately sick of this servant.

"That's correct," her father said. He spoke coldly, and Mara had to fight to keep a humble expression on her face as the servant's mouth opened in mild outrage.

"Well," he blustered, "Overseer Hayne is waiting within. Please wait in the lobby for the guide to take you further."

Her father said nothing in response. The massive doors opened seemingly of their own volition, and Mara followed her father inside.

The Hayne's property took up almost a third of Ironhaven, including the gardens and grounds. The mansion itself was absolutely massive. Even the lobby was intimidating in its size. Where the lobby of the Watson's home was barely even a room, the lobby in the Hayne mansion was huge enough that Mara wouldn't have been able to hear someone talking if they were standing on the opposite side.

As the servant at the door had said, shortly after they entered another servant appeared to take them further into the mansion. The second servant was dressed exactly the same as the first, down to the arrogant expression. Mara followed the servant and her father through endless corridors, twisting and turning until she was completely lost. Eventually, they reached a giant pair of exquisitely decorated wooden doors at the end of a long hallway. *This is it,* she thought, *Riffolk Hayne is behind these doors.*

Riffolk Hayne stood at the far end of the library, hands behind his back, motionless. He watched them enter, standing motionless as they crossed the massive room. He was tall, slim and elegant. High cheekbones framed his handsome face, and his bright blue eyes shone with an intimidating intelligence. Dark, thin hair sat neatly combed atop his head. He wore an expression of quiet certainty, a confidence which bordered on arrogance but was tempered with experience. He was beautiful. Mara's breath caught in her throat, and she almost stumbled as she approached her husband-to-be.

Her father noticed and quietly cleared his throat, a subtle reminder of the punishment that would follow were she to make a fool of herself or him. She lowered her eyes and concentrated on walking; *One foot in front of the other, please don't fall,* she told herself. *You can do this. You* will *do this.* Riffolk simply watched, his face a beautiful but unreadable mask. An energy came off him, even from the other side of the library, that spoke of immense talent and limitless intelligence. He somehow seemed... more than human. The thought brought an uncomfortable feeling to her skin, a cold flush that made her a little scared of him.

Finally, they reached the opposite side of the room, and Riffolk took his hands out from behind his back to greet them properly.

"Mr Hannibal Watson," he said quietly, "it is a pleasure to meet you." he took her father's hand in his own, staring intently into his eyes as their hands moved smoothly up and down.

"I am Overseer Riffolk Hayne. I apologise for the formalities; purely for my father's satisfaction, I'm sure you understand."

Her father was speechless. It was the first time Mara had ever seen him so. He was usually the type who walked into a room and commanded the attention of everyone in it, and who intimidated others into silence. But Riffolk's quiet confidence and casual dismissal of the 'formalities' had apparently taken him aback. Mara felt a blossom of genuine love for her future husband in that moment. Then his eyes flicked to hers and an electricity she never knew existed sparked between them. His eyes widened and she gasped. Both their lips parted slightly at the same time.

"Mara..." he breathed her name, and she melted. "My, you are beautiful. Your father didn't mention... but of course he wouldn't. It's an honour to meet you, my dear." He swept her hand into his own, bowing as he brought it to his lips. Her heart thumped painfully, so loud she was afraid he would hear it. He kissed her hand tenderly, almost lovingly, and her love for him grew. He straightened and let go of her hand, his grip lingering long enough to hold her fingers in an unmistakably erotic embrace. His eyes were locked on hers. She realised he was waiting for her to speak, but she couldn't find any words. Her father cleared his throat again, and she stammered for something to say.

"I – you're – I mean... umm."

Her cheeks flushed so hot she feared she would start a fire, and she felt another panic attack grip her throat. And then Riffolk smiled, gentle, kind and loving, and her throat eased back to normal. She took a breath, ignoring her father's repeated "ahem" sound, and returning Riffolk's intense but lovely stare.

"Thank you, Overseer Hayne, you are far too kind," she managed, "the honour is all mine."

His smile spread into a grin, and she found herself grinning too. They stood like that, grinning at each other, until her father moved uncomfortably and cleared his throat again. Riffolk glanced at him, straightened, and actually blushed a little.

"I apologise again, Mr Watson, I simply was not prepared for your daughter's stunning beauty."

Every word he says makes me love him more, Mara thought. Her father again seemed at a loss for words, and Riffolk clapped him on the shoulder and turned to the other corner of the room, gesturing to the quiet man who stood there waiting. Mara gasped again, almost screamed. She'd had no idea there was someone else in the room.

"Hannibal, I believe you know my father?" Her father nodded and gave a short wave.

"Mara, let me introduce my father, Sir Isaac Hayne. Father, this is Mara Watson."

"A pleasure, Mara," Sir Isaac said. His tone suggested otherwise.

The rest of the day passed in a mostly pleasant blur for Mara. She didn't understand the contracts, and their words washed over her in meaningless waves, but Riffolk glanced at her every few moments and smiled, and that was all she cared about. Once the business was out of the way, a servant appeared with tea and bread on a gleaming silver platter, and the four of them sat in a pair of comfortable lounges. Riffolk sat next to her, and their fathers sat next to each other. The three men spoke for a while, and after the tea was gone the servant brought a bottle of whiskey and three glasses. Riffolk shuffled closer to her after reaching for his glass, and their legs touched. He glanced at her again, smiling, and he was the only person in the world.

Riffolk

Watson and his offspring snuck timidly into the room. They might as well have been shouting "we are poor and uncultured!" as they took step after ginger step. The Watson family was well respected, of course; otherwise Riffolk would never have consented to this match. The Haynes gained nothing from the union, other than a slight increase in social standing by joining with one of the oldest families in Ermoor. He didn't care about social standing in the slightest. He didn't care about the Watson family, or the girl, or any of this pointless nonsense. Still, images had to be maintained, if his goal was to be achieved.

When the two finally reached him, he introduced himself. He charmed them immediately, of course, and the girl looked absolutely smitten. They signed the contracts, talked over whiskey, and a few lingering glances and some brief physical contact was all it took; the girl was his. He saw it in her eyes. She was beyond smitten, she was in love. Most people were born to be controlled. It was pathetic how easy they were to manipulate. Even Riffolk's father could be moved if he was careful. Of course, he was always careful.

Arthor

Lord Commander Arthor Symond stood tall, his hands clasped imperiously behind his back as he stared at the blueprints on his desk. Overseer Hayne stood nearby, smug and self-assured as ever. His underlings, a handful of engineering graduates, stood nervously behind him. Arthor's right hand, Commander Mathys Corby, sat casually on a comfortable chair against the wall. He didn't look it, but Mathys was the most dangerous man in the room. He had a talent for being utterly inconspicuous, so much so that most people other than Arthor himself routinely forgot his name, and often overlooked his presence. Despite this, Arthor would not have picked anyone else to be his Commander. Mathys was honourable, talented, intelligent, and discreet.

Overseer Hayne watched Arthor patiently, a smirk tugging the corner of his thin lips. Arthor let him wait. The blueprints were undeniably impressive. They shared the same goal. The Twelve Crowns deferred to Arthor on military matters, so he had no betters to convince; it was entirely his project, his responsibility. If only it was entirely his *choice*.

But still, there was something about Hayne that made his skin crawl. The man was incredibly intelligent, and had contributed more to Ermoor's society than any other living person; but there was an endless well of cold, pure cruelty sitting underneath the surface. What the Overseer had designed and built pushed well beyond the limits of ethical science. If their goal wasn't so important, Arthor would have scoffed and told Hayne to burn the blueprints and never speak of them again. But he couldn't. Not any more.

An unnatural form sat in the centre of one of the blueprints, stark against the otherwise straight lines and plotted curves of the other plans. It tugged his eyes toward itself, forcing him to think about what they had done. *What Riffolk has done,* he tried to convince himself. But it was no use; he couldn't sidestep responsibility for this monstrous design just because he didn't draw the plans himself. He sighed heavily, and looked at Hayne's cold eyes for as long as he could bear.

"It worked, then?"

Hayne's smug smile broadened, turning into an almost childlike grin.

"Oh, yes," he said quietly, "it works."

"What *is* it?"

"You wouldn't believe me if I told you."

Arthor was not easily troubled, but Riffolk Hayne was an exceptionally troubling man. His eyes seemed to say *I know what you are thinking... I have seen your very soul.* Still, he maintained eye contact and pushed the conversation along.

"And with this... thing, you can manufacture enough units for a full-scale invasion?"

"Of course."

"Time frame?"

"Two years."

Arthor couldn't stop his eyes from going wide. Hayne had to be bluffing. It was a full eight years ahead of his original estimates, which already halved the time frame that would have been in place without Riffolk's technology.

"That's impossible," Arthor stated flatly, "we're talking about a full-scale project here, Overseer Hayne, not just Shanaken; we need enough units for a full battalion on each continent. The original time frame was *twenty years*; there's simply no way two years is enough-"

"I can guarantee it, Lord Commander. Look through the blueprints again. You will see I have put measures in place to expedite the manufacturing process significantly. Power will no longer be an issue, money is no longer an issue, and personnel levels are insignificant once the process starts."

Hayne stared at Arthor. He had never looked so smug.

"You ordered this project, Lord Commander. I have delivered, and far above expectations. Unless you have any additional requests, I will take it you have approved the blueprints and begin within two weeks."

Arthor could think of nothing to say. The project was going ahead. It was what he wanted, what the Twelve Crowns wanted, and yet... He knew the implications. They were crossing not just one line, but many. This moment was pivotal; there was no turning back once the project began. Besides; it wasn't entirely up to him. Not any more. *Stop thinking like that,* he told himself, *of course it's up to you; nobody is controlling you.* And it was true. Nobody was controlling him. But some*thing... something* was. Unless he was simply insane. *Stop! Stop thinking like that. Get Hayne and his lackeys out of here, then you can deal with this properly.*

"Fine, Hayne, of course. It's approved. Begin as soon as you can. I want regular updates and access to all information regarding the project."

Hayne gave him a knowing look – an eerily certain smirk – and strode from the room, leaving the blueprints for one of the assistants to scoop up. Once the room was empty but for himself and

Mathys, Arthor sat heavily in his chair. Mathys watched him, expressionless.

"What do you think, Mathys?"

"You know what I think."

Arthor sighed, nodding his head slowly.

"This is wrong," he whispered.

Mathys left his office shortly after. Arthor wanted to delay his leaving, and tried a handful of empty conversational topics; he couldn't stand to be alone any more. But it was no good. Mathys had never been one for small talk, and his disgust at the project was only just held in check by his respect and loyalty for Arthor. Once he was alone, the voices started again.

Mara

They were to be married next year, on the tenth anniversary of Riffolk being named Overseer of Scientific Advancement. Mara couldn't believe she would be part of such a monumentally historic event. Her father's mood had lifted ever since the day they'd met Hayne. She thought it had something to do with the contracts, but it wasn't her place to know. Her own mood had improved drastically too, and that was what she cared about.

The church service went back to lifting her spirits instead of feeling oppressive as it had just before she'd met Riffolk. She joined in the songs, responded with "for the good of all" whenever prompted, and prayed with everyone else that God would cleanse the world of the faithless and deliver them all to a perfect world.

Her friends were jealous, none more than Millicent, and Mara laughed and teased her after she'd told them the news. Abigale and Audrey squealed and hugged her, giggling and remarking on how handsome Riffolk was. Millicent had stared at her as though she'd thrown a bucket of ice cold water at her face.

"Congratulations," she'd said coldly. Mara felt an incredibly satisfying swell of pride and victory. *You might be a Duchess,* she thought while staring into Millicent's eyes, *but I'm going to be the wife of the most intelligent and powerful man in the world.*

"Thank you," she responded.

Mara saw Riffolk once a month after their first meeting. Her father would drop her off to the Hayne mansion after lunch, and they spent the afternoon together until just before sundown when her father would collect her and bring her home. The time she spent with her future husband was incredible. He knew so much about so many things, and dazzled her with facts about his inventions and the world around her.

He kissed her hand every time she arrived at the mansion, his hand lingering in hers for far longer than would normally be appropriate. She didn't mind at all, in fact she found herself thinking about the way his hands felt after sundown, when she lay in bed with the lights off. She wondered how they would feel running down her shoulder, her neck... up her thighs. Every time her thoughts went to that thrilling, terrifying place, she had to shake her head and think of something else. She couldn't bring herself to think about what her body wanted. Not until she was married. Simply knowing that it would happen, that Riffolk wanted it as badly as she did, would have to do.

His eyes assured her that he wanted her. They seemed to push images into her head that made her blush. But despite the intense suggestions in his eyes, he never said anything inappropriate, nor even acted inappropriately beyond holding her hand a little too long. He was the perfect gentleman, and she couldn't wait to be his. Each month dragged on until the day she got to see him again, and after a few months she could think of nothing but him.

The wedding was absolutely breathtaking. Every noble family was present; from Lords to Governors, all the way up to the Lord Commander himself. Representatives from each of the Twelve Crowns showed up as well, which was almost unheard of. The representatives wore rich black jackets with gold trim, luxurious silk blouses and fitted black trousers. They stood as still and composed as the most intricate statues, and they spoke to no one.

Mara wore a pure white dress, as was the custom, and it had been made by the most sought after dressmaker in Ermoor, Cordelia Parkes. Cordelia was almost seventy years old, never married, and though lovely to talk to, was wildly inappropriate. Very unladylike; it must have been all that time spent without a husband. Mara had spent all of her time with the old woman covering her mouth with a hand, either to stifle a laugh or to cover her shock.

When she had first walked into Cordelia's dress shop, with her father of course, the old woman had grabbed her by the wrist and dragged her into a separate fitting room, muttering "a father shouldn't see his daughter fitted, you'll be naked as the day you were born for God's sake." Mara managed a shocked and terrified glance at her father, who returned her look with bafflement of his own.

Once in the fitting room, Cordelia had been true to her word; she had all but ripped Mara's clothing off, no niceties, no 'please' or 'thank you'. No modesty. Mara had been terrified, standing naked on top of a short stool, while the strange old woman pottered around her with a measuring tape, grabbing and moving her body without the least bit of concern for Mara's shame.

As soon as the measurements were taken, Cordelia had disappeared from the room without a word. Mara stood on the stool, naked and scared but unsure if she was allowed to put her clothes back on. She had never felt so vulnerable in her life; the fitting room was only separated from the main room by a thick red curtain, and anyone could have yanked it aside at any time. As if to illustrate her fears, the curtain was suddenly swept open, and Mara screamed. Cordelia had stopped, stared, then rolled her eyes, leaving the curtain open. Luckily there had been no one in the main room but her father, who had dutifully averted his eyes and cleared his throat.

"Why aren't you dressed, silly girl?" Cordelia had said, with a touch too much humour in her voice.

"I – I didn't – CLOSE THE CURTAIN!" Mara had screamed in response. To her credit, Cordelia did as she was bid and left her to get dressed. It had taken two months to make her dress. When she first tried it on, she could see why. It fit her like a second skin, flowing over her body in flattering curves, layers of beautiful fabric that made her look like one of God's angels. The design looked simple at a glance, but the fabric was pleated and folded beautifully in certain places, with different layers of different textured fabrics merging into one gorgeous garment. Luckily the first time she'd tried it on was in one of the fitting rooms, with only Cordelia for company; she'd wept when she saw her reflection, her hands over her mouth and her tears sliding down her fingers.

"Careful, silly girl!" Cordelia had grumbled, rushing off to get tissues for her, "the fabric will be ruined by tears!"

Now, standing on the stage in Rookfell Square, where Riffolk had been named Overseer, Mara saw the looks of awe, desire and jealousy painted on the faces of everyone in the massive crowd. She felt like the most beautiful woman in the world. She felt like an angel. When she walked up the aisle with her father beside her, she had to focus to avoid weeping again. Gasps and appreciative murmuring followed her all the way up the aisle.

When she glanced up and saw Riffolk staring at her with unmasked love and lust, she couldn't stop the tears. They flowed down her cheeks, and to her utter shock, her father had pulled a handkerchief from his pocket and dabbed her tears dry while they walked. She stared at him and he smiled back, caring and loving and totally unlike him. A feeling of unreality swept over her then, as she walked towards her soon-to-be husband in front of almost all of Ermoor. Her father had never looked at her that way before. Ever.

The ceremony itself was a blur for Mara. She remembered saying "I do" in a small voice and hearing Riffolk say it too. She remembered his face, and especially his bright blue eyes as they stared at her, making the crowd disappear and the priest's words meaningless noise in the background. After the ceremony, the crowd dispersed and those rich or highborn enough were invited to the reception where giant trays of absurdly expensive food were walked between the guests as they stood with glasses of equally expensive alcohol.

The reception was held in Atkins Hall, a massive banquet hall in Emberwatch, the richest part of Ermoor. Lavish banquets and parties were held in Emberwatch every night, and the Hayne's marriage to the Watsons was one of the most lavish and extravagant the country had ever seen.

Just like the ceremony, the reception ended up being a blur to Mara. Music, food and alcohol were abundant all through the night, and the laughter of the guests mingled with the music and constant chatter to create an almost physical cloud of noise. An unending stream of richly dressed men and women congratulated Mara, most of them so drunk they slurred their words while swaying on their feet, and stumbled away giggling.

She was the centre of attention for the entire night. She felt like royalty. She even indulged in a few glasses of sparkling white wine, which she'd never been allowed before. When a servant first offered her one of the gleaming crystal glasses, she had raised her hand to take it entirely out of impulse, then stopped and glanced guiltily in her father's direction. Their eyes caught, and he had raised his own mostly empty glass, smiling and nodding. Shocked, she took a glass and stared at the golden liquid in wonder. This was what it felt like to be an adult. *I'm married now,* she thought with utter joy, *I'm a woman! An adult!* Her father had never been so accepting, so supportive.

The first sip was like something out of a dream. It tasted like fruit, but with an odd sour bite that seemed to burn her throat all the way down to her stomach. And the bubbles tickled her mouth and nose. It was a sensation she had been wholly unprepared for, and she coughed and spluttered just as Riffolk walked up beside her.

"Woah," he laughed, "slow down Mara! Maybe take a rest from the drinks?"

She had tried to tell him that it was her first sip but ended up spluttering again before the words could come out. He'd laughed again, took the glass from her hand and placed it on a nearby table. The burning in her throat got much worse with her coughing, and she had to hold onto Riffolk's arm as she tried to get herself under control. She was mortified, but Riffolk stayed with her, steady and patient. His hand patted her back gently, and when her coughing died down it went from patting to rubbing. When the coughing finally subsided completely she stood upright again, and his hand slid gently down her spine, brushing over her backside so briefly and gently that she couldn't tell if it had been done on purpose.

She blushed fiercely, staring at Riffolk with a hand over her mouth. An electric tingling spread from the place where he'd touched her throughout her whole body, and her skin erupted with goosebumps. He stared back, and just when she started to convince herself it had been accidental, he'd winked at her and a sly grin had broken through his composure. She couldn't believe it; he *had* done it on purpose! And right in front of everyone!

She glanced around wildly, hoping no one noticed. She couldn't imagine the shame she'd feel if one of these wealthy families thought of her as a hussy. A small, timid smile crept over her lips as her and Riffolk stared into each others eyes. She couldn't tell him off here, it would only draw attention to what had happened. And besides, truth be told, having his hand on her had been thrilling.

The night went on, and Mara drank several glasses of wine. Riffolk spoke with every guest, gracious and charming and handsome. Mara watched him, thanking each guest who congratulated her and making polite conversation here and there. As the reception started drawing to a close, Mara suddenly realised what would happen when Riffolk took her back to his mansion as his wife. Although she'd wanted it since they met, the knowledge that it was happening tonight was somehow terrifying. She really *would* be a woman now.

Riffolk

There was a spy in Ermoor. He was almost certain. Someone was trying to find out about his project. The signs were subtle, almost imperceptible, but definitely there; notebooks in the document storage room were slightly out of place, tiny muffled sounds occasionally came from unoccupied rooms. The only thing Riffolk didn't know was how the person moved from place to place. He knew the project itself was safe from prying eyes; the security system protecting it was one of his latest inventions.

Still, there was always a way. He stood in his secret lab, looking over the blueprints of the building. He kept all the blueprints he'd ever drawn, including early drafts and scrapped projects, even mundane plans like the building itself. One never knew when the specifics of a design would need to be revisited. His blueprints were incredibly detailed, leaving nothing out. He scanned the building slowly, his eyes settling on every individual line and measurement before moving on to the next.

He shook his head, angry with himself. So many weaknesses! The building was easily accessible by a skilled spy. When he first designed it, he'd been too excited by the layout of the interior and the equipment that would fill it to consider protecting from espionage. No one in Ermoor would dare risk the punishment that would come with trespassing on an Overseer's property; and he'd never considered that a spy might be able to sneak into Ermoor from Tarsium or Shanaken.

He took out a fresh piece of graph paper, a pencil and a straight-ruler; it was time for some upgrades to the lab's security.

Riffolk was a careful man; he always had been. His lapse with the security of the lab was a very rare mistake in an otherwise spotless career. Security upgrades would need to be done subtly. He needed to trap the spy, and to do that they couldn't be made aware that he was trying to catch them in the first place. He left an entry in his journal saying the lab's equipment needed an upgrade; he knew the spy would read it before long, and he wanted any activity to appear to be part of a standard upgrade. In his private lab, he started building small traps which could reveal, restrain, and even kill an intruder incredibly quickly, without Riffolk needing to be present.

To make sure the traps worked as intended, Riffolk ordered one of his assistants into a small storeroom containing spare vials and containers. The room had no air duct vent and no sensitive information, meaning that even if the spy had managed to sneak into it, they would have dismissed it as unimportant immediately. Riffolk had cleared a space at one of the walls and set his trap against it, with the trigger pointing to the centre of the room. He'd set the range at two metres, almost the entire length of the storeroom.

After he told the assistant to fetch him some vials, he waited a few minutes before following. He stood outside the door for a moment, savouring the sounds of the assistant struggling against his bonds. *Perfect,* he thought. He entered the storeroom, smiling in satisfaction at the trapped figure before him. The assistant couldn't move a muscle. Riffolk looked at the remote he'd designed, lightly fingering each button in order from top to bottom:

Trap
Hurt
Kill
Release

The first button clearly worked. The last one was essentially in case a trap misfired and caught someone it shouldn't have; Riffolk didn't anticipate using it often. He tried the second button; it worked. He tried the third button; it worked too.

He set the traps in places his assistants weren't allowed to go. The secret lab was almost certainly safe, but to cover all possibilities, he set traps all throughout it too. The air ducts were the biggest weakness in security, but were necessary for a scientific laboratory. He couldn't set traps in them, as much as he wanted to; if the spy was captured in the air ducts they would be incredibly difficult to retrieve, and if the spy was present while Riffolk was setting traps, they would see them being set and would know to avoid them.

The next best option was to set traps at the opening of each vent in the ceiling. He covered the secret lab first, then moved up to the normal lab, telling the assistants he was setting new smoke alarms as a safety precaution for the soon to be upgraded lab equipment. They accepted his words with absolutely no doubt or suspicion, as they always did. His work didn't take long.

He wrote another journal entry, this time focusing entirely on his success with the project and his upcoming meeting with the Lord Commander. If the spy thought he was distracted by victory and becoming complacent, he might lower his own guard and make a mistake. Far from guaranteed, of course, but he would use any advantage he could gain over the spy.

From this point on, Riffolk would need to simply wait, perhaps planting a few more clues and withdrawing into his private lab to draw the spy in closer. He smiled to himself; no one had ever gotten this close to his work without his permission before. It was almost as exciting as the project itself.

Pera

T*hree hundred seventy four,* she thought as she trudged around another rotation. Her hands fit the thick handlebar perfectly. A long time of holding the handlebars every wake-time had stretched and moulded her hands. They were oddly reassuring, almost comfortable; the simple but hard work kept her busy, and the wheel's continued turning kept her safe. Workers left and were replaced, keeping track of their own rotations. There was no talk but for the workers sitting around the edge of the room; those who hadn't yet expended all of their energy.

Synchronised footfalls thudded through her mind. She used them to keep pace. Workers all lost themselves in the echoing footsteps of their walking group, it was a sort of meditation. Pera found it relaxing, despite the brutally hard work. She closed her eyes and stepped in time with the others.

Four hundred ninety six. Almost there. Pera didn't know how long it took to complete five hundred rotations, all she knew was that by the time she was done, she could think of nothing but the comforting embrace of sleep. Keeping count towards the end became a chore unto itself; almost as difficult as the physical work. Her hands were numb, her back screaming, her shoulders throbbing. She kept her eyes closed. *Thud, thud, thud. Shuffle, shuffle, shuffle.* The footsteps of the workers echoed in her mind, through her body. *Four hundred ninety seven.*

Pera woke, cold and alone. She knew she was alone instantly; the sounds of snoring, breathing and moving were constant in the bunk rooms. Cold was a familiar feeling, but alone certainly wasn't. She stood, dressing out of habit, checking her things out of habit. *Nothing missing,* she thought, *except all the people.* Creeping through the dark, she felt for the doorway and sighed as its familiar rough stone greeted her hand. She turned out into the corridor leading to the wheel room. No candles, no people.

A sinking feeling dragged her heart down to her stomach. A small part of her knew what had happened. The rest of her didn't want to admit it. *A wheel stopped turning. The monsters appeared. Everyone's dead.* Surely she would have heard something? Her head throbbed savagely, reminding her. *You drank before sleeping,* the gritty pounding of her head seemed to say, *nothing would have woken you.* She picked up her pace, feeling sick and weak and stupid.

The wheel room was so far away, her legs were trembling halfway down the corridor. *Please,* she begged the Creator as she ran, *please let everyone still be alive!* No response came, but then again no response ever came to Pera. The others spoke of soft voices, faint touches, vivid dreams. Pera had never experienced any of that. There was light spilling softly into the corridor from the wheel room. Pera's heart soared briefly, and she sprinted the last few steps.

But the room was empty. The wheel stood silently, unmoving. Silence battered her ears and crushed her heart. She had never seen an empty wheel room before; there was something horribly unnatural about it, something evil. Then she saw the doorway.

A section of the wall, in the far corner, was gone, leaving a gaping black hole. Like the solid inky blackness she'd seen in that secret part of Tyra as a child. *A portal,* her mind screamed, *it's where the monsters come from; a portal from Hell!* Her legs gave way, not quite numb enough to stop the jolt of sharp pain when her knees hit the stone floor.

It's done. The monsters came and took everyone. But she'd seen it before, and this was different. The monsters didn't take people; they slaughtered them. But they always left most alive, to continue turning the wheels. This time there was no blood, there were no bodies. There were no people at all. Not even signs of a struggle.

Candlelight flitted over the wheel room, and other than the fact that she was utterly alone, nothing was out of place. Something was terribly wrong. Pera sat where she'd landed on the floor, trying to think of something to do. But there was only one option; as terrifying as it was, and as much as she didn't want to... she had to enter the portal. She had to walk into Hell.

Mara

Mara lay in her massive, comfortable bed, surrounded by pillows and blankets as soft as clouds, and wept. She hadn't seen Riffolk in almost a month. He was very busy of course, but he didn't even sleep in her bed. She'd taken to calling it *her* bed since she was the only one who slept in it, even though it was in the master bedroom and technically Riffolk's bed.

Everything changed after they were married. Six months had passed, and Mara cried almost every day of it. Without him around, she was unable to leave the mansion, and despite its size, Mara felt trapped and claustrophobic. She had taken to drinking the same wine she'd tried at the wedding, just to calm herself down. The maids and servants wouldn't talk to her except to serve her food and wine, and the mansion had no visitors unless Riffolk was hosting. Not even her father visited. The only time she felt okay was on Wednesdays and Sundays, when either Riffolk or a servant took her to the church service.

God made her feel much better. The priest's words settled her. She knew that God was looking after her in His own way, that He had a plan for her.

"The savages in the desert, and in the forests, and everywhere else," the priest was saying, "are angering our Lord with their Godless ways. They do not pray, they do not believe. Their very existence is taking away our ability to remain faithful to God!"

The service always made Mara incredibly grateful to have been born in Ermoor. She couldn't imagine how horrible it must be to live in a desert or in the middle of the jungle, especially among people who didn't even believe in God. The idea itself was terrifying; how could these people not believe? Did they not see the beauty of God's love in everything around them? She hoped Ermoor could teach these savages the priest spoke of to love God. Otherwise, as he said, they would need to be destroyed. She didn't want anyone to die, but what choice was there if they refused to accept God's love?

Ermoori missionaries had been trying to teach the forest people God's way for years, but were consistently and brutally attacked each time. Mara couldn't even imagine the kind of savagery it took to viciously attack missionaries who were simply trying to teach enlightenment and love to the world. She prayed every night for them to see reason.

"God loves us all," the priest said, "even the faithless. But His anger is boundless and He must be feared and respected by all."

Riffolk spent almost all of his time in his laboratory in Darkpoint, the district over from Ironhaven. Mara wasn't allowed, of course, unless Riffolk brought her with him. But he never did. She thought about asking him to take her one day, but she was afraid he would get angry or laugh at her. "You're just some silly girl, you wouldn't understand a single thing you see in the laboratory," she imagined him saying.

Imagining conversations made up a large part of Mara's day. In her head, she spoke with her friends, Riffolk, her father, Uncle Lewis, and even the priests sometimes. The conversations were often unpleasant, except for Uncle Lewis of course, and she usually ended up in a dark mood after each one. She wasn't sure if it was purely her imagination, but she thought she had an accurate idea of how the people close to her would speak.

Her friends never visited, although they each had servants who could accompany them if they chose to leave the house. Mara had servants of her own now too, although she couldn't bring herself to leave the mansion; she wanted to stay just in case Riffolk showed up during the day. He kept strange hours, and could appear at home at any time. Besides, most days she had at least a bottle of wine while waiting for her husband, and it wouldn't do at all to let others see her drunk.

She walked through the immaculately tended gardens some days, wandering aimlessly and staring at all the exotic trees and flowers. Usually a half-empty bottle of wine hung from her hand while she wandered. The servants never mentioned the wine unless they offered another bottle, and she was surprised to find there was never a hint of judgement in their voices. Two of them consistently kept a respectful half-dozen paces behind her when she walked through the mansion and the grounds, and they were always quick to offer help whenever she needed it.

It was a good life, at least in theory; she had nothing to complain about, and it would have been the perfect life but for Riffolk's absence. Still, Mara found herself growing more and more numb as the days passed by.

Riffolk's grunting filled her ear, his lips pushed against the side of her head. Her hair pulled back painfully with his thrusts, held in one of his fists. His other hand gripped her hip like a vice, pulling her into him roughly. Tears flowed freely and she bit her lip to avoid crying. He didn't like it when she sobbed while he took her. "If you have to cry, do it silently," he'd said the first time he'd been rough.

He never seemed to care if he was hurting her. Their first time, on their wedding night, had been loving and slow. It had been painful of course, but only for a little while. He'd stared into her eyes and kissed her deeply, and after the pain stopped she felt a pleasure she'd never imagined. Their lovemaking continued like that for maybe a month or so, and then suddenly, he had changed. He grew distant, spent far more time at Darkpoint, and started taking her roughly, forcing her in ways that made her cry for hours afterwards.

She couldn't speak to her friends about it; after she'd stuck it in Millicent's face, what would they say about her awful marriage now? They wouldn't be any help. If anything, they would laugh at her. And her father would offer no solace, either. He'd only started being remotely friendly to her after the contracts had been signed; if she displayed any unhappiness now, he would think she was threatening the marriage he was so pleased with. So she suffered in silence, with only the servants following her around for company.

Pera

As soon as she crept through the portal, everything changed. It was warm, much warmer than Pera had ever been in her life. The air itself was different; a different smell, and a different *feeling* in her lungs. Cleaner, sharper, dust-free. She walked as slowly and carefully as she could through a small dark room into an equally dark corridor, braced for an attack. Nothing happened. It seemed to stretch forever in the same direction. The darkness was complete. Her hand slid across the wall as she moved, but it was utterly different to the stone she'd felt her whole life. The wall in this place was so smooth it felt almost like water, and completely seamless. There was no echo; her footfalls simply fell flat in her ears, disappearing almost as soon as the sound was made.

Suddenly a voice boomed from somewhere nearby.

"No! You're too late!"

Arms as strong as metal rods scooped her from the smooth floor, and then she was moving along the corridor at inhuman speed.

"We won't make it all the way out," the voice said gently. It was female, definitely not a monster. "But I'll get you somewhere relatively safe."

The woman's accent was strange; otherworldly. Her strength and speed were unbelievable. A sudden thought hit Pera as she was sped through the blinding corridor; Was this the Creator? A rush of other thoughts followed immediately after: Were the monsters destroyed once and for all? Did her people survive? Where did the corridor lead?

Too terrified to ask anything of this being, Pera simply let herself be carried until her eyes adjusted to the darkness; it didn't take long. When she could see, she glanced up at the woman carrying her, and screamed. *It's one of the monsters, one of the monsters has me, I'm going to die.* It was a bright orange and red demon, with a snarling, inhuman face. Pera's screams startled it, and she used the surprise to begin kicking and fighting until the thing dropped her onto the cold floor.

She sprinted back the way they'd come, screaming and knowing she couldn't outrun it. Suddenly, more of them spilled from another portal in the corridor wall in front of her, shouting and pointing. She tripped and fell, screwing her eyes shut and screaming. She hit the floor hard, and the flat thudding of heavy footsteps grew louder, still curiously without echoing.

The demons reached her, and she was kicked and grabbed in a chaotic frenzy from every direction. Shouting surrounded her, and heavy boots slammed into her back, her legs, her face, her stomach. Her screams turned to tortured sobs, and she prayed to the Creator to save her.

"Please," she choked out between vicious kicks, "save me!"

The shouts turned from anger to sudden fear around her. The kicking stopped, and for a few seconds the air filled with thuds, grunts and screams. Pera kept her eyes closed, praying to the Creator through the chaos, dimly thinking *it's working!* The sounds halted abruptly after no more than a few seconds, and Pera was left in a heavy silence that felt even scarier than the shouts and kicks of her attackers.

She opened her eyes slowly, coming face to face with a dead monster. She scrambled to her feet, backing against the wall away from the thing's corpse. But her foot caught on another dead monster, and she looked around her. The corridor was full of corpses. Somehow they had all died in a matter of seconds. *The Creator*. It had to be. There was no other explanation.

Her thoughts ended there as her gaze reached the other side of the corridor. Another monster stood there, staring at her.

"No," she said. "No, no, no!" she bolted down the corridor, back towards Tyra, towards safety. Thudding footsteps sounded behind her, inhumanly fast and growing close. She screamed, closing her eyes just as it reached her. It snatched her mid stride, yanking her forcefully backwards and sprinting back towards wherever it wanted to take her. She screamed, but could do nothing to break its grip. Dead monsters appeared on the ground below her, growing smaller as she was sped away.

"*Please,"* She prayed again, "Please save me!"

"I am," the monster said.

Riffolk

He moved into the room carefully, gun up, eyes scanning every surface. The underground lab held no mysteries to him; he knew every inch of it as well as he knew each of his inventions. He knew there was someone here; he'd suspected a spy for a little while, and a sudden drop in energy output from the lab meant that the spy was tampering with equipment. He was constantly monitoring his project via a hand-held controller; it was connected to his main lab, the underground lab, and his mansion. They'd gotten past his traps and detection equipment, but he was ready now.

"I know you're in here," he said. "I have many security measures in place. Whoever you are, you will not escape with your life. You've just – Ah. Hello."

He'd been searching intently as he spoke, and spotted a dark, unclear figure hunched upside down on the ceiling.

"One of the Shenza assassins, I presume?"

"I'm no assassin," the figure said, "but I will kill you if I have to."

A woman. Interesting. He knew women were treated equally to men in many places outside Ermoor. Then again, there were many places where they were below men as well. He didn't trouble himself with learning the cultures of savages, so he hadn't realised Shanaken was in the former group. A woman assassin wouldn't pose much of a threat, although her ability to stick to the ceiling was a surprise.

"Feel free to try," he said, and when she didn't reply, he fired the gun.

She bolted to the floor so quickly that for a second she simply disappeared. He trained the gun on her again, but she'd already unsheathed her blade and stood ready.

"What... *are* you?" she asked, her face showing genuine confusion.

He didn't bother answering, and she refocused, shaking off whatever had bothered her.

"I will kill you if I have to, but murder is not the mission."

What game is she playing? He thought. First the odd question, then denying her reason for being there in the first place... Riffolk found himself intrigued, if not a little annoyed.

"What else would you be here for?"

She pointed her blade at the tank in the centre of the room, and the movement almost made him fire again. Instead, he smiled.

"Do you know what it is? What it will do to your people?"

She didn't react at all, just staring with blank stupidity. *Of course,* he thought, *I expected too much from a savage Shenza.* He sighed.

"No, of course you don't. Well, it seems we have a decision to make."

He offered the choice between a fight, or safe passage. Then he toyed with her a while, letting her know he'd known about her presence the entire time she'd been snooping around. When he left the choice to her, he watched her closely, and she moved into a combat position.

He moved first, reaching into his pocket for the security remote he kept for emergencies. A pitch black circle appeared in front of the Shenza woman, and he fired at her. He grabbed the remote and pressed the button just as the circle smashed into him, sending him flying backwards into the door behind him. For a few seconds, bright spots invaded his vision, and then there was nothing.

Mara

Fog smothered the quiet streets of Ermoor. Colourful lights blurred and mixed together, turning what would have been an ominous dark alley into a beautiful cascade of colour. Mara gripped her cloak, pulling it closer over her shoulders. As beautiful as it was, the fog was still freezing cold. Her steps tapped lightly on the smooth pavement, seeming to fall flat on her ears instead of echoing through the night. Glancing around, she snuck down another alley, moving as quickly as she dared through the fog.

She was alone. Outside. The thought still hadn't quite settled in her mind, but blared behind her eyes like the colourful lights pulsing through the fog. Sneaking out like this was incredibly dangerous for a girl, but the thrill of imagining herself outside in the dark without a man for protection had made her stomach flutter and her heart thud in her chest. It had been imagination at first, of course; pure fantasy brought about by boredom and inebriation. But it kept returning to her mind, until finally the thought alone wasn't enough to excite her any longer.

She had put on the darkest and warmest clothing she owned, dressing in the dark so the servants wouldn't notice. The balcony that came off the master bedroom faced Riffolk's private gardens; no guards or servants patrolled there. She had lowered herself gracelessly to the dew-covered ground, grinning and trying to stifle giggles as she imagined her mother and father's face if they ever saw such an unladylike display. Running through the gardens had been a thrill on its own, the trees and plants that were so beautiful by day turning to dark, aggressive shapes reaching at her through the gloom as she ran.

That had been the first time. She snuck into the gardens every night that week, simply running breathless through the gloom, terrified and ecstatic. The fear and excitement dwindled with each night however, until she decided to try wandering the streets.

Getting out of the Hayne property was far more difficult than simply walking into the private gardens had been. The only way out was through the front door, the rest of the grounds closed off from the public by a high metal fence. Most of the servants slept the night through, but some were always up and about. Avoiding them was fairly easy. The servant guarding the entrance to the mansion wasn't so easy to get by. He remained alert, drinking coffee and staring out into the night. Mara had paused in the massive lobby, stuck and wondering what to do, when suddenly a crash had shattered the silence, echoing through the lobby and scaring her almost to death. If she hadn't thought to dash behind one of the pillars lining the outside of the room, she would have been seen and questioned. But from the safety of her hiding spot, she heard the servant come in from outside and rush to the source of the sound.

Angry but quiet whispers floated through the lobby, and when she was sure the servant was quite occupied, she snuck out from behind the pillar. The main door had been left ajar, and, smiling at her good fortune, she had left the mansion.

Now, rushing through the fog, she realised she had no idea where to go. She couldn't visit anyone without a man to escort her. She couldn't be seen by anyone. With limited options, she was confined to alleyways and quiet streets. Cold, damp, alone and scared, she suddenly realised how stupid she was being. The excitement of only a moment ago vanished, and she stopped walking in the middle of an empty street.

The beautiful street lights, which created fuzzy halos in the fog, went out. Mara gasped, staring desperately in every direction. All she could see was the now dim fog. She'd turned around too many times, and not a speck of light told her where the streets lay.

Panicking, she decided it was time to return to the mansion. She took a few tentative steps, then stopped again, tears filling her eyes. Without excitement pushing her forward, the thought of walking through the city alone at night was suddenly overwhelming. She wrapped her arms around herself tightly and lowered her head, trying to think clearly. She stood that way for a while, and the cold slowly chewed through her layers of clothing, biting first her skin and then through to the bone. Shivering, she started moving just to try to warm up.

A deep, loud grating sound sprang up from somewhere nearby and Mara screamed. She backed into a wall and slid down until she sat on the cold paved street, huddled and crying. A loud clang followed the grating sound, echoing through the fog, and Mara whimpered. Nothing happened for a few excruciating moments, and then, to her utter horror, footsteps beat the smooth streets. Footsteps that were growing unmistakeably louder.

Pera

The corridor gave way to another dark tunnel, then the tunnel turned straight up into a tight circular shaft. The monster's breathing remained regular despite its speed. The vertical tunnel seemed to go for miles. Stuck in the monster's arms, facing down, Pera could only stare in horror as the ground disappeared into an endless black void. They sped up the tunnel for what felt like far too long, until finally a loud grating sound assaulted Pera's ears directly behind her head, followed by an overwhelming clang.

She was swept up into a nightmare; a wide open space, cold and alien. It was bright, horrible jarring twinkles of colourful light stabbed through the air from above; but that wasn't the worst of it. What made it nightmarish was the air itself; thick, white, and horribly cold, it obscured her vision and filled her lungs. The monster kept running, its footsteps now thumping on solid ground. After a short time, they slowed to a stop, and Pera heard panicked breathing in front of the monster. Then she was dropped to the freezing ground. A frightened, tiny voice spoke up out of the gloom:

"What are you?"

The thick white air pressed in on her, speeding her heart up and clogging her throat. She pushed herself to her hands and knees, glancing around in fear; but the monster was gone. Instead, a young woman sat against a wall, staring at her in astonishment. She was dressed all in rich black clothing like nothing Pera had ever seen. This place had to be the afterlife. There was no other explanation for the ghostly air, the monster, the woman in such strange black clothing. She had literally been carried by a monster into death.

But this woman... she was obviously not Tyran. Was she some kind of servant to the Creator? A dead soul from some other world or time? Or worst of all, was she simply one of the monsters dressed in human skin? The terror was building in her mind and her heart, and she felt herself losing grip. She forced herself to ask the one thing she was terrified to know.

"Are you one of them?"

But the thick air finally took her breath completely, and blackness seeped into the edges of her vision. She saw the woman's lips moving, but the black swept in and took her before the words reached her ears. She didn't feel herself hit the ground.

Mara

A demon flowed out of the fog, dragging a filthy, emaciated woman effortlessly in one hand. It wore jagged red and orange armour that seemed to be made out of fire. Its face was the same colour as its armour, glaring at her with a vicious, inhuman snarl. Mara had never seen anything like it; wouldn't have been able to even imagine it. The demon ran straight to where Mara crouched against the street wall, and dropped the woman at her feet.

"What are you?" Mara regretted asking the question the moment it left her lips, when the demon's eyes bored into her own. It pointed to the woman on the ground, stared intently at Mara for a moment, then abruptly disappeared.

The woman moaned and struggled to her hands and knees, looked around her quickly, then up at Mara as though she were as strange and terrifying as the demon that had brought her here.

"Are you one of them?" the woman whispered.

"One of who? Who are you? Mara said, but the woman slumped to the smooth cold pavement and lay still.

After wandering the streets for what felt like years, Mara brought the woman to Riffolk's mansion, finding the main entrance curiously unguarded and none of the lights on. She remained undisturbed through the entire mansion, despite the noise she made trying to half drag, half walk the woman through the corridors. By the time she reached a spare room near her bedroom, she was sweating and breathing heavy. She lay the woman on the bed, aghast at the filth and smell. Bringing some water in from the closest bathroom, she filled a pitcher and left it next to the unconscious woman. Then she returned to her bedroom, removed her dark clothing and underclothes, and washed herself until the woman's smell was gone. She threw the clothes in the bin.

A soft knocking woke her up the next day. She sighed, blinking, and made sure she was covered by the bedsheets.

"Enter," she said. A servant slipped through the crack in the door and took a few tentative steps into the room.

"My lady, I'm terribly sorry, but your visitor is quite unwell," he said. The servants all had the uncanny ability to balance fear, respect, and a prim sort of arrogance in their voices at all times. Mara frowned; she never had visitors. The only time a stranger had ever come into the house who wasn't there to see Riffolk was the disgusting woman from her odd dream last night. It had to have been a dream, of course; demons weren't real. Neither was magic, except for the miracles performed by God himself. The Devil, though... He was real. Mara pushed the thought away.

"I don't understand," she replied to the servant, "I don't *have* a visitor."

The servant looked terrified; they were trained never to question their lords and ladies, but he was clearly under the impression that she did indeed have a visitor. She sighed again.

"Very well, what is wrong with this visitor?" She asked. The servant fidgeted, remembered himself, then stood straight again.

"She is starving, my lady. Living in conditions too poor to maintain good health. We must summon a doctor at once."

"The... the woman from last night was real?" The servant's face turned as pale as Mara's must have been.

"Yes, my lady, she is real. And... she is dying."

Riffolk

He woke before the Shenza did, groggy and furious. The remote had done its job; when he stood and cast his eyes over the room, his robotic sentinel stood directly in front of the assassin, her blade in one of its multifunctional claws. She was trapped by the snare he'd set at the ceiling grate. The roof traps were set up to automatically extend downwards after being activated, bringing the victim close to the floor.

Taking her sword from the sentinel, he stared up at the open grate on the roof. She had to have come in from there, but the trap didn't go off on her way in. She'd clearly done something different on her way out, but Riffolk had no way of knowing what it was. Perhaps the spell that turned her into a shadow... Or perhaps there was some other kind of Shenza magic involved.

Either way, he was going to find out. He had her now. Whatever it took to understand their magic; he would question her, torture her, test her limits, and then dissect her. He was looking forward to it. She stirred, and he waited until he was sure she'd seen the sentinel before speaking.

"I did warn you. I may not have a magical sword, but I can assure you the weapons I've designed are far more deadly."

"You have no idea how deadly Shadow Magic is, Hayne."

Her confidence was ridiculous. He'd seen reports of the Shenza's capabilities in battle, of course, but most of it could be put down to fear and adrenaline. A lot of the feats he'd read and heard described could also be achieved through technology. Or deception. He had no doubt they were formidable on the battlefield, in their home country; but a single Shenza, bound and unarmed? And a woman to boot?

Riffolk didn't laugh often, but the Shenza's empty threat was too much, and he couldn't help himself. But as he started laughing, she burst out of her bonds, the black circle shield appearing on her arm again; in an instant, she dropped, rolled and sprinted past him. She moved so fast he barely felt the sword get snatched from his hand.

The sentinel reacted faster than he did, stepping around him and firing at the woman as she ran. A heavy thunk sounded as her magic shield buried itself in the sentinel's triangular eye. She leapt in an impossibly high arc straight over it, bringing her sword down with both hands. The sentinel collapsed, completely dead; years of hard work and dozens of separate inventions, destroyed in a matter of seconds.

He pulled his gun and fired, over and over, reloading as he went. She leapt up to the ceiling and launched off it in one motion, streaking over him faster than he could keep up with. He saw a brief spray of blood as she flew though, and triumph joined with his fury for a moment.

His victory lasted until the Shenza landed somewhere behind him, and before he could turn around, she smashed into him with the magic shield. He stumbled to the floor, whipping around to face her as quickly as he could, and catching the shock on her face as he raised the gun.

He'd lost focus on the weapon and forgot to reload. Its dry click ignited a storm of helpless fury in his mind which threatened to drown his vision in a sea of burning red. He threw the gun away, disgusted at himself and the woman. Staring into her eyes, he prepared to die.

"What you do here today will make no real difference," he said, "Shanaken will fall. All of Pandeia will fall."

She stepped close, raised the shield, and smashed it into the side of his head.

Mara

The woman thrashed and muttered in her sleep, sweating and breathing hard. Not only was she emaciated, her skin was pale, her clothing worn to shreds, her hands so calloused they resembled ruined leather. The doctor hissed a shocked intake of breath upon first seeing her, and would have recoiled if he wasn't a professional.

"What happened to her?" The doctor whispered to Mara.

"I'm sorry, Doctor, I have no idea," she replied. He shooed her out of the room, closing the door behind her. She ran to her room, worried for the woman but terrified for herself; what was happening? Where had this stranger come from? Ermoor was spotless and beautiful, all its citizens properly dressed and bathed as God demanded. To be dirty and dishevelled was to be disrespectful to God. Did this woman want to bring God's wrath down on Mara? On Riffolk? A horrible thought occurred to her then; what if this woman was some kind of trap? Some kind of awful test of her faithfulness? Or even worse, an attack on Riffolk?

Despite his distance and violence, Mara found herself desperately wishing her husband was here with her now. He would know how to handle the situation. He was a genius, after all. She couldn't get the woman's feral appearance out of her head, nor the stench from her nostrils. It clung to her as though she was still in the room. She wanted to shower again, but with a doctor and servants rushing around just outside her bedroom, she didn't have the privacy.

And the thing that dropped the woman at her feet... Its evil, horrifying face kept swimming into her mind's eye, glaring and snarling. It wasn't human, she knew that. It was evil, and demonic, and the woman it had thrown into her life was going to cause trouble. She knew this was either a test or a trap; but had no way of knowing which. If it was a test, it could be God Himself testing her. But if it was a trap, it could only be the Devil. Just as her heart starting speeding up, faint, shouting voices echoed from the lobby. *Riffolk!*

She knew his voice. Her fear suddenly vanished, she left the bedroom and waited for her husband in the corridor outside the spare room. He swept into the corridor, his mouth set in a grim line. His eyes sparkled when he looked at her, and his features softened. She couldn't wait another second; she ran to him. He embraced her, kissed her briefly, then glanced towards the spare room.

"Why didn't you send for me?" he said.

She blushed, suddenly embarrassed. "I thought... I thought you would be too busy. I thought your work would be more important than – than her."

He stared at her for a moment, with an expression Mara couldn't read.

"Yes, well my work is far more important, of course," he muttered, more to himself than her, "but when it comes to inexplicable strangers in my home, I would prefer to be told as soon as possible."

She nodded quickly, although she had no idea what inexplicable meant. Riffolk often used long words that soared over her head. He stepped past her and strode to the spare room. He disappeared from her view, entering the small room and closing the door behind him. Mara stood for a few moments, then returned to her bedroom. The need to bathe returned, this time overwhelming; she hated feeling unclean while her husband was in the mansion. She wasn't allowed to lock doors while Riffolk was home, so she stood shivering under the cold water of the shower, staring at the closed bathroom door and straining to listen for any noise beyond. The power hadn't come back since the night before when she'd snuck out, otherwise she would have set the water on the hottest temperature possible. She hated being cold.

After her shower, she dried herself and slipped into a silk robe. She meant to dress herself in the bedroom; she'd forgotten to pick new clothes out from one of her wardrobes and hang them in the bathroom the way she usually did. But when she opened the bathroom door, Riffolk was sitting on the edge of the bed, waiting for her. The silk robe was partially see through, and barely covered her nakedness. She suddenly felt exposed and vulnerable, and his eyes wandered slowly over her entire body.

He stood, beckoning to her. She went to him immediately; she had learned to obey him without hesitation in the bedroom. His temper was short when he was aroused. He pushed her to her knees. Without waiting to be told, she unbuckled his belt.

As soon as Riffolk was done with her, he strode from the room, leaving her still on her knees feeling used and sick. There was a small part of her which felt exhilarated by the experience; each time he used her this way, that part grew a little. It still felt wrong, and scary, but that growing part of her seemed to get some thrill out of it. Her stomach seemed to flush and churn with different feelings; disgust and fear, but also an odd satisfaction. Then there was a sickening excitement. It made her feel as though she was about to throw up, while at the same time flooding her with a tingling sense of desperate anticipation; as though being used by Riffolk sated some deep, unknown hunger.

He'd left her a mess, as he usually did. Mara showered again, hugging her arms around her body as the cold water froze her skin. It was shockingly cold, but it still felt better than the sticky mess her husband left on her body. Her stomach still roiled with conflicting emotions.

She knew he wasn't doing anything *wrong*. She was his wife, and using her this way was his right. But it still felt... off. Of course she couldn't talk about it with her friends; if it was normal for men to behave this way, they would make fun of her ignorance, and if it wasn't normal, she would be seen as a disloyal wife for speaking ill of her husband.

Besides, the sick feeling was much weaker now. He loved her, she knew he did; he'd said it on her wedding day with tears in his eyes, and he'd said it once or twice again since. He wouldn't do anything to hurt her. It was just her inexperience clouding her mind. After her shower, she dressed in a modest slip and sat on the bed for a while. When her heart wouldn't settle, she got to her knees and prayed, clasping her hands with her elbows resting on the soft bedsheets.

God did not speak to her. Suddenly, being on her knees felt awful, and she wondered why she must take the same pose to pray as she did to pleasure her husband. In that moment, a sliver of doubt pierced her perfect faith, and it was enough to bring her to tears. She sat on the bed, thought about her husband and her God, and wept.

Riffolk

Riffolk stood slowly, sore and furious. The Shenza woman was far more talented than he'd anticipated. Miscalculation left a bad taste in his mouth. She knew a lot, he was sure, but he'd planted the seed of doubt in her mind, and she would be second-guessing everything she had found. It was a small victory, but all he could do in the circumstances. Even in failure, however, Riffolk found opportunity. He would be upgrading his security systems using what he'd observed of the Shenza assassin.

For now though, he got to work repairing the cage. Energy output from the tank was at a dead zero. For a savage who lived in a tree, the Shenza had done a remarkable job of sabotaging his equipment. And her fighting ability... surely there was a way to harness whatever magic the Shenza used. He made a mental note to look into it. His sentinel, now a pile of scrap metal on the floor, could well do with an upgrade if he could find and secure one of those black swords.

He had a lot to think about. The delays to his project were going to set him back with Symond; he'd had to fight just to get it this far without being shut down. Symond's state of mind was clearly compromised; the Lord Commander wavered between ruthless ambition and moral crisis on a daily basis. The man had no drive, no backbone, and no sanity.

If there had been a way to remove him permanently, Riffolk would have done it years ago. But his hold over the Twelve Crowns was tremendously convenient for Riffolk's work, and besides; despite his obvious insanity, he was intelligent and talented. Riffolk hated giving the man praise, even silently within the confines of his own thoughts; but credit had to go to Symond for his decades of military service. He was a good leader.

The wires drawing power from the creature were utterly destroyed. The Shenza had even done a half-convincing job of making it look like pests were chewing on them. It might even have convinced him, if not for two glaring facts: the lab was not at all accessible to pests, and the wires were made of a material that could not be damaged by anything short of magic. She had no way of knowing exactly how difficult it was for him to acquire some of his equipment, but her goal had been to stall his work and she had done just that.

She was using the air ducts, as he'd surmised. And his trap worked perfectly too; only the mysterious magic she used could cut through even the re-enforced metal armour of his sentinel. But her magic had a weakness. He saw the hand gestures she needed to make to activate it. His next trap would focus on restraining hands. Crushing them, maybe.

Mara

Mara woke slowly, the silk of her bedsheets slipping over her skin as she turned with her eyes closed. These were her favourite moments; half-awake, superbly comfortable, the worries of the day ahead as murky and ethereal as the dreams of the night before. She remained in this state for as long as she could every day. It was over a week since the woman appeared in front of her from the fog, and the stress of having a wild stranger stay only a room over from hers was taking its toll.

It had taken a few days for the power to come back on, and that only added to her stress; cold showers were absolutely awful, almost as bad as not showering at all. But one comfort which couldn't be taken from her was the half awake bliss she felt before she had to rise in the mornings. Occasionally she would be forced to get up early; a party in the afternoon she would need to prepare for, or a visiting representative from one of the Twelve Crowns. This morning it was the sound of her bedroom door opening. No knock had preceded it; it wasn't a servant. Her mind drew the only conclusion it could.

"Riffolk?" She asked sleepily, turning once again and opening her eyes. The horribly skinny woman from the street stood in the doorway nervously, staring as though Mara was made from food. She shot upright, crawling backwards and slamming into the headboard behind her hard enough to bring bright pinpoints cascading over her vision. The woman moved towards her slowly, and Mara screamed in horror.

"What do you want?"

The woman stopped close enough to the bed to reach out and touch it, marvelling at its softness.

"What... is this?" the woman asked.

"It's silk," Mara replied without thinking, "obviously. You've heard of silk, haven't you?"

The woman shook her head absently, stroking the bedsheets in wonder. "It's so soft. I never knew anything so soft existed."

Mara frowned. Silk was everywhere in Ermoor. Everybody knew what silk was. She moved cautiously to the side of the bed, slipping off the side while keeping her eyes on the woman. She was no longer filthy, but she still looked... wild, somehow. Like she'd grown up in a forest. *Dear God,* she thought suddenly, *what if she's one of the tree people?* She circled wide around the woman, who was still preoccupied with her bedsheets, and made towards the light switch closest to the bed.

"Let me turn on a light for you, and we can-"

"NO!"

Mara flinched, freezing mid step with her eyes wide.

"Please, no. There's enough light in this place. I don't know how you can stand it."

Mara glanced around the room, wondering if she was going blind. Her curtains were quite thick, and other than a thin bar of golden sunlight slanting through the top, it may as well have been the middle of the night. She could see across the room, but everything was layered in shades of grey, the shape of the furniture foggy and uncertain.

"Stand it? The curtains aren't even open, there's almost no sunlight in here."

"Sunlight?"

"What? Yes, sunlight... light from the sun."

The woman looked incredibly nervous.

"What's the sun?"

Mathys

Something terrible was happening in Ermoor. Mathys felt it as surely as he felt the ground beneath his feet. First a murder spree, then an attack on Dreadhold and a total power outage throughout the city. The Twelve hadn't told him much of the attack, and their secrecy made alarm bells chime in his head; they were notoriously secret about most things, of course, but an attack like that fit squarely into his jurisdiction; covering it up from the Commander of Security made no sense.

It was almost enough to make him want to investigate further, even if the Twelve clearly didn't want him to. But he had enough to worry about. The clean up from the Gilded Goblet was still going, and there was some damage and some unrest as a result of the power outage, especially in the poor districts.

He was also dealing with some retaliation from thugs who were previously in Massey's employ; apparently whatever he was paying them was enough to inspire an incredible amount of loyalty. Usually the thugs just stuck to whoever paid most, or friends and family, but Massey stood out among the criminals of Ermoor. It was going to be a difficult few months.

Most of the civilians from Ermoor's upper districts had never even been south of Riverford or Dawnton; as far as they were concerned, Ermoor was perfect. Mathys was different. He grew up in the lower districts, before he'd enlisted; he knew them, and the people who lived in them, well. He'd never fit in with the rich and powerful.

When he was far younger, before he joined the military, he wished more than anything to have a house in Riverford, or even Ironhaven. He would have given almost anything for the chance. After he was promoted to Commander after serving honourably in the exploratory force at Shanaken, he was given exactly what he wanted. He hated it. The mansion itself, a cosy little place in Dawnton, was perfect; the lifestyle, the people... not so much.

After a couple of years spent trying to fit in, and only being judged and misunderstood, he'd finally resigned to spending his time alone. He'd always enjoyed his own company, so it wasn't a particularly difficult decision; but he remained disappointed with the "upper classes" of Ermoor.

So he spent as much time as he could in the city's southern districts, where both his job and his heart belonged. But even so, there was a sense of not belonging. Ever since his promotion, he had to use a disguise when he wasn't there on duty; to everyone who lived in the poor districts, he was now one of the rich and powerful.

He didn't belong with the rich, and was no longer accepted by the poor. But at least he still had a friend or two; solid contacts he'd built over decades, people he could rely on. It felt good, and despite the animosity, and the danger, and the filth; the poor districts of Ermoor still felt like home.

Looking at it now, Mathys almost understood the disdain on the faces of Ermoor's wealthy when they talked of the southern districts. After the power outage, there had been chaos.

Arthor

Arthor thought of himself as a good man. He took care of his wife, he was loyal to his country and God, and he worked hard every day. He wasn't perfect of course; nobody was. But he was clearly a better man than many. Certainly he was a better man than Overseer Hayne. Wasn't he? The project was going ahead, approved by him. Ermoor, in the name of God and for the good of all, would be butchering thousands, tens of thousands. Maybe even more.

In the name of God. For the good of all. Lately, the phrases had lost their meaning. They sounded empty to him, but something worse; they had become ominous. Almost menacing. They were thrown around by all of Ermoor's leaders to justify any decision. He would never say it out loud, but laying in the comfort of his bed, with Ellie asleep next to him, he could think freely.

Thinking was all that was left to him most nights; he never got much sleep any more. Not since the voices had gotten worse. He knew he was crazy. Nobody else heard voices in their head except for their own thoughts. But it felt to him like a *real* voice, not just some errant crazy thought. It spoke to him, gave him information he couldn't possibly have otherwise known.

Arthor didn't believe in magic. He barely believed in God, if he was honest with himself. He followed the scriptures, attended church services, and made sure to repeat the sacred words whenever it was required; despite all that, the belief in an actual real God slightly eluded him. But the voices he heard were definitely something else. Almost certainly not magic, but something out of the ordinary. And if he were to believe the things those voices said...

The air shifted, close to his face. His eyes sprang open. Pitch black greeted him, soft smudges of grey showing the tops of the walls between the furniture. A heavy silence hung in the room. He'd lived in this mansion his entire life; his family owned it going back five generations. He'd slept in the master bedroom for twenty years, since his father had passed away. It was his sanctuary, the place he felt safest and most comfortable. Now it felt different. He rolled slowly onto his back, and saw the thing on his roof.

It stared down at him, a demon made of shadow. He knew instinctively this was the thing that had been talking to him. He glanced over at his wife; Ellie slept on beside him, undisturbed. Part of him was tempted to wake her and ask if she could see what he saw.

"Don't wake her."

He looked up at it.

"It's you, isn't it? The one who speaks in my head?"

The shadow shifted slightly.

"Of course," it snapped, *"I am here to tell you that your goal has changed."*

Arthor's skin tingled, suddenly cold. It had never changed its mind before.

"What must I do?"

"Stop the scientist. He meddles in things he does not understand."

An intense wave of relief washed over him, almost as strong as his fear. Finally, he had a reason to put Hayne's inhuman project down. But the shadow was the one who originally told him to approve the project in the first place; and it had been terribly convincing. He couldn't question it's motives directly. Whatever it was, it was powerful. As confusing as the change was, his new goal aligned perfectly with his moral compass, and he was glad to obey.

"Of course, anything you wish."

He blinked and the shadow was gone, empty grey ceiling staring back at him. He realised he would need to explain the project being shut down to the Twelve Crowns. The conversation wouldn't be pleasant. He didn't answer to them, not technically, but their approval by vote was required by Ermoori law on military matters. Arthor rolled to his side again, thinking. The voice didn't come again, but neither did sleep.

Mara

As soon as the curtains were pulled open, the woman screamed. Mara recognised the scream right away; It wasn't shock or fear, but pain. She quickly yanked the curtains closed again. The woman was on her knees with her hands pressed firmly against her eyes, moaning in agony.

"Please," she gasped, "don't ever do that again."

Mara stared at the woman. "What are you?" she breathed. But the woman was already asking questions of her own, and didn't hear.

"Where does that much light even come from? How can it be so powerful?"

Mara hesitated. She knew about the sun, of course, but she was no scientist; she wouldn't be able to explain how it worked or where it came from the way Riffolk probably could. Women weren't allowed to study academics beyond primary school. Instead they were taught cooking and cleaning, etiquette and ladylike behaviour.

"The sun is a... sort of giant ball of fire and light, I think. It's what makes day and night; when the sun is up, that's day, and when it's gone, that's night."

The woman was staring at her blankly.

"Didn't you ever wonder why day is bright and night is dark before?" Mara asked slowly. She had wondered the very same thing when she was a child.

"We don't have the sun where I come from. Or day, or night. I've never seen that much light, or even heard of it."

Mara shook her head.

"That doesn't make sense. The sun goes around the entire world, everyone knows that. There's nowhere that the sun doesn't touch. It was made by God, so that plants could grow and people could see and feel the warmth of His love."

The words of the Priests always comforted her, and reciting them now filled her with certainty again. And miraculously, the woman was now looking at her with surprised elation.

"God? You mean the Creator?"

"Yes!" Mara almost squealed it. "God is the Creator of everything, He is our lord and saviour!"

The woman closed her eyes in relief, and Mara finally relaxed her fear and suspicion a little. If God's name brought this much happiness to the strange woman, she couldn't possibly be a demon, or a test, and certainly not one of the Godless tree people.

"It must be," the woman said to herself, "thank the Creator, it *must* be!"

"Must be what?"

"This is heaven, isn't it? I've been brought to the Creator's Kingdom after Tyra was attacked by the monsters?"

Tyra? Monsters? Mara had never heard of Tyra, but the woman's mention of monsters brought a shudder down her spine. Something finally occurred to her.

"What is your name?"

The woman glanced up at her, looking vulnerable and alone.

"Pera," she whispered, "what's yours?"

"My name is Mara Wats- Hayne. Mara Hayne. I'm very sorry Pera, but this is certainly not heaven," Mara said quietly. She finished the thought in her head. *God would never let someone like Riffolk into His Kingdom.*

They spent the rest of that day talking. Pera knew nothing at all about Ermoor, or Pandeia for that matter. Mara knew nothing about the mysterious land Pera came from either, and she was fascinated by it. It was called Tyra. It was a cold place, in perpetual darkness. As Pera spoke, Mara's fascination turned to shock, and then eventually to horror.

The Tyrans spent all of their time turning gigantic wheels that they called "wheels of life". If the wheels stopped, monsters appeared from nowhere and attacked, killing anyone in their path. Mara interrupted quietly.

"What do they do?"

Pera stopped talking, frowning at Mara.

"I told you, they kill us. As many as they can until we start turning-"

"No, the wheels. What do they do?"

"They... must be turned, they are the wheels of life." Pera looked as though she couldn't think clearly.

"They must keep turning to appease the Creator."

"But turning them must *do* something. That's how machines work."

"Machines? What are machines?"

Mara closed her eyes, trying not to get frustrated with the woman. She knew nothing about the world; nothing at all. At the same time, she wasn't sure she knew enough to explain things to Pera in a way she would understand.

"Machines make things easier for people. Things like lights, showers, carts, teleradios, ovens. They work on their own, powered by electricity that goes through pipes, which come up from-"

Mara almost choked on her own words as a sudden, horrible realisation swept through her mind. The night Pera had appeared; she mentioned the wheel rooms were empty, no one turning them; and the street lights had gone out...

"Oh, no. Oh no, no, no!"

Pera looked as horrified as Mara felt, her eyes wide and her already pale face ghostly. Mara got herself under control, but couldn't look Pera in the eyes as she voiced her fears.

"I think... I think I know what the wheels of life do."

Every building in Ermoor was powered by electricity. None of the citizens knew where it came from, and almost none of them cared. They were content in their comfortable lives, and taught to be grateful to God for what they had. Who in their right mind would question God for His gifts? Mara had previously been one of the people who didn't care where her comfort came from. More accurately, she had been too terrified to question it. God had seen fit to give her a life of luxury; if she asked why, He could just as easily take it away from her.

As she explained what she knew of electricity, which wasn't much at all, Pera's face grew stony. It had to come from somewhere, she had explained, and the cables which carried it always began and ended in the ground. Pera had come up from underneath Ermoor, in a world with no power or light, from a life of turning gigantic cogs. Mara had seen cogs turning inside a few of Riffolk's inventions. She was far from a genius, but she could put all of the information in front of her together, and it painted a horrifyingly clear picture.

"Riffolk Hayne is the Overseer for Scientific Advancement. He invented pretty much every modern machine in Ermoor. He designs and builds it all in his laboratory in Darkpoint. He couldn't possibly have designed the wheels of life, but he must surely be aware of them. How else could Ermoor have so much power?"

Pera shook her head. "No," she said, "I don't believe it. All of Tyra, all of my people, just to give you power? That's insane!"

Mara desperately tried to think of some other explanation, another way to link all of the clues together. Could they really be unrelated? Maybe Riffolk and the other Overseers didn't know where the power came from either? She hoped so, for their sake. Using people like that, a whole population, for electricity, was evil. God would punish those responsible. Riffolk was smarter than to defy God in such a horrific way. The thought that he might be aware of Tyra terrified her. But there was no other conclusion she could reach.

"I'm so, so sorry, Pera. I truly hope it isn't so. But I can't think of any other explanation."

Something happened suddenly within Pera's pale, squinting eyes; a complete change. Pera sat up straighter, her mouth hardening into a straight line, her eyes shining with something scary.

"I need to know," she said. Her voice was strong and even. She sounded like a different person.

"I need to see for myself. Take me to Riffolk's laboratory."

Elana

Kaizeluun were the best of the best. Legendary even among the Shenza. Elana was among the best of the *Kaizeluun*; she was aware of this. From the moment she passed the shadow trials and forged her *Kaizuun*, she was given the most secretive and most pressing missions by the *Duulshen*. Her current mission, to the grim and awful land of Ermoor, was easily the most important so far. *Find out what they're planning,* the *Duulshen* had told her, *Gather as much information as you can, and then stop them by any means. But above all, do not be seen!*

She was crouched inside a barrel, alongside others just like it full of luduk, the fish found around Shanaken. Luduk were exported to almost every country in Pandeia, except Ermoor. But Tarsium had open trade agreements with the Ermoori, and the Tarsi bought plenty of the fish from Shanaken. Elana simply had to accompany the fisher's boats to Tarsium, oversee the transaction and the loading of fish to a barge bound for Ermoor, then slip inside one of the barrels before it was loaded. Easy enough, especially since she could wrap herself in shadow and become almost invisible. She had been *Kaizeluun* for almost ten years now, and such magic was second nature to her. Each tattoo still tingled when she used the spell that corresponded to it; despite the years, she wasn't used to the feeling.

The journey to Ermoor took about a month by sea. She would be able to eat a little bit of fish when she needed to, but she didn't want to make the Ermoori suspicious. Her barrel had been snuck in and didn't appear on the barge's manifest, and by the time the barge arrived in Ermoor, she would be long gone; hopefully, they wouldn't think too much of an extra, empty barrel. But missing fish that they'd paid for? That would invite questions and investigation.

Luckily, there were spells which could help her survive the journey with little to no food or water. She had used them before, but only in her training. This journey would be a perfect test of her survival skills. She remained in the barrel, unmoving, for three days. No one had come to check on the cargo, and on the fourth day she finally pushed off the lid and climbed out. The cargo room was pitch black, long, low and narrow. Elana traced one of the tattoos next to her eye with a finger, and the darkness opened to her, hiding nothing. Satisfied that she was alone, she replaced the barrel's lid and walked down the cargo room to the very back. She shuffled some barrels around to create a narrow space between them and the wall where she could comfortably lay down, and prepared for the long journey ahead.

Pera

The words burned into her heart as fiercely as the sun's light had burned into her eyes. Tyra, her home, her entire life and people, were nothing but a source of power for the people living above them. It didn't make sense, but at the same time there was some small part of her that understood it was true. How long had this been happening? How had it started?

Even worse, this woman's husband seemed to be some sort of creator of machines, using the power taken from Tyra to build things that gave the people of Ermoor comfortable, luxurious lives. It made her sick, and furious. A deep, aching rage trembled through her body from her very soul. The power of it darkened her vision, inky red bleeding into the corners of the beautiful bedroom.

She would kill this man, and anyone else who had dared take so much from Tyra while keeping them in the dark. There was no one she could trust, that was clear. This woman, who's husband was central to the exploitation of her people, was no exception. For some reason she seemed to think they were on friendly terms, and that was fine for now; it would be useful. But Pera had a mission; and she would do anything to complete it.

She turned to the woman, hiding as much of her rage as she could.

"I need to know," she said. "I need to see for myself. Take me to Riffolk's laboratory."

"I – I can't," Mara said, "not right now. Not until after dark, and we'll have to be careful."

"What are you talking about?"

"Well without a man to escort us, we can't leave the mansion. I've snuck out a few times though, and if we're careful, we can-"

"A man to escort us? Why would we need a man?" Mara looked confused. Her brow furrowed.

"It's... the rules," she hesitated, "God says that a woman's rightful place is below a man. It's how things have always been; how things *must* be. A woman's purpose is to serve, to clean, and to bear children. We must stay in the house, we must stay quiet, and we must do as we're told. It is God's will, for the good of all."

She added the last sentence in one breath, her eyes down, the words dry and automatic. As though she'd said it a thousand times before. As though she'd be punished if she didn't. Pera felt sick. She almost pitied Mara; would have if not for her people using the Tyrans as unwitting labourers for generations beyond count. For a while, she had assumed the Creator her people worshipped was the same as the God Mara continually talked about, but it simply could not be true.

"What kind of God forces half of His subjects to be inferior to the other half?"

Mara stared at her in horror.

"God loves us all! He does not force us, he gives us life and love and comfortable lives! But there are rules to follow if we are to be allowed into Heaven; only the pure can live for eternity in His arms."

Now it was Pera's turn to stare, horrified, as Mara spoke. It was nothing like what she'd been taught about the Creator. She couldn't help but wonder which version was correct; The Creator who loved all His people equally, or the Creator who demanded rules and restrictions in return for His love. There couldn't be more than one God... could there? The idea was somehow terrifying. Mara talked for a while, teaching her about the Ermoori version of God. The more she spoke, the more scared Pera became.

Ermoor's streets were cold and far too bright, the twinkling lights stabbing at her eyes. Pera was slowly getting used to it, although she didn't enjoy them; but the fog made her uncomfortable. It felt oppressive somehow, as though it was set on purpose to stop people wandering at night.

As they walked through the streets, she felt claustrophobic, despite being outside. There was something wrong with Ermoor. Everything wrong with it. So many subtle things, small uncomfortable things like the way Mara spoke about God and the fact she had servants to do her bidding.

She glanced at the girl walking beside her. She still seemed scared to be walking outside without a man present. It disgusted Pera; there was no part of the concept that made sense to her. It was almost as though women were seen as belongings, not real people but some sort of decoration, to be carried around on the arm of a man like an accessory. The more she thought about it, the more furious she became.

Mara wasn't just accepting her place in Ermoor's society, either; she embraced it. Totally believed it. There seemed to be no doubt at all in her mind that Ermoor was perfect just the way it was. She believed that women were underneath men just as fervently as the men of Ermoor believed it.

Riffolk's lab was a little while away, and Pera found the walk just fed her rage, where usually a walk through Tyra's corridors helped calm her down. She was certain Riffolk knew about the Wheels, and that he was intentionally exploiting Tyra. Mara seemed genuinely unaware; her sudden realisation about the Wheels was believable. But was this girl really innocent? How innocent could a person be, if they loved a society as broken and corrupt as Ermoor? Her belief in the Ermoori God was terrifying; so many of the "rules" of her religion were absolutely repulsive.

She suddenly realised this could easily be a trap. Mara could be just as awful as the rest of Ermoor, could be in league with her husband. Pera might have been manipulated into wanting to search the lab in the first place... *No,* she decided, *this girl is genuine. Naive, stupid maybe, but not plotting against me.* They walked silently, and Pera occasionally caught glimpses of Mara staring at her. She walked a little too close to Pera, and though the cold was brutal, the closeness was worse.

Antony

Antony dried off the last vial in the set, placing it in the second drawer down in the cabinet in the lab's corner. Gurgling filled the lab's silence as the basin drained of soapy water. He was the last assistant there, and he'd stayed back more than two hours after the others had gone home. Overseer Hayne was a miserable prick. He'd picked on Antony since day one of the internship, and for no reason other than his surname happened to be Fleming. It wasn't Antony's fault that his great grandfather invented the light bulb. He didn't understand why Overseer Hayne was so jealous and petty over such an invention when he'd personally revolutionised all of Ermoor's technological advancement since.

Almost everything had been cleaned, packed, and stored. Since Overseer Hayne's project was shut down almost two weeks ago, the assistants had been tasked with shutting down the lab. It was a monumental task; the lab was complex and busy, with hundreds of instruments performing dozens of experiments. Today was the final day, and for the first time Antony had ever seen, the lab was empty, dark and silent.

He wiped off the suds and water from the basin until it gleamed, each swipe of the cloth making him more angry. He shouldn't have to stay behind when all the other assistants had left. Despite his anger, there was a savage victory in the act of cleaning the lab; Overseer Hayne had been shut down. His work, his precious projects, all of it stopped. Antony wasn't aware of the details of most of the projects being worked on. Just like the other assistants, he was given small individual tasks with no contextual information, and no understanding of how his work fit into that of his colleagues.

A few boxes sat on one of the smooth benches in the room's centre. They had to be put in a storage room, the room locked, then he'd have to make a final sweep to make sure everything was packed. He walked to the bench on which they sat, laying a hand on either side of the top box.

A scuffling sound echoed down one of the corridors, clear in the heavy silence. *The courtyard?* There was no way into the courtyard except through the lab itself. Antony frowned. Maybe one of the other assistants hadn't left after all. He took a few steps towards the courtyard door before his mind caught up. *It could be Overseer Hayne.* The assistants all knew there was a secret lab, though none of them knew where the entrance was. The courtyard made sense...

If it was Overseer Hayne, Antony didn't want to be present when he entered the lab. An assistant went missing not long ago, and as far as Antony was aware, the Overseer hadn't even particularly disliked the man. If Antony ran into his superior this late, completely alone, with no witnesses, he may go missing too.

But the scuffling sound occurred again, and it sounded like two sets of feet. Maybe even three, but certainly more than one. Overseer Hayne never let *anyone* into his secret lab. His frown melting slightly, Antony went to check which of his fellow assistants had decided a late night party in the lab's courtyard was a good idea.

He opened the door, but the courtyard was empty. He'd expected two or three assistants, maybe a smuggled cask of Omati wine, but the courtyard was as dark and silent as the lab itself.

"What -" he managed to say, and the door slammed back into him, knocking him to the floor. Before he could get his bearings, a dark creature was on top of him, hitting and grabbing. He tried to stop it, tried to grab its hands, but he was caught at an awkward angle between it and the ground. It smashed his ribs, his shoulder blade, and then the back of his head.

Blackness exploded through his vision, points of twisting white light glaring at random until he faded with them into nothing.

Mara

It took a while to explain to Pera that women weren't allowed to leave the house without a man escorting them. She didn't understand why women were underneath men. Mara tried explaining that it was God's will, that things had always been this way, that it was taught in the church, but still she didn't understand.

Eventually she dropped the subject, agreeing to sneak out after dark as Mara had done on the night Pera appeared. Mara was terrified, but Pera wanted to go as soon as possible. They agreed on the night after next, to give them some time to prepare and make sure they had as much of a plan as possible.

Their plan consisted of wearing dark clothing, sneaking out the way Mara had before, and taking the shortest possible path to Riffolk's lab. Darkpoint was only one district over, right next to Ironhaven, so the journey wouldn't take more than a couple of hours. Mara had never been there before, so their plan ended there. Once they arrived, they would have to find a way in without being spotted.

The weather was on their side. It was awful, cold and foggy, but that was what they wanted. They snuck through the darkened streets, huddled together in thick black coats. Two weeks had passed since the monster had brought Pera to the surface, but they already trusted each other beyond doubt. It felt good to Mara. Even through the terror of trying to sneak into Riffolk's lab, and walking through the dark city at night, having a friend to trust felt good.

When they reached it, Riffolk's laboratory loomed over them through the fog, as though it knew they were coming and had been waiting. Lights glared through several of the windows like monstrous glowing eyes. The thought that she didn't really know Riffolk only occurred to her in that moment. Before now, he was her husband first, and a reclusive genius second. But there was so much she didn't know about him, and it suddenly terrified her.

They stood together, Pera and her, staring at the laboratory. What actually happened in there? Mara had always pictured bubbling vials of chemicals, complex machinery with countless moving parts, and sparking electricity shooting in every direction. But what if it was worse? What if Riffolk really was doing something awful within those walls?

Pera cleared her throat and glanced at Mara.

"What now?" she whispered.

Mara looked from her to the lab and back again. She shrugged; their plan ended here. They knew as much about this building as each other. Suddenly their situation caught up with her, and she started giggling. Pera looked at her as though she'd thrown her clothes off and screamed at the top of her lungs. Then she started giggling too.

"Should we at least look at the front door?"

"Yes, let's go."

They wandered closer. The front door of the laboratory looked like a hunched monster built from steel, its heavy door barring the way like massive, terrible fangs. A small box jutted from the wall next to the door with numbered buttons; they would need to know some kind of code to enter this way.

The back of the laboratory was almost unreachable. They circled around it as much as they could, but it backed onto a group of factories and other buildings on three sides. By the time they'd squeezed through a dirty narrow alley, scrambled over a tall fence and climbed up a high brick wall, they were filthy and exhausted. From the brick wall they perched on, they could see a back entrance which opened onto a small courtyard. The door was much smaller, and Mara couldn't see any code box next to it.

"This is it," Pera said, "we can get in this way."

Mara nodded, her eyes scanning the courtyard for a safe way down; nothing. It would be just as difficult getting into the courtyard as it was getting to where they were now. They rested for a while, sitting in silence in the fog. Pera occasionally broke the silence with a long, heavy breath. The fog seemed to effect her lungs somehow, and she sounded as though she could barely breathe at all. Still, she had kept up with Mara and never complained. When Mara felt her energy returning, she touched Pera's arm and pointed at the courtyard. Pera nodded. The fog was starting to recede, the back door into the lab becoming clearer with each passing minute. It was time to move.

Pera lowered her as far as she could reach down the wall. Her feet were still dangling more than a metre above the ground. She counted down in short, sharp breaths, and Pera dropped her. Hard pavement slammed into her feet, and she crumpled to the ground. Her left ankle had rolled slightly, but overall the fall was harmless. Pera was carefully lowering herself over the edge of the wall, hanging by her hands. She was higher than Mara had been, but when she let go, she kicked against the wall, landing and rolling with some forward momentum. She sprang back up to her feet, ready to continue. Mara had never seen anything like it, let alone from a woman.

"Where did you learn that?"

"Tyra is full of secret places to climb. I was a very curious child... I guess I'm still too curious for my own good." She smirked and gestured to the lab's back door.

"Shall we?"

They made their way to the door, Mara limping slightly. As they approached, the doorknob rattled. From inside the courtyard, there was nowhere they could go. Pera grabbed her wrist and yanked her towards the door. Her ankle pulsed, hot and sudden, as she was forced to run, and the pain forced a low hiss from her lips.

The door opened, and Pera dragged her behind its swing before they caught a glimpse of whoever entered the courtyard. Pera shoved her against the wall hard, holding her hand over Mara's mouth and her face close enough their noses almost touched. A sudden image of Riffolk entered her mind, and despite the dangerous situation and the fear scattering her thoughts, that same disturbing exhilaration welled up deep within her.

Pera was strong; incredibly strong. Mara couldn't move, pinned against the rough stone wall by this mysterious woman. She suddenly felt more excited than any time she'd been with Riffolk. He was a monster, using her when he wanted and discarding her. But Pera wasn't using her strength to take anything from Mara; she was protecting her. She looked into Pera's eyes, seeing the deep well of strength there. Courage and sadness pooled within her eyes too, and something much darker; a pure, unfettered rage lurked behind her pale eyes.

But it wasn't directed at Mara, and knowing that stoked the fire of her excitement. She felt safe. For the first time in her life, she felt as though someone was on her side. It didn't even matter who came through the lab door, Pera would protect her.

One of her hands was free. Without thinking, she placed it on Pera's hip. The Tyran woman recoiled a little, a look of confusion bordering on disgust slashed across her face. Mara's sense kicked back in, and her stomach roiled. *Oh God,* she thought as Pera stepped away from her, w*hat was I thinking?*

The door was almost fully open, close to touching the two women, and Pera stepped into it as she backed away from Mara.

"What -" a voice said.

Pera shoved the door as hard as she could and bolted around it. Thuds and grunts followed, but Mara remained against the wall, scared and ashamed. When silence settled into the courtyard again, Mara took a tentative step around the door. Pera was kneeling over the unconscious man, looking through his pockets.

"I don't know what that was," Pera said without raising her eyes, "but it won't happen again."

Mara gave a ragged sigh that sounded even to herself like a sob. Pera finally glanced up at her, eyebrows raised.

"I'm sorry," Mara said.

She didn't know what else she could say. It seemed to be enough. Pera took whatever it was she needed from the man, and they entered the laboratory together.

Elana

Ermoor was massive. It was crowded, both with buildings and people. The streets were organised and perpetually clean. All the people dressed richly; extravagant fabrics, bright colours and lavish metal buttons, clasps and jewellery. It was utterly different to anything Elana had ever seen before. She had been to Tarsium of course, but where the Tarsi countryside and even the districts featured grass and trees, Ermoor was a stark, lifeless landscape. Beautiful, but without any natural life other than the people themselves. She was horrified. The *Duulshen* held a dim enough view of Tarsium, with its buildings that squatted on the ground and its lack of giant trees. They'd given her no indication of what to expect, and now she realised why; they looked at Tarsium with idle disdain, but they *hated* Ermoor. If they had told her what they really thought of this lifeless place, even she might have questioned their choice in sending her here.

But it is *necessary,* she thought, *regardless of how I or the* Duulshen *feel about it.* Tensions were high between the two countries, and the most recent attempted invasions were becoming even more brutal for both sides. Elana had to find out more about the Ermoori; how their technology worked, whether they had weaknesses, any critical information she could gather to bring an end to the fighting. The *Duulshen* hated Ermoor, but the Shenza were a peaceful, life-loving people at heart, and they abhorred battle and killing.

Elana slept in a small bedroll on the roof of a tall building in the middle of the city. Standing on its wide ledge, she could see everything. It wasn't quite as tall as the trees in Shanaken, but considering the fact that it had been built by people, it was breathtaking. Still, despite its impressive scope, Ermoor had a dead weight about it, a feeling that pushed down on Elana's spirits. It was the exact opposite feeling she had when walking through the forests. There, she could feel the presence of Amalus, the God of life, flowing through everything. Here, there was no flow at all, no sense of life or magic or soul. After a week, she was certain without needing to investigate: there was no God in Ermoor. The realisation left her more upset than she would have believed.

Riffolk

Riffolk stared back at Symond with barely repressed rage. Moments like this tested his self control. Symond had the gall, after all Riffolk's work, to shut down the project.

"It's just too dangerous, Overseer Hayne. I took another look at the blueprints. There are too many inconsistencies, too much left to chance."

Riffolk took a long, steadying breath. He was too close to losing control. Symond had no idea how much danger he was in, and far too much faith in his own safety.

"I leave nothing to chance, Lord Commander."

"It seems to me, Overseer Hayne, that you've placed the safety of the entire city in the hands of an unknown creature, without proper study, and without a full understanding of what it can do."

Symond's hands were clenching, his eyes jittery. He took shuffled half steps in place. Riffolk had seen the lower class citizens act the same way; the ones who were addicted to chemical stimulants. Symond wasn't stupid enough to get himself addicted to drugs, but there was clearly something happening to his mind that didn't bode well. He looked Riffolk straight in the eyes, and his voice took on an oddly personal tone.

"Please, Riffolk. Surely you understand how insane this is. What is that thing? Do you even know?"

"I know more than you could possibly imagine."

"I *need* to shut this down, Riffolk! I'm sorry, but I just don't have a choice."

That struck a chord with Riffolk. Symond had a lot of power over military matters, almost total authority. Additionally, he'd always been supportive of the project; at least vocally. This sudden change was obviously triggered by something. Someone had influenced the Lord Commander. It was no mystery who had the skill and motive. *The Shenza woman.* Letting her go had been a mistake, but at the time he didn't have a choice.

He didn't have any way to hunt her down and destroy her without causing irreparable damage to the city and, more importantly, to his reputation. Still, even though Symond allowing himself to be used as a pawn was pathetic, and certainly not ideal, it wasn't enough to slow Riffolk's work down. As always, he had several plans in place to mitigate setbacks such as this. Arguing would be pointless; whatever the Shenza woman had done to convince Symond was obviously quite effective.

"I see," he said, "I'm sorry too. I live to serve the Twelve Crowns, of course. If my project is no longer in their best interests, I will step down."

As predicted, Symond faltered at Riffolk's meek acceptance. He'd be suspicious, no doubt, but his suspicion wouldn't last after the project was shut down. The only concern now was how much more the Shenza woman would try to meddle in his affairs. Her mission clearly wasn't over, and it was clear she could be quite a threat. He needed to catch her again, find out more about the magic she used, and get his hands on that black sword of hers.

In the meantime, he would focus on the project. After the shut-down, he would have no assistants and none of the city's resources. It was annoying, but amounted to nothing more than a minor inconvenience; he was the wealthiest man in Ermoor, and if he needed to spend his own money to keep the project going, he gladly would. And with the project officially shut down, the Shenza woman may not actively pursue him any longer, if he kept his activities quiet.

"You'll step down? Just like that?"

"Yes, of course, Lord Commander. I disagree, strongly, with your assessment of the situation. But I am a servant of Ermoor, and if the project must be shut down in the best interests of our country, I will obey and shut it down."

Symond simply looked at him, utterly baffled. Riffolk was done with his stupidity; there was nothing to be gained by dragging the conversation out any longer.

"If that is all, Lord Commander, I would ask your leave to attend to my own matters. Shutting down a fully functioning laboratory is quite a task."

"Oh, yes of course. Very well." Symond paused, frowning, and managed a few seconds of eye contact. "Thank you, Riffolk," he said in that same strangely personal tone.

Riffolk left without another word, barely containing a smile as he reached the door. Symond was barely even a pawn any more; the Lord Commander of Ermoor's military had been overtaken by a Shenza savage. His good humour carried him all the way to his lab, and affecting a sour expression as he broke the news to his assistants was more of a struggle than he anticipated.

The lab took a while to clean out – almost two weeks. Riffolk spent most of it yelling at his assistants, keeping up the appearance of the slighted scientist. They bought it, of course. When he wasn't completely silent, yelling at them was common; they made many mistakes. When the cleaning and packing started nearing completion, he retired to his underground lab. The assistants suspected its existence, but had no proof and wouldn't dare report it to the Lord Commander, even if they could somehow get the message to him.

On the last day, he ordered the Fleming boy to stay after the other assistants left to finish off the last of the cleaning, for no other reason than it was fun to watch him fume. That done, he returned to his own lab, and its still fully functioning equipment. After the Shenza woman's meddling, he was siphoning far less energy from the creature than he should have been able to. Obtaining more of the energy cables would be incredibly difficult, so he'd had to make do with a makeshift repair that was nowhere near as effective. He was just glad the Shenza either hadn't known or hadn't thought about sabotaging the ingoing wires; if she'd cut off the system that kept the creature sedated, he'd be dealing with a very different disaster.

He was able to run the lab from the power he was siphoning, but he had to ration the energy to only the most important instruments. Remaining off the main lab's power grid was absolutely essential, even if it meant compromising on the speed of his work. The one real obstacle was mass production of weapons and armour; with the project shut down, he would be unable to use the factories that were previously at his disposal.

Perhaps he could replace the Lord Commander somehow, with someone more compliant. It wouldn't be a stretch to prove Symond's mental state was compromised; he was clearly insane, after all.

Mid-thought, the proximity alarm for the back courtyard lit up, pulsing red and lancing through his concentration. Dismissing it as Fleming mucking around, he went back to his work. He was close to calibrating a much more portable energy battery for his new weapons, and meant to have the prototype completed within the next few days. Whenever he came this close to finishing a design, everything else became background noise.

The problem was energy displacement. He could transfer and store more than enough power, but the excess tended to either leak or overload the energy housing matrix and corrupt the battery. He'd discovered a new lightweight material that could absorb and retain energy, but that just introduced a new problem; once the energy was absorbed, drawing it out again was almost impossible in a portable system.

The addition of another material may help; a catalyst, that when connected to the stored energy, may cause the energy to transfer naturally... Riffolk was sure he'd seen something similar, in his travels. He'd seen a lot of impossible things, things even he couldn't explain. The difficulty was leaving Ermoor again.

Another proximity alarm went off; this time for the storage room that served as the secret lab's hidden entrance. Unlike the courtyard, this alarm pulled him right out of his creative trance. He left his equipment, grabbed a scatter gun and his new prototype dart gun, and headed for the entrance.

Pera

What the hell was that? She thought as they entered the lab. Mara had touched her like a lover, caressed her hip as though she was about to kiss her. Ermoor just became more and more strange. Pera had barely even been friendly to her, but Mara obviously took it as a deep and meaningful connection. The girl was a mess. She was just glad the door opened when it had; she had no interest in girls in that way, let alone a naive little rich girl from a corrupt, horrible place like Ermoor.

The lab was nice and dark, and even better, completely empty. She strode into the corridors, ready for anything. The lab was the complete opposite of Tyra; it was clean, warm, and everything was straight lines and perfect angles. Tyra was a mess of rough stone, odd curves and cold, feral darkness. But the feel of walking through a maze of corridors was familiar enough that it brought the two worlds crashing in on each other like a terrible dream merging with real life.

Tyra was huge, with hundreds, if not thousands of corridors reaching every little corner of the city. Pera, unlike most other Tyrans, had spent a lot of her childhood exploring the lesser used corridors. Darkness, mixed with the fact that every corridor in Tyra looked essentially the same, forced every Tyran to develop an uncanny sense of direction. But where most Tyrans ended up relying on the bump-and-line markers on the walls to navigate, Pera could map any building or room with her eyes closed; with one cursory sweep of her hands on the walls. Although the lab was dark, compared to Tyra it may as well have been illuminated by the Ermoori sun, and with sight on her side, mapping the corridors was easy.

The layout of the building made sense to her. It wasn't quite as efficient as Tyra, but it was logical and tidy. The fact that the lab was totally empty was odd; not the lack of people, as it was late at night according to Mara, but the total lack of equipment and furniture. One room they'd passed, close to the door they entered through, contained a pile of boxes, but other than that the entire place was deserted. Combining that with the fact that Riffolk wasn't at the mansion and spent most of his time at his lab told Pera almost all she needed to know. A quick walk up and down each corridor confirmed the rest.

Every space was accounted for in the lab; any free space used for storage, rooms, or utilities. Every corridor led somewhere specific, or joined another corridor. The rooms were laid out more or less in orderly fashion, evenly along every corridor. Every space account for... except one. Behind a small storage room at the end of a corridor, there was enough space to fit a large cupboard or even another small room. The back wall of the storage room was made from slightly separated large panels.

When she was younger, she'd stumbled upon several different surprising rooms and features of Tyra. But they all paled in comparison to this; she'd found something that the greatest scientific mind in Ermoor was trying to keep hidden.

Mara

Dark corridors snaked through the lab, all cold smooth surfaces. Mara moved slowly, letting Pera take the lead. She listened for sounds further ahead and only heard her and Pera's footsteps. No one else was in the lab. Locked doors lined the corridors. They reached an open door, and Mara glanced inside. It looked as though it was the main lab room; it was massive, full of metal benches and lined with basins and cabinets. But it was utterly bare, no equipment at all. Nothing except for a few boxes sitting on one of the benches.

They moved on. Each corridor looked exactly the same, and it wasn't long before Mara felt lost. Pera seemed comfortable with their whereabouts, however, and walked slowly but surely through the lab. Mara followed Pera through endless corridors for what felt like hours. Almost every door was locked, and behind those that weren't were more empty rooms.

Pera spent a lot of time looking around at the walls at random, stopping and staring at nothing Mara could identify. They doubled back a lot, and for all Mara knew, they could have kept going up and down the same corridor dozens of times. Pera mumbled under her breath a lot as they walked. Mara couldn't understand a word of it.

Finally, Pera led them to a corridor that ended in yet another storeroom. She stared at it, mumbled some more, then moved close. Mara couldn't see what she was doing, but she heard a clicking sound and then the storeroom door opened. The room beyond was small but mostly empty. A few storage boxes sat on shelves along the walls either side of the room. Opposite the door, a blank wall stared back at them.

Pera strolled to the blank wall without hesitation. She leaned in close, her head turned to the side as though the wall was whispering to her. She ran her hands over its surface, frowning. Moments passed in silence, Mara growing impatient as Pera aimlessly inspected the wall.

"What are you doing?" Mara said. Pera gave no response, but shook her head slightly, her frown deepening. Just as Mara was about to ask again, Pera's eyes grew wide and she grinned, glancing back at Mara.

"I knew it!" She said, then turned back to the wall. Her hand pushed against a small section, one of many square plates set against the wall at random. It bent inwards under her palm, made a clicking sound, then swung out. Underneath it was a number pad. Mara stared as Pera leaned in close to inspect the pad.

"How... how could you possibly know that was there?"

She grunted and continued staring closely at the number pad. Running her fingers over the buttons slowly, she whispered to herself. A quiet click sounded from the wall. Mara couldn't believe it; Pera was figuring it out, unlocking whatever the number pad was hiding! But Pera turned, face pale and eyes wide. She shook her head, but before either of them could run, the wall slid away silently.

Riffolk Hayne stood in the now open space, pointing a gun directly at Pera's face.

"*Mara*?" Riffolk's face twisted, rage mingled with bafflement. He looked nothing like her husband in that moment; he barely even looked human.

"What are you doing here?"

Before she could answer, he pulled a very different looking gun from his belt with his free hand, and shot Pera in the chest. She recoiled and fell to the floor, and Mara's vision drained of colour. Nothing made sense any more. She wanted to ask Riffolk what was happening, why he'd shot Pera, why he looked so angry, but he raised the odd weapon to aim at her. The bang of its discharge sounded hollow and distant, but she felt a thud in her chest and a cold swept over her body. When it reached her head, she was dragged into darkness as though a thick, cold blanket had been pulled over her face.

Elana

Travelling through Ermoor was much easier than she thought it would be. Their tall buildings were almost as plentiful as the trees in Shanaken, and far easier to walk and run on. The only problem was that after several weeks, her magic seemed to be dwindling. She felt weaker. Slower. The food she was able to steal was drab and flavourless, as dead as the landscape from which it came. There were no fruit-bearing trees or bushes, no naturally growing food of any kind that she could find. The people were pale, rigid, and formal. They seemed to be obsessed with wealth and clothing, and worshipped a God which they had named simply "God". Worshipping their God was done indoors, in ornate buildings where they gathered in an eerie, mournful silence.

Has their God died? She thought to herself. *It makes sense... I definitely don't feel the presence of Gods or magic here.* An entire country ritualistically mourning a dead God several times per week... Elana shuddered. These people were disturbingly morbid. *Why not just worship a different God? Amalus could give them so much knowledge...* But even as she thought it she knew it would never happen. The Ermoori had been fighting to destroy Amalus and Shanaken for thousands of years. They would never worship her God.

She discovered more every day about their way of life. More importantly, she had located the head of their military, and the source of their technological power; the two most important people in Ermoor. Her priorities now were to take as much information as possible from them and return to the *Duulshen* to report, as well as sabotage their work as much as possible to slow Ermoor down.

Lord Commander Arthor Symond, leader of the Ermoori military, was insane. Elana realised this within minutes of seeing him for the first time. He was older, his hair slightly greying, his no doubt formerly impressive figure slightly sagging. Despite his age, he held an unmistakable air of unquestioned authority; a very dangerous amount of power for a madman to wield. He managed somehow to retain the illusion of sanity in the presence of his inferiors, which only made him that much more dangerous. But the first time Elana snuck into his office, he had been alone. He was muttering to himself, his tone swapping from rage to sulky humility and back again with terrifying suddenness. The whole time he spoke, he had been staring at a blank wall.

"Are you there?"

"Hmph. Why do you never respond then?"

"Yes of course, I apologise profusely, it's not my place to... Yes, of course!"

"They will! I will make sure of it, even if I have to gut them personally!"

"Oh please, please have mercy, I only meant that I... Oh my lord."

He stopped talking then, mumbling incoherently instead until his voice trailed off into silence. Elana perched in the shadows on a high bookshelf in a corner of the room. It was one of the only places a person could hide, and even Elana had to twist uncomfortably to fit. Every other room and building in Ermoor was ostentatiously decorated, but this man was simplistic and utilitarian. His office contained only that which he needed. The bookshelf was massive, but simple and sturdy, and filled with thick tomes that seemed to each be relevant to Ermoor's military and history in some way. No rich carpets, no hideously expensive artwork, no ornate furniture.

He mumbled again, then sat in a chair against the wall. The chair behind his desk, which was large and comfortable-looking but otherwise as plain as the rest of the office, sat ignored by its owner. He hunched forward and put his head in his hands, breathing slowly and deeply.

"Why me?" he said.

She stayed in his office until he left, then rifled through everything she could find. Mostly routine reports on soldier training and weapon production, as well as summaries of previous 'explorations' to Shanaken. She saw a recent file and stopped. *5,000 men sent on exploration to Shanaken, 7th month of 1772.* She knew that by whatever measurement the Ermoori used, 1772 was the current year.

They're invading right now, she thought, *and I'm rifling through some office across the sea.* Trembling with the injustice of knowing her people were fighting without her, she put the file back where it came from. She let out a ragged sigh, closing her eyes and trying to focus. *They can handle it,* she thought, *there are many* Kaizeluun *in Shanaken right now, and tens of thousands of* Daishen. *They need me here more than they need me on the battlefield.*

It felt weak, even to herself, but it still helped. She'd fought the Ermoori many times, and the Shenza always won. They would win without her too. As much as she wished she was back home fighting, she had a mission to complete. Failing the *Duulshen* was not an option.

After Lord Commander Arthor Symond, Elana watched Overseer Riffolk Hayne. Much younger, with black hair and deep, intelligent eyes, Hayne was in his prime; though still nowhere near as physically intimidating as Symond. Elana suspected the Overseer was also insane, but in a cold, calculating, and much more terrifying way. He was always composed, always quiet, and always ten steps ahead. Being around him made Elana feel as though she was being watched, as though he knew she was there and was simply playing with her. She'd never felt so unsettled in her life. Shadows wrapped her in darkness, and she had never been so glad for the comforting invisibility of Shadow Magic. Hayne's laboratory was almost as stark as Symonds' office, although there were far more places to hide.

Hayne's assistants scurried around the lab constantly, scattering around Hayne as he walked through them thoughtlessly. He treated them the same way he treated the upper class nobility of Ermoor, and while that would normally indicate a humble sense of equality, in Hayne's case it simply meant he spared no thought for anyone but himself.

His eyes scanned over his terrified assistants in the same dispassionate way he studied his scientific equipment. Elana was certain that if a fire were to break out in the room, Hayne would attempt to save the most expensive or most useful equipment well before the assistant's safety even occurred to him.

Just off the main laboratory, a small office branched off from the corridor. Elana swept into it from an air duct in the ceiling. She was becoming accustomed to the odd Ermoori architecture, and had found useful ways of navigating the insides of buildings without being spotted. Boxes of neatly bound notebooks filled most of the office, and a small desk with a reading lamp took up one corner. Lining the walls were metal sets of drawers with locks set in each. It was cramped and stuffy, and filled with secrets.

Elana dropped silently to the floor, leaving the metal panel leading into the air duct open; escape was always on her mind in these closed-off Ermoori buildings. She scanned through the notebooks as quickly as she could. The Ermoori language was relatively simple to learn, and although she was far from fluent, Elana could read most basic words. She could understand and speak Ermoori at a conversational level too, and although it was an ugly language, she'd found it fascinating to learn.

The *Duulshen* possessed knowledge of the history, language and political landscape of each of the countries of Pandeia, and quite often ordered infiltration missions to obtain more up to date information. Most of the time, the information they held was simply kept for historical purposes. But it could also be used to win wars, and in Ermoor's case, the information the *Duulshen* held was the key to the Shenza repeatedly defeating the invasion attempts of the oppressive country.

Most of the notebooks contained complex scientific language that Elana didn't understand; her knowledge of the Ermoori language only stretched so far. Some were simpler, detailing the goings on of the laboratory in a diary-like fashion. The words were neat, concise, and somehow cold. It was clearly Hayne's handwriting.

She read the diary notebooks much more closely, trying to remember as much as she could. Luckily, the entries were dated, and she was able to find a notebook written within the last year. Most of the entries just described laboratory conditions, progress made on some unexplained project, and kept a record of dates and times of any significant events. One entry glared at her from the page, stopping her breath as suddenly as if her throat had been cut:

SUCCESS! Taranos lives. Energy output exceeds expectations. Progress now ahead of schedule. Mass production to begin within a fortnight. Estimated full delivery of working units is 2 years. Meeting with LC in 3 days to discuss logistics of invasion.

It was dated two days ago. Elana stared at the entry, committing the words to memory. So there was yet another invasion planned. *Taranos lives. What does that mean?* Some kind of new, undoubtedly horrible weapon was being built in large numbers. The good news was that Elana had plenty of time to try to stop it, and a meeting she could eavesdrop on the next day. 'LC' obviously stood for Lord Commander. It was a meeting she definitely needed to see.

Riffolk

Riffolk had seen things that shouldn't exist. He'd seen magic, and Gods, and technology that made his own inventions look like ancient relics. He was very difficult to surprise. But when the hidden entrance to his lab slid open and he came face to face with his young, naive wife, he was honestly baffled.

"*Mara?* What are you doing here?"

She looked just as shocked as he was, though he noted a healthy amount of fear in her expression as well. *Good*, he thought, *she's right to fear me*. It was immediately apparent that Mara wouldn't answer his question; she was frozen with fear. The other woman, the Tyran, looked to be a fighter. Before the situation could escalate, he shot them both with the dart gun and dragged them into the lab once they were unconscious.

His metal binding traps, though almost useless against the Shenza assassin, were incredibly effective on normal humans. The two girls were held in place, totally unable to move. He went back to his battery and worked until he heard them stir. He turned to see Mara staring uneasily at the creature.

"I'm surprised, Mara. And disappointed. What exactly were you hoping to achieve by coming here?"

The other one spoke for her. He greatly enjoyed the subservience of his wife, but when it came to talking, she seemed unable to when nervous, and was perpetually nervous around him. He preferred her remaining silent most of the time, so it usually didn't bother him, but when he asked her a question he expected an answer. The Tyran, however, was all fire and rebellion. She would be interesting to break.

"I'm here to stop you," she said, "and so is she."

He ignored other the girl, keeping his eyes on Mara. Provoking both of them at the same time; Mara hated his stare, and the Tyran was desperate for an emotional reaction. He kept his voice soft, low, and familiar, as though the married couple were alone sharing a private conversation.

"Is this true, Mara?"

She nodded, terrified. He expected her to deny it, beg and plead, but the slight nod of her head was resolute. Even through her terror, she'd found enough strength to defy him. Fury enveloped him, and for a moment, even though he remained totally still, his vision disappeared and all he saw was a wash of red. When the rage subsided enough that he could see again, the two girls were staring at him in horrified anticipation. He managed a smile, just to push them further into unease. He decided to show them some of his real work; the project that was shut down by Symond and the Twelve Crowns.

A whir sounded from the metal arms as they released the two girls. Riffolk's scatter gun and dart gun were in his hands again; they didn't dare move. The Tyran eyed him, pure defiance painted on her features. Tyrans, though naive enough to have been unknowing slaves for over a thousand years, were undeniably tenacious. He'd read reports of the recent escape attempt; "the uprising", as it was being referred to. They'd put up quite a fight, according to his contacts in the military and Symond's office.

They were beaten, of course, and put back underground. Their situation must be so much worse; now that they knew they were slaves, their work moving the energy mills would be robbed of its previously glorious purpose. Riffolk found the idea particularly amusing. Having a whole people unite against their oppressors, rising up together to fight; only to be crushed and swept back into servitude within a matter of hours.

Luckily, the military had contained the fight to the district where it had started. The entrance to the Tyran underground was within the military district of Dreadhold anyway, of course, where it could be under constant surveillance and instantly defended. The general population had no idea Tyra even existed, let alone that its people had just staged a revolution.

Riffolk knew it was the Shenza woman, even if no one else in Ermoor was aware of her existence. The Tyrans themselves could never have figured out how to leave their dreary little world. The girl with Mara was looking at him as though she was just waiting for her opportunity to strike. From the look in her eyes, she had no idea her people were already back in captivity. Telling her would be delicious, watching the fire stutter and die in her eyes, savouring her grief and observing her reactions afterwards. Were he a betting man, he'd put his money on her giving one last rebellious attack, giving up her life to try to take his. He looked forward to it.

Now that they were free, he watched them keenly. He was confident he could handle them, but lapsing into carelessness would get himself killed. Riffolk had always been a careful man. He gestured to one of the benches in the lab.

"Come, I'd like to show you my work." He kept his voice light, conversational, and he saw the confusion and unease in both of their faces. Mara moved first, wanting to enter his good graces. The Tyran continued to stare, sensing a trap. As worthless as she was, her survival instincts couldn't be faulted. He raised the scatter gun to point at her face, raising his eyebrows just slightly. She moved slowly, keeping her eyes on him but glancing briefly at the bench as she drew closer.

The bench he'd motioned to was fairly large, and covered in several projects. One of them was a technology he'd seen in his travels, which he was certain would be a great source of income once he could reverse engineer the design effectively. It wasn't dangerous or "evil" at all, but its purpose today would cause an incredible amount of pain to the Tyran girl. It was a glass screen with some machinery attached which could receive and project moving images sent by a transmitter which captured those images from a distance. It was beautiful. The concept was very similar to the teleradio device he'd built years ago, but with images instead of sound.

This screen, his prototype, was currently displaying a large room from a high angle. The room contained a gigantic horizontal wheel, slowly turning under the efforts of a hundred Tyran slaves. The girls both gasped when they saw the moving image, their eyes equally wide, disbelieving.

"What... is this magic?" Mara said.

"How are you doing this?" the Tyran said at the same time.

Riffolk smiled.

"This is a projection device. There is a transmitter in one of your wheel rooms, capturing this image, right now. What you're seeing is Tyra at this very instant."

She stared, and he waited for the realisation. It didn't take long; she wasn't as stupid as she looked.

"That's – they're alive. They weren't killed... the monsters didn't get them after all." Stunned. Relieved, but only for the barest second. He smiled as he watched the flash of hope twist into grief.

"Monsters? You still have no idea, do you? There are no monsters, girl. Not in Ermoor. The 'monsters' that attack you and your people are simply soldiers."

She didn't answer; he kept pushing.

"I don't know how they escaped, but it didn't take long to get them back under control."

"They escaped... But they were recaptured?"

"Oh yes. Did you really think a bunch of emaciated slaves with no weapons or armour would stand a chance against the might of Ermoor's military? Come now, surely you're not that naive."

He watched her carefully, and the emotions played out as he predicted; her spark of rage flickered, died, and her shoulders hunched. Grief and dismay washed over her face. He sighed gently, savouring her defeat. Now he just needed to watch out for her inevitable last stand. Mara, to his surprise, looked just as grief-stricken as the Tyran. He didn't understand it, but that could complicate things;

bringing her back under his control once the other girl was dead would be difficult if she'd built up an emotional connection to the slave.

"It's a great invention, don't you agree?"

There. The spark of fury inside her wasn't completely dead after all. She looked up at him, not bothering to hide the hatred in her face. Her lips curled, baring filthy teeth. Her fists clenched at her sides, white and trembling. She was ready to fight, which meant she was ready to die. He'd only let her live this long so Mara would have an interesting new pet to keep her entertained. His servants had told him of her depression, her wandering the gardens and sneaking out of the mansion at night. The night she'd come back with this one, this animal, Riffolk had informed the servants to make themselves busy elsewhere, so Mara could bring the Tyran in through the front doors. She hadn't even questioned her "good luck".

He was tired of the game now. The Tyran was nowhere near as interesting as he'd hoped she would be. Her passion was intriguing, but beyond that she was just like the others; all the playthings in Ermoor were just so boring. Mara would hopefully be a challenge after tonight, but her loyalty was almost unquestioning, and it wouldn't be long before she was his again. At least he still had his inventions to focus on; were it not for them he would have gone insane from boredom years ago.

His scatter gun was loaded, resting in his right hand, heavy and lethal. *Not here though,* he thought, *I want to see their reactions to the creature.*

"There's one invention far greater, however. Over there, both of you. Now."

He gestured with his left hand, empty now that he'd holstered the dart gun. Both girls walked towards the tank, though the Tyran stared daggers at him before moving. She was close to the edge, close to attacking him like the animal she was. He relished the turmoil in her eyes. The scatter gun felt as though it was buzzing in his hand, the potential energy of the explosion mounting as his finger itched to pull the trigger. These moments were his favourite; the anticipation of bringing someone to the edge, building their hope, their rebellion, and then crushing it all.

Riffolk stayed behind them as they approached the tank. Their fear and discomfort was palpable. He watched the Tyran intently, ready for her to attack. She kept her head straight, staring at the creature in the tank, and didn't try anything. When they reached the thick glass wall, she glanced back at him. His finger, anticipating resistance, twitched and almost ended her; but she still didn't attack.

"Do you know what this is?" He asked her.

"A monster," she said. He smiled.

"No, though it is certainly monstrous. And what I will achieve with it... Very much so. But would you call this weapon a monster?" He shifted the scatter gun slightly. "Or merely a tool?"

She shook her head, dull and defeated.

"What's your point? If you're going to kill me, I'd rather you do it before I have to listen to you talk for hours."

Mara let out a whimper at the mention of possible murder.

"I want you to know exactly what I'm doing in this lab. You see, Ermoor has been harvesting energy from Tyra for over a thousand years. That power has sustained our great city for all that time. But now, I've developed a much more powerful energy which will make your filthy little city obsolete."

He could see her fuming. Her hatred thrilled him, lifted his spirits. Knowing she was so close to death at his hands made the moment all the sweeter.

"This creature creates energy almost without limit, much more than Tyra. Once I have perfected long term and portable storage devices for that energy, Tyra will be of no use to Ermoor, and its people will be culled."

She moved. Much faster than he would have believed. She ducked underneath the scatter gun's muzzle, and his first shot missed her entirely, slamming into the thick glass of the tank. She dove to the side. His second shot clipped her legs and she grunted as a splash of blood painted the smooth floor. He reloaded, fast and smooth, but she'd already rolled to her feet and dived behind a console. Mara hadn't moved. No screaming, no running; she just stood there staring at Pera's blood on the sterile floor.

"You won't be able to wipe out all of Tyra," Pera said from behind the console, "Ermoor's leaders would never let you get away with it."

He turned his attention to the Tyran. She never peeked around the console at him. Too clever, this one. Cunning, like an animal, cornered and desperate.

"Fool," he said, "The Twelve Crowns gave their blessing on this project. They know full well what the fate of Tyra will be."

Not the whole truth, but she didn't need to know that. There was no reply. Riffolk knew it was only a matter of time; he just needed to press the right buttons. He waited, letting the silence build. Her emotions were high, and silence would only push her further. But he was calm, and they were trapped in his world; he had all the time he needed.

Pera

He was waiting behind the secret door. Like he knew they'd be there. Now, held in place by immovable metal arms, she felt like a child who'd been caught exploring the darkness and was about to be punished. If she got the opportunity to move, she'd fight back, hopefully kill him; but in the restraints that held her now, she didn't stand a chance.

Her first impression of Riffolk was that he was terrifying, but not in a physical way; she could definitely defeat him in a physical fight. What made him terrifying was his composure, and his eyes. He was still and patient, and he moved slowly and only when necessary, like a shadow viper. Pera had almost been bitten by a shadow viper when she was younger; they curled up in corners and against walls, just out of the light of candles, waiting for someone to step near them. They remained motionless for huge periods of time, until just the right moment, and then struck within the blink of an eye.

She'd found one once, as someone in front of her moved past it in a corridor holding a candle. She stopped nearby, lighting her own candle and simply watching. Fascinated, she edged closer. It didn't move at all. She couldn't quite tell because of the flickering candlelight, but it didn't even look as though it was breathing. Feeling bold but nervous, she edged closer still. A couple steps away from it, she had leaned in a little, moving the candle closer. Then it struck, faster than Pera could think. The candle vibrated in her hand. She dropped it and ran as fast as she could through the darkness. After that she'd been banned from carrying her own candles for a while.

Looking at Riffolk now, watching her and Mara with a cold and utterly emotionless stare, she felt as though she was edging closer to that deadly viper again. Only this time, she was stuck, and the viper was the one edging closer to her. He asked Mara what she was doing in his lab. The girl was terrified; just as terrified of him as Pera herself. In that moment, she knew that Mara could actually be trusted. Her terror was no act. She didn't answer the question, just stared at the lab's floor, frozen. Pera's fear of him was briefly overtaken by rage, and she spoke for Mara.

"I'm here to stop you, and so is she."

He didn't react at all to her voice. Continuing to stare at Mara, he asked her to confirm instead. She gave the slightest of nods, and finally Pera saw a flash of something primal and lethal in his eyes. She knew then that neither of them would make it out of the lab alive.

Mara

The last thing she remembered was darkness, and smooth surfaces, and Riffolk. Bright lights bit into her eyelids as her mind slowly cleared. Blinking the last of the darkness away, she opened her eyes and saw another huge laboratory, this one still full of equipment. In the centre of the room, a giant glass cage held something horrible-looking. She couldn't see it clearly, but she saw enough to be terrified.

Riffolk stood nearby, facing away from her, paying attention to a series of dials and lights. Her mind was still cloudy. A low groan sounded beside her and she almost screamed, but it was Pera waking up. Metal bindings were wrapped around her, and Mara glanced down at herself to see the same restraints keeping her in place.

Pera squinted, the lights obviously painful for her. Mara realised this was the first time Pera had come into contact with full lighting other than when she pulled the curtains back in her room at the mansion. She was obviously badly effected by the light, but forced her eyes open anyway, taking in as much of the lab as she could.

The women glanced at each other, and Mara saw that same look of controlled fury in Pera's eyes. Somehow, even in their current situation, it made her feel safe. Protected. She had faith in Pera. She looked again at the glass cage; now that she felt a little safer, taking in her surroundings was easier. The thing inside was massive, made from metal and flesh, and clearly alive. It twitched occasionally, and a low humming vibrated from it, not only in her ears but through the metal holding her still.

"I'm surprised, Mara."

Riffolk's voice cut through the humming, colder than Mara had ever heard it.

"And disappointed. What exactly were you hoping to achieve by coming here?"

He was staring at her, his bright blue eyes boring holes through to her very soul. She was helpless around him. Even Pera's presence, so comforting only seconds earlier, was totally forgotten under the cold stare of her husband. He owned her; she knew it as well as he did, but knowing didn't help her break his spell. She was his.

Words eluded her, and she simply stared back at him, terrified. Her lungs shrank and her throat tightened. And he continued to wait, as still and implacable as the metal vice holding her in place. His patience was inhuman. Pera scoffed, breaking Mara's frozen, panicked trance.

"I'm here to stop you," Pera said, "and so is she."

Riffolk's gaze never moved from Mara. He didn't even blink. His voice became soft, almost intimate, and Mara's mind conjured the image of a silent, terrible monster waiting to strike from the shadows.

"Is this true, Mara?"

She nodded, barely coherent, no longer in control of her body. She would have stayed perfectly in place even if the metal arms weren't holding her there. She would have done anything he said.

His expression didn't change, didn't budge at all, but something in his eyes whispered rage and death directly to her heart, and she felt a wave of icy cold wash over her body. This man could kill her and wouldn't feel a thing. She knew it suddenly, and with an intense certainty that choked her. She glanced over at Pera again, and Pera looked back.

The look in the Tyran woman's eyes matched her own, and she knew Pera had felt that awful cold wave too. For the first time, the unshakable confidence and rage in Pera's eyes was replaced by pure fear. They were both utterly at the mercy of a monster.

Elana

Hayne's meeting with the Lord Commander took place in the latter's office. Elana, already familiar with the layout, was in place and shrouded in Shadow Magic well before Riffolk showed up. Even without a *Kaizuun* unsheathed and in hand, a well trained *Kaizeluun* could make themselves utterly invisible. The Lord Commander leaned with both palms on his desk, waiting. A nondescript man sat nearby, on a small chair against the wall. For the briefest moment, his eyes scanned over her, and his brows creased almost imperceptibly. Neither man spoke.

She adjusted her stance slowly, making sure she was covered in the natural shadow of the room; the invisibility spell only worked when used within actual shadows. In daylight the spell was still effective, but turned the user into a blurred dark shape.

This high up on Symond's massive bookshelf, she'd be safe even if there was no shadow to hide in, but Elana still didn't want to take the risk. Just as she settled silently into place, Riffolk strolled through the heavy doors of the Lord Commander's office, a small group of assistants trailing meekly behind him. The unknown man stood, and the Lord Commander straightened to his full height.

The men greeted each other somewhat coldly, surprising Elana. The atmosphere in the room was one of thinly-veiled hostility. Hayne's face glowed with confidence and victory, and he looked at the Lord Commander as though he were looking at a defeated enemy. He motioned to his assistants, and one of them scurried forward with an armful of papers, spreading them onto the large desk in front of Symond before scurrying back to stand with his colleagues. The nondescript man sat down again, and the meeting began.

Pera

T*here were no monsters, this whole time; except for him. No human could be this cruel.* Her mind raced as she saw the Tyrans working once again at the Wheels, tiny and blurred on the glass panel of Riffolk's invention. She wanted to look away, wanted to deny it, to think that it was an image captured before the Tyrans escaped, but she knew. Somehow, she knew it was real. Her people were slaves once again, after a brief glimpse of freedom.

But simply showing her wasn't enough; he taunted Pera, gloating at the misery and slavery of her people. She'd never felt such rage in her entire life; she trembled with it, her entire body cold and tingling. *I'll kill him,* she vowed to herself, *even if I have to die too.* He could see her rage, and his eyes danced with amusement, which only pushed her further down that dark corridor.

After he had his fun with the glass screen, he gestured to the massive tank in the centre of the lab. They could see something within the glass from where they stood, but as they drew closer the thing became clearer, and Pera's heart beat faster. She'd thought of Riffolk as a monster, but the thing in the tank fit the word literally.

It was huge, and its body was half animal half machine, or so it seemed. Its face was utterly inhuman, other than its cold, pale yellow eyes; something about those eyes was eerily human. It was clearly alive, but was kept in a permanent sleep, its eyes half closed. Occasionally it twitched, and Pera found herself wondering what kind of beast it was when free and alert.

She wondered if it was as scary or as deadly as it looked; if it could be as destructive as its appearance suggested. Looking at its razor sharp metal-looking claws and jagged, muscular body, she thought it likely. She glanced at the weapon in the scientist's hand, and a plan formed in her mind like the sudden glow of a newly lit candle. When the time came, she moved as fast as a shadow viper.

Pera dove behind the console, the wound in her leg burning. She'd never seen a weapon like the one Riffolk carried, but she'd assumed it could only make a single shot at a time; the second one took her by surprise. *Foolish,* she thought, *don't assume anything with a man like Riffolk Hayne.* Trapped now, but at least out of range of his gun, she was still at the mercy of his taunting. He kept at it, and though she knew he was simply trying to provoke her, it was working. Every time he spoke, that tiny hint of amusement in his voice, she told herself not to reply, to simply say nothing. And every time, she shouted back at him from behind the console, her voice growing emotional.

She knew her time was almost up. There was no way out; Mara was utterly useless, the door out of the lab was in the far corner past Riffolk, and there was no way of knowing how many more shots his gun could fire before it was empty. All she had was the console she hid behind. She wasn't even close enough to get to him before he could shoot her.

"You will die today, Tyran. And your people will follow soon after. Or maybe... Maybe I should press that button now, so you can watch your people die right in front of you."

It was too much. She knew she would die, and she knew she couldn't kill him or even reach him before she did, but it didn't matter any more. Tyra was lost, there was no way out of the lab, and Riffolk was going to win. She screamed and bolted around the console. Time felt slow and heavy, and she saw him raise the gun. Its barrel pointed directly at her face, and she could see the tip of the projectile in its depths. Still running, she saw a flash, then darkness, and heard just the very beginning of a deafening boom.

Mara

Pera dashed just as Riffolk fired his gun. For a single second, Mara thought she'd been hit. She dived and Riffolk fired again, but this time blood splattered the floor and her heart froze. She couldn't fully process what was happening. Pera rolled and ran to cover. She disappeared behind a bench before it occurred to Mara that she hadn't died. Her breath was uneven now, her heartbeat even worse, and the lights somehow became brighter as her husband reloaded the gun. Pera spoke up from behind her hiding place.

"You won't be able to wipe out all of Tyra... Ermoor's leaders would never let you get away with it."

Riffolk looked bored. He glanced at Mara, and the total lack of emotion in his eyes plunged her into further confusion. The whole situation felt like a dream; had she hit her head at some point? Was this some awful nightmare? Tyra, the lab, Riffolk being a monster... God wouldn't allow any of this. The Twelve Crowns wouldn't allow any of it. Ermoor was a perfect society.

"Fool," Riffolk said, "The Twelve Crowns gave their blessing on this project. They know full well what the fate of Tyra will be."

He kept taunting Pera, and she argued back, but Mara couldn't focus enough to hear the words. Her head was swimming in a haze of terror and denial. She started praying silently, sure that God would do something, anything, to fix things. But, as always, her prayers were ignored. Pera remained out of sight, Riffolk's gun trained on the place where she hid. For the first time, Mara really thought about God. The scene unfolding before her slowed, and she felt something give way inside her. It felt like a corset finally being untied after a long dinner party. She could breathe, and think. Pera's words came back to her;

"What kind of God forces half of His subjects to be inferior to the other half?"

She remembered thinking Ermoor couldn't possibly be heaven, because God would never allow Riffolk into His Kingdom. What little schooling she'd had never discussed anything outside of Ermoor other than to say how Godless everywhere else was. She'd heard of

Shanaken, Tarsium, and Omas, and possibly one or two more countries from ancient times. Why would God create so many people who were condemned to hell? Why not just create Ermoor itself, if it was the perfect society?

She remembered every time she'd felt a slight doubt about God, and had buried it deep down, listening to her father and the priests and believing the scripture. Every time she had a question about why things were the way they were, why God did the things he did. She realised she still felt all those questions and doubts, and had never been given a real answer. Out of her new focus, an old memory from a church service rose up:

The Priest paced the stage, glaring around at the children in the front pews.

"When you have a problem, and you pray, do you know who is listening?"

"God is!" all the children shouted.

"Yes! And do you know who is responsible for fixing your problems?"

"God is!" all the children shouted again.

"No!" the Priest stopped pacing, his glare growing more intense. The children were utterly silenced.

"It is your *responsibility! God will not heal your scraped knees and elbows, or stop a bully from pushing you to the ground. He gave you the strength you need, it's up to you to use it! He listens to our*

prayers, but he will only help in the most dire of circumstances, and only for the most devout of his servants."

Mara had been ten years old. She remembered thinking that if God listened but refused to act, He wasn't very good. She'd said as much to her father after the service and received a swift slap to the back of the head for her attitude. Now, hearing those words again, she thought *if he ever would help, it would be now.* She was devout, though she had her doubts. She prayed every day, went to church whenever her father or another man took her, and knew her place. Her circumstances were dire. But God didn't do anything. Had never done anything.

He gave you the strength you need, it's up to you to use it! Two tools came flying from behind Pera's hiding place, pulling her attention back to the present, but they missed Riffolk. The gun went off again and she screamed. Riffolk stayed where he was though; Pera seemed to still be alive. He stepped closer to her, his eyes trained intently on Pera. The gun he'd put them to sleep with rested in a holster on his belt, on the side closest to Mara. Riffolk taunted Pera again, she screamed and jumped out from her hiding place.

A loud, awful cracking sound came from somewhere, and Mara took her chance. She snatched the gun from its holster, stepping back just as Riffolk fired his gun again. She tensed, thinking he'd shot her, but there was no pain. Pera toppled to the ground, a red, jagged mess where her head used to be. Mara's mind emptied, her heart tore, and she screamed. Pera was the only safe person, the only person who'd genuinely helped her, and she lay mangled on the cold metal floor.

Riffolk started reloading his gun. He hadn't seen her yet.

"Stop!" she shouted.

He completely stopped moving. The effect was terrifying, and intoxicating. This powerful man, the wealthiest man in Ermoor, the man who had used her countless times and discarded her afterwards, had instantly obeyed her command. His eyes rose to meet hers, and a deep, boiling rage radiated from him in an overwhelming wave.

He snapped the gun closed with a loud clack, and she almost fired the gun in her hand. The awful sound she'd heard before happened again, like something gigantic slowly breaking, and she knew it was some trick or gadget Riffolk was using. Was it just a distraction, or was something about to kill her?

"What is that? What are you doing?" she said.

"I don't know."

He looked around, distracted. *He might be telling the truth,* she thought. The idea was somehow even scarier than him using some sneaky trick to kill or catch her without warning; what could be happening in Riffolk's own secret lab that he didn't know about?

Riffolk was staring at the glass tank. It was covered in massive cracks. A grating, electronic sound started from it. She felt the blood drain from her face. *That thing is awake. Riffolk woke it up!*

"What are you doing, Riffolk?" she whispered.

His eyes softened, just for a moment, and her heart fluttered for him, even after everything that had happened. The giant, deep cracking sound filled her ears once more, and then the thing in the tank let loose a horrible roar, and the glass holding it in exploded.

The creature bolted out of its cage. Riffolk fired his gun twice at it, but it roared and kept moving. Mara's first instinct was to fire at it, screaming as she pulled the trigger, but the dart pinged off its metal skin. She fired again, this time at Riffolk; *it's under his control after all... isn't it?* He took a stumbling step away from the creature as it reached him.

"Stupid..." he said.

It grabbed him, and he screamed as it lifted him off the ground and threw him across the lab. It stared at her, and she fired the gun again. She couldn't tell if it hit, but the creature was unaffected. Too late, she realised she was between it and the only door out of the lab. With terrifying speed, it ran. She wasn't fast enough to get out of its way, and it grabbed her the same way it grabbed Riffolk, its massive claws covering her entire shoulder and neck.

Immediately, an intense, buzzing pain arced through her body from the point the creature touched. It felt as though lightning and fire had replaced her blood. Rhythmic thumping shook her, and she realised the creature was running with her still in its hand. After a few seconds that felt far longer, she was flung across the room, and heard the beast smash its way out the door. A bare second later, her head cracked against a wall and she toppled to the ground. The lab swam through a murky grey cloud and then slipped away.

Riffolk

Riffolk's lab had been designed to his exact specifications, under his strict supervision. The underground lab had been completed by a much smaller team, and Riffolk himself had done a lot of the work. The builders who'd worked on the underground lab all mysteriously vanished just as it was completed. Nobody knew they were working for Riffolk, and nobody realised work was being done underneath the main lab. The secrecy allowed him to install equipment and technology that would never have been accepted by Ermoor.

The creature he siphoned energy from was immoral enough, but at least the Twelve Crowns and Symond could see its necessity. Until the Shenza woman got to Symond. Now there was nothing in the lab which could be seen by anyone other than Riffolk. He loved the isolation of course, and had no problem with staying out of the public eye. It meant fewer distractions for his work.

It also meant killing the Tyran of course, which would have been fine on its own. But Mara was another matter. He couldn't easily explain her sudden disappearance; as her husband, he was solely responsible for her. Even though everyone knew he spent all of his time at the lab, her disappearing would bring unwanted attention onto him at a time when he needed to remain inconspicuous.

A few moments slid by in the heavy silence, Riffolk enjoying the build of tension as the Tyran girl's breathing became irregular.

"You can't hide forever, girl. You and your people are done."

"We'll fight. We'll find a way!"

Her voice was tight, emotional. Weak. She was close to snapping. He had two quick shots, and more ammunition on his belt. She was fast, but he could take her. The distance between them would allow him to take both shots before she reached him, and as long as one connected, he should be able to reload quickly enough to take her down if the first two shots didn't end her. He pulled two rounds from his belt and held them ready in his left hand.

His gun, which was one of his own inventions of course, worked by hurling small lead ball bearings at the enemy using a controlled explosion within the barrel. His personal weapon was a new prototype; the guns he sold to the military had to be reloaded after every shot, and while reloading was relatively fast and easy, it could still slow a soldier down. His gun held two rounds at once, fired them one at a time, and then ejected them for even faster reloading.

The console she hid behind was tall, too tall for her to easily jump over. She could only run around if she was going to attack. And the door out of the lab was behind Riffolk, to his left; even if her plan was escape and not combat, she'd have to go through him. He moved silently, towards Mara. She stepped away, quick, as though he were a deadly snake. Her fear was satisfying, and more importantly, useful; he needed her out of the way. Too bad he was too busy to truly enjoy it. He made a mental note to play with her later, to enjoy her fear properly; maybe even straight after he killed the Tyran.

The thought brought a smile to his lips; he couldn't help it. Mara's fear was always entertaining, but he'd never brought her to this level of terror before; now she would see him in a whole new light. Controlling her from now on would be interesting. He was looking forward to the challenge. But he was getting ahead of himself; he focused on the girl again. Her breathing was still ragged; not only fear but pain. The wound in her leg must have been bad. It would slow her down even more.

She was more interested in the welfare of her people than of herself. And justice. She seemed to think the world would provide fairness and justice to people who deserved it. People like that sickened Riffolk. Such weakness. Her naivety was painful. But it was a weakness he found exceptionally easy to exploit.

"You don't understand," he said, "Tyra can be wiped out without any Ermoori soldiers being present. I installed poison canisters in dozens of key locations, all linked to one button in this lab."

Her ragged breathing stopped, and silence filled the room. A heavy wrench hurtled over the console, passed by two metres to his right, and clanged to the floor. A deep, loud crunch sounded from somewhere behind him, and another tool flew towards him, again missing him by a few metres. She was aiming for where he had been, and was surprisingly accurate; if he hadn't moved, both tools would have hit him.

Her eyes peeked briefly over the top of the console, and Riffolk fired. Mara screamed, and sparks flew off the console, but there was no splash of blood.

"You will die today, Tyran. And your people will follow soon after."

He watched closely, waiting for her move. She'd marked him, and her aim was disturbingly precise; he moved again, towards Mara, feeling her presence nearby without looking. His wife didn't back away this time, but he was focused on the other girl. The trap was set, and he knew she wouldn't be able to stop herself.

"Or maybe..." he said slowly, stretching the thought out into silence, "maybe I should press that button now, so you can watch your people die right in front of you."

She screamed before he'd even finished his thought, and bolted from behind the console. Another deep crunching sound filled the lab, and Riffolk felt something tap his left side. But the Tyran was running toward him, fast. He fired, and her head exploded as she ran. Her momentum carried her through another two steps before she spilled to the ground, and Mara screamed. He reloaded out of habit, but before he'd finished Mara screamed at him.

"Stop!"

Pure shock stopped him. His wife had never once raised her voice at him like that. When he glanced up from the Tyran's corpse, his shock grew deeper, and a wave of fury splashed through his thoughts. She held his dart gun, pointed at his chest. Her face was pale, her lips set in a grim line. He finished reloading, closing the gun's barrel with a sharp clack. Mara flinched, and stepped back slightly.

The crunching sound broke the silence again, deeper and louder this time.

"What is that? What are you doing?"

Mara's voice was shaky, terrified. The barrel of his dart gun shook, her tense finger pulled up against the trigger.

"I don't know," he said, looking around the room. It seemed to come from everywhere now.

As another crunch echoed in the lab, he realised what it was.

Thick, reinforced and insulated glass contained the powerful creature. It was designed to contain the immense power created by the creature, and to stop any attacks from within if something went wrong with the sedation. A direct blast from his prototype firearm, which was more powerful than the standard military weapons, was enough to form a scattered web of deep cracks in the glass. Each crunch was another massive crack shooting out from where Riffolk shot the tank. The cracks had spread too much already; most of the glass on his side was irreparably damaged. A pair of eyes stared back at him from behind the broken glass, pale yellow and just as emotionless as his own. They were no longer half-closed, staring listlessly at the lab's wall; they stared directly at him, aware and alert.

A dull grinding emanated from within the chamber, and he realised the creature was growling. Mara's skin was ghostly, her eyes wider than he'd ever seen them.

"What are you doing, Riffolk?" she whispered.

For the barest second, he felt a pang of something towards her. Not love, surely. Pity? He couldn't tell, it was an utterly alien feeling to him. One more crunch filled the room, the creature's growl turned into a roar, and the tank exploded.

It swept out of its prison with a speed that shouldn't have been possible. Riffolk fired both rounds but it didn't slow, only roared louder. Mara screamed and fired the dart gun. Riffolk was almost impressed by her instincts, until she fired again and he felt a thump in his side. He grew weak immediately, trying to stumble out of the creature's way.

"Stupid girl," he said as the creature reached him.

It grabbed him by the shoulder in its huge claws, pulsing with energy and growling. His shoulder burned violently where the creature touched him. A buzzing vibrated through his entire body, searing in its intensity. He screamed, and despite the pain, the dart kicked in and he fell away into merciful oblivion.

Elana

Full-scale invasion. The words flashed in her mind. Things were much, much worse than she had thought. Possibly even worse than the *Duulshen* realised. Every country in Pandeia was at risk, not just Shanaken. The Lord Commander seemed hesitant to agree to whatever Hayne was working on. She briefly considered making direct contact with him, trying to persuade him to change his mind; but the idea was as ridiculous as it was brief. He would never listen to an enemy, let alone one who appeared from nowhere with knowledge of his secrets.

After Hayne left the office, the nondescript man, whose name was Mathys, stayed behind for a short time. He said almost nothing to the Lord Commander before leaving the man to his own devices. Once he was alone, Symond spoke again.

"I know you're there."

Elana's heart skipped a beat. He couldn't know. She'd remained perfectly still and silent the entire meeting. She didn't move. Holding her breath, she prepared to spring into combat; her muscles tensed, her hand open and ready to sweep her *Kaizuun* from its sheath. But Symond placed his head in his hands again, and continued talking. He sounded tired and old, definitely not as though he expected a dangerous intruder.

"Please, talk to me," he said, "I've given you everything. Please just tell me I'm doing the right thing."

A few moments of silence stretched between them. Elana was still deciding whether or not to reveal herself when Symond gasped.

"No, no I wasn't – I merely meant that..."

He leaned back in his chair, his eyes glassy and red. *Is he crying?* He truly believed he was talking to someone in the room. Someone controlling his actions. Silent as a breeze, Elana raised her left hand to the tattoo next to her eye, tracing its mark on her skin. When she finished the simple shape, her vision sharpened, brightened, eliminating the few shadows of the room. The tingle of magic made her blink once, but she saw clearly, and the room was unchanged other than the lack of shadows; no magic was present but her own. It meant there was no one manipulating Symond. He was simply insane.

After the Lord Commander left his office later that night, Elana headed straight for the laboratory. Hayne mentioned he'd already built something that worked, and that would allow them to mass produce some kind of weapon. She had to find it, and sabotage it. She couldn't simply destroy it, as Hayne would just make another, and it would also alert him and Symond to an intruder's presence. The *Duulshen* were clear that she must remain unseen and unsuspected. Anything she did had to look like it happened without the interference of the Shenza.

It was why she couldn't assassinate the two men outright. She'd been tasked with eliminating the most powerful members of Ermoor's military and technological networks, but secrecy remained her priority, and the *Duulshen* had left it to her to figure out how to complete her mission without being seen. She was still unsure of how to eliminate them both inconspicuously. But she'd handle one problem at a time.

The laboratory was quiet, but several rooms were still lit. As she expected, Hayne was working into the night. He often did. Elana had observed his home several times, and he was almost never present there, not even to sleep. He had a young wife, who seemed to miss him dearly, but still he spent all of his time in the laboratory. The wife, Mara, was perhaps the only decent person Elana had come across in Ermoor, though she was hopelessly naive. She had no clue what Hayne was doing and probably wouldn't have believed it if she did.

Elana snuck in the same way as she usually did; a vent on the roof which led into the air ducts. The building's layout had become a vivid map in her mind, and she barely needed to think about where she was going. Hayne had a secret second laboratory underground which no one but him was allowed to access. Luckily for Elana, there were still air ducts winding through the roof of the underground room. She'd only seen glimpses of it, as it was a much more open space and Hayne was almost always there. There was nowhere she could hide while he was in the room.

As Elana crawled through the air ducts, odd sounds emanated from one of the sections of the main laboratory. They were the sounds she now associated with science; bubbling liquids, the rushing sound of intense directed fire tools, the whirring of machinery. A lot of work was being done for such a late hour. Making sure she was wrapped in shadow, she peeked through one of the vents into the main lab. Hayne was working alone, as he usually did after dark. Her heart sped up a little; this was her chance to see the underground laboratory.

Mara

She woke in darkness, cold and sore. Her head pounded. A few moments of disorientation dragged by before she remembered where she was. She glanced up, wincing as her body screamed pain all over, and looked into the dull grey dark of the huge lab. A hulking wreck sat in the centre of the room; the broken tank. It was even more terrifying empty than with the creature still inside. She stood, shaking, trying to move slowly. Her entire body hurt.

The worst pain was her shoulder, where the thing had grabbed her. At the time it felt like both fire and lightning, but now it just felt like a deep, intense buzzing. As though a giant clamp was holding her shoulder tight and vibrating.

The room looked different somehow; not just the darkness, but some other quality she couldn't define, a sort of energy pulsing within the lab. It felt alive, almost like the entire lab itself was a massive creature, and she was standing inside its living body. But there was a deeper problem; the energy she felt was weakening even as she became aware of it. As disturbing as the sense of life within the room was, the feeling of it growing dim unsettled her more than she could say.

Feet shuffling against the cold floor, she left through the massive hole torn by the creature as it escaped. Above the secret lab, the path of destruction continued through the corridors and out into Ermoor itself. One wall of the main lab was destroyed, and Mara stared down the creature's trail as far as her vision allowed; it had simply smashed a straight line through the city to the west, never deviating regardless of obstacles.

Mara walked for a while, through the creature's wake, thinking of nothing but her buzzing shoulder and the cold morning air. The eerie sense of life returned, coming from all around her. She glanced up and gasped; the coloured lights lining the streets danced through the morning fog, brighter and more vivid than she'd ever seen before. *But it's daytime,* she thought, *they can't be that bright.* She'd been outside in the early morning before, for early church services, and the lights were always turned off as soon as the sun rose enough to see by.

The light was different now. Not just glowing but *moving;* living. The buildings around her felt full of life as well, and the ground beneath her feet was an endless well of powerful energy. She didn't understand it. She'd heard of people seeing things that weren't there after a horrible head injury; perhaps she was suffering from visions after being thrown against the lab's wall. Or perhaps she'd simply gone mad. She found it incredibly hard to focus, and stopped thinking as she walked. The buzzing in her shoulder remained constant, never growing or fading, and it kept pulling her mind away.

Somebody shouted, and she frowned at the noise. Her head ached. Another shout pierced her mind, and then an incredibly loud bang shattered the still morning air. Pera's mangled corpse appeared in her mind's eye, blood spreading over the smooth lab floor. Mara stopped walking, and finally noticed the soldiers surrounding her. Dozens of them, all pointing their guns at her. She realised too late what she'd done wrong.

"I'm sorry," she said, "I don't think my husband can escort me."

The soldiers moved closer, their guns still raised. Tears started running down her cheeks, and the numbness of a moment ago was swept away by fear and loss.

"I think he might be dead. They're both dead."

"Where is your husband?"

"Who is your husband?"

"Where did you just come from?"

"Who else is dead?"

"Do you know what happened here?"

"Did you see the beast?"

Every soldier threw questions at her, until a storm of shouting drowned her mind. She couldn't think, or speak, or feel, except for the ceaseless buzzing in her shoulder. One of the soldiers was close, and reached for her wrists with one hand, a pair of restraints in the other. He grabbed her, and her mind flashed with an image of Riffolk grabbing her, forcing her, pushing her. Riffolk restraining her and Pera. Riffolk shooting Pera in the head.

The life around her reached out, like a protective arm to hold her, and she embraced it. There was no malice in that embrace, she simply felt whole. It touched her, whatever it was, and the soldier grabbing her melted away into dust with a buzzing, whooshing sound. Just like that, in an instant, he was gone. And Mara felt power for the first time in her life.

A soldier facing her fired his gun. A sharp crackle of lightning arced from Mara, and though it was too fast for her to see, she knew the metal pellets had been vaporised. She remained unharmed, staring into the now terrified face of the man who tried to kill her. She reached out to him, and the new life flowing through her arced again, this time ripping the man's flesh and bone into dust from a distance. She felt the power as it left her body and destroyed his, but it didn't harm her at all; it buzzed under skin, tingling and cold.

The soldiers started screaming at her, moving to try to hide from her new power. She reached out to another one as he ran, watching as he crumbled into ashes mid step. A thump jolted her thigh, and a pink cloud sprayed out into the cold air. Her leg gave way and she dropped to her knees, seeing the jagged hole where she'd been shot and wondering why her power hadn't saved her. Footsteps slapped the street behind her, and she realised the shot had come from behind. As the soldier approached, she gathered more of the buzzing energy inside her, focusing it in her hands. It was surprisingly easy. Before she could turn around and grab him, something heavy and solid smashed into the back of her head. Pinpoints of light exploded in her vision, then spread and engulfed her in painful white infinity.

She woke suddenly, snapping from sleep to total awareness within seconds. Pera was shot again in her dreams, and there was so much blood, too much blood. She could see the ruined place where her head should have been in far too much detail; even still, after waking. Bone and brains and blood mixed together. Mara threw up onto the floor, and only after she was done did she notice her surroundings.

She was in a cold, empty room, which looked uncomfortably like Riffolk's lab. The only furniture was the hard slab bench she lay on. Her shoulder still buzzed, and now there was another feeling, even more unpleasant; *there's something in my head.* As she thought it, she became even more aware of the sensation. *What is that?*

What am I?

Who is that?

Are you one of the Others?

What is happening?

I saw you. You were outside my cage. You wanted to help me.

Mara's head split, a white blade of searing pain forcing its way into her mind as her voice and another voice fought inside her thoughts. *The creature.* Somehow their minds were connected. It should have been impossible. *Only God can hear my thoughts!* She screamed at the thing in her mind. It was gentle, and patient, and she knew it didn't want to hurt her. But the fact of its presence was terrifying on a deep, spiritual level; if this creature could speak in her mind and hear her thoughts, what did that say about God?

Perhaps I am God.

She shook her head, stomach churning. It couldn't be. God wasn't some grotesque creature in a lab. God couldn't be captured or contained by a mortal, even one as intelligent as Riffolk.

What are you really? She thought.

I... don't know. My memory is gone, only coming back very slowly.

Mara had assumed Riffolk created the being in the tank, but now she chided herself; of course Riffolk couldn't create life. The very thought was dangerously close to sacrilege. Only God could create life. She was suddenly fearful. Conversing with this creature was surely against God's will... if it could read her thoughts, it had to be some kind of demon or similar creature, and those were the enemies of God.

Please, she thought desperately, *leave me alone!*

But we are connected. You are joined to me now.

I don't want this! I don't know what you are but you can't be God, and talking to you is wrong!

Did your God tell you this?

Mara faltered. She remembered the doubt she felt in the lab. The fact that God had never spoken to her, or answered her prayers, or even made His presence felt. The scriptures were very clear, and very specific, but still... She suddenly wondered if anyone else had actually heard the voice of God. The Priests had an answer ready for every question about God's lack of communication with the general population, but what if they'd never heard him speak either? It occurred to her that as well as never hearing God speak to her, she'd also never been punished for any sins she'd committed. Other than by the Priests and her father, and only after admission of her guilt. She couldn't bring herself to consider the answer just yet, but the question came to her mind anyway; *What if there is no God?*

Arthor

"You know why you're here, Lord Commander?"

"To explain why the project was shut down."

"Yes. So?"

Arthor sighed. He still didn't know what to say. The invasion was wrong, and many people would die; but the Twelve Crowns possessed the same moral compass as Overseer Hayne, so that argument was invalid. Neither could he admit to being controlled by a shadowy figure that whispered into his head. Even worse, he himself had been given control of overseeing the planning and military aspects of the project, and up until now had never displayed any arguments against it. What could he say now?

All but two of the Crowns were present for the meeting; it was fairly normal for some or even most of them not to show up to meet the Lord Commander. The Crown who'd asked the question spoke to him as though he was one of the lower class citizens, the ones living in group houses and indulging in God knew what drugs. They could see his uncertainty, and they were losing respect for him by the second. His power and authority were on a level with their own; their disdain, though possibly warranted in this situation, made him furious.

"After careful consideration, it became apparent to me that the invasion-" each of the Crowns reacted to the word – "will not benefit Ermoor as much as we first thought. You underestimate the Shenza, and the Thearans. The Tarsi are a total mystery, for all we know they could be the most powerful of all. Our technological power is immense, there's no doubt of that, but we are fighting against magic. Forces beyond our understanding. If we can send out some agents and gain more knowledge of-"

"Enough!" One of the Crowns shouted.

Too late, Arthor realised his mistake. The Crowns were in complete denial about the existence of magic. At the same time as crusading to destroy it in the name of God, they refused to accept that it existed in the first place. Not that Arthor believed either, but fearmongering was perhaps the only language they understood.

Another dead end. The Crowns all shouted at him simultaneously, drowning the large room in echoing, hateful voices.

"Do you really expect us to believe such nonsense?"

"Nothing but baseless fearmongering!"

"None can withstand the might of Ermoor!"

The Twelve do not deserve their power.

"We will crush those savages!"

"You have no faith!"

Arthor shook his head; the voices were overwhelming. He tried to think of some way to argue with them. He had the authority to shut the project down anyway, but if he made enemies of the Crowns, eventually he would be retired. Forcefully retired. He had to play things carefully. The being that spoke to him had given him no reasons, nothing he could use to justify the sudden change.

"Enough!"

The Crowns stopped immediately; Arthor had never raised his voice to them before. When he spoke again, he kept his voice as low and even as possible.

"You haven't seen this thing. No one has but Riffolk. We don't know what it is, or what it's capable of. I'm sure Riffolk is capable of keeping it contained, but if there's even the slightest chance of something going wrong, the consequences would be far more severe than you or Riffolk are willing to admit. Ermoor could be crippled instantly."

An uncomfortable silence filled the dark room. It felt to Arthor as though the Crowns might finally be listening to him; but he doubted it. They were incredibly resistant to change, especially anything that halted progress; or their version of progress, at any rate. But, when faced with no other alternative, they could occasionally set aside their stubbornness and bring about change to Ermoor. Arthor had only seen it once or twice in his lifetime, but he knew it was possible.

This was going to be a tough argument to have though. The Crowns had been intent on "liberating" the other countries of Pandeia for decades. They claimed it was to bring the light of God to all the Godless savages in the world, but Arthor suspected there was something else driving them. All their actions within Ermoor were motivated by financial or technological gain. Despite their adamant faith, Arthor had never seen them do anything purely for the love of God.

"Has Overseer Hayne ever failed us before?" One of the Twelve said.

"Do you have any real proof to back up your belief that something could go wrong?" Another said.

They want proof from you for doubting them. They never demanded proof from Riffolk. They never demanded proof from you when you gave them what they wanted.

Arthor's head dropped; he knew then there was nothing more he could say. These hidden men, ruling from the shadows, were utterly out of touch with Ermoor. It just made no sense to him. Their refusal to even consider the potential consequences was baffling. And their demand for proof pushed him over the edge, from anger to rage.

"Proof?" He yelled. "You demand proof that something *could go wrong?"*

More stunned silence met his sudden outrage.

They would never demand proof for their own beliefs. Where is their God in all this?

The thought was quick, quiet, and deadly. It left his mouth before his brain had fully processed it.

"You've never asked for proof when it suits you. What if I demand proof from you? Prove you're doing God's work. Prove to me that what we're doing is *right.*"

This time, after he spoke, the atmosphere of the entire room changed instantly. He saw the posture of every one of the Crowns straighten, becoming aggressive and combative. Their faces were hidden under deep, thick hoods, but their hands either balled into fists or drew back into claw-like shapes. He'd done it now; Arthor wouldn't survive to see next month. The Twelve wouldn't care if it slowed

Ermoor's invasion down by ten years, they would kill him for questioning them as surely as they'd kill some low-born drug addict.

"Lord Commander Arthor Symond," One of them said, "You are found to be in contempt of the Twelve Crowns of Ermoor, and will submit yourself for retirement in two week's time."

Without a word, Arthor strode from the dark, echoing chamber, battling the urge to scream at them again. Under his rage, an overwhelming terror was growing. Not only was he an enemy of the Twelve Crowns now; he'd also failed the being that spoke directly into his mind. He had no idea what it was or what it was capable of, but he supposed now he would find out. His heart didn't slow down until he reached his home, surprising his wife with a tight, long embrace. He held her until his emotions calmed; it took a long while.

Sleep eluded him even more now. After the meeting, he'd officially shut down Riffolk's lab. He knew it meant effectively signing his own death warrant, but he had to heal his own conscience, as well as obey the thing that spoke to him. He couldn't keep the secret from his wife, although he'd wanted to protect her from it. So they lay next to each other each night, terrified and motionless, waiting for some professional assassin, or an explosion, or something worse. Although Arthor hated himself for telling Ellie and putting that burden on her, sharing their fear and finding comfort in each other made him feel even closer to her. A couple of weeks passed, and Arthor heard nothing more from the Twelve.

Riffolk had more or less dropped off the face of Pandeia. Arthor, like many others who'd dealt with him for a long period of time, suspected that he had a secret lab somewhere in Ermoor. There was no way to find it, let alone stop him from using it, but at least he couldn't use the city's resources for his sick work any longer. Despite his fear of disobeying the Twelve Crowns, Arthor was glad he'd been able to stop such a monster from working, even if it was a temporary obstacle.

The idea of a secret lab, and Riffolk working even now, unsupervised and completely free of morals, terrified Arthor even more than whatever punishment the Twelve had in store for him. He tried to convince himself that the rumours of a secret lab were just hearsay and speculation. He almost succeeded, but a small part of himself was certain Riffolk had a hidden facility somewhere. He was full of back up plans and secrets.

After another week, he awoke to a servant knocking desperately on his door. His eyes shot open, sore and tired, and he groaned as he got up. Glancing over at Ellie to make sure she was covered, he called for the servant to enter. The moment he saw the expression on the man's face, he knew something terrible had happened. His heart stopped, his face growing cold. *The Twelve have done something awful,* he thought. But when the servant started talking, even his thoughts stopped cold.

Elana

Elana stared in shock. She was expecting weapons; terrible weapons, granted, but nothing like what hung behind the massive glass case in the centre of Hayne's secret laboratory. *It's alive,* she thought, *for the love of Amalus, it's alive!* Living flesh melded with metal and wire, creating a hulking beast unlike anything she'd ever seen. Even the most horrific animals sneaking through the depths of the forests of Shanaken were less terrifying than this monstrous creature.

A deep humming sound filled the room; Elana wasn't sure if it came directly from the creature itself or from the machinery all around the room, but she had an awful feeling it was the former. The creature twitched occasionally, startling her each time. Its glassy, half-closed eyes stared lifelessly straight ahead, at a point just next to her head. Each twitch moved its eyes slightly, and for the barest second, the thing stared directly at her. Chills ran down her spine, and the cold stark room around her suddenly felt like the most dangerous place in the world.

It's alive, she thought again. Its arms ended with horrible, jagged metal claws which looked like pieces of some exploded machine. As she stared, its claws closed partway, forming a loose fist. It relaxed again after a few seconds, but it seemed more than just a twitch. She frowned, looking for more signs of consciousness, but the creature remained in its horrifying state of twitching sleep.

She scanned the room, her eyes never too far from the creature, her back never totally facing it. She was utterly on edge in this room; she had a hunch that Hayne suspected her presence, and she knew there would be security measures in place. She'd kept her shadow spell up when she first entered the room, and luckily it seemed to work against whatever device he'd planted next to the vents in the roof. When she first opened the vent, the small machine had beeped and whirred right in front of her face. She'd stared, terrified, waiting for some awful attack. But the machine had calmed once more, and she dropped silently to the floor.

Nothing else looked like a weapon or security device. The room was silent. Elana didn't believe it at all; didn't trust this room or the man who spent his time here. Turning her attention back to the creature, she examined its cage and the equipment around it. There had to be some way to sabotage it.

The thought made her sick; she'd expected some machine, a weapon she could tamper with. But a living creature? *Taranos lives.* She remembered the words Hayne wrote in his journal, and her stomach heaved. She should have known what to expect. Her mission couldn't change, however; the *Duulshen* would tell her that it didn't matter what the Ermoori were using as a weapon. *Stop them at all costs,* the elders had said, *and if you can't stop them, slow them down, put up as many obstacles as you can.*

Ermoor had invaded Shanaken countless times, as far back as recorded history could stretch. The vast majority of the time they used a relatively small force, though combat still dragged on, sometimes for years. Lately, in Elana's lifetime, the attacks had grown far more serious; more soldiers, deadlier weapons, and better armour. Invasions lasted longer, and the Shenza lost more warriors each time.

The *Duulshen* had been sneaking *Kaizeluun* into Ermoor for years, but now they were truly worried. At the rate the weapons and armour of Ermoor were improving, it wouldn't be long before the Shenza would be unable to defend themselves.

The creature, whatever it was, had to be stopped. It hunched inside the transparent walls of its cage, lifeless yet somehow pulsing with energy, as though it was simply waiting for the right moment to strike. What was it? What would it do when it woke? Elana took a few tentative steps towards it, alternating her gaze between the creature and the machines attached to it. There were consoles built into the cage on every side, facing outward at waist height and brimming with complicated buttons, dials and gauges.

She stopped a step from the creature's cage. Within arm's reach of the closest console. A small light blinked in steady pulses, its bright green glow bouncing off the glass and the creature's skin. A gauge measured some mysterious thing, the needle wavering nervously on the high end of whatever scale it used. Buttons lined one gleaming section. Nothing was labelled.

Elana drew her *Kaizuun*. The shadow blade filled her with energy and magic, responding to her body and mind like an intuitive lover, and she saw the creature in a new light; through the filter of magic. Most animals gave off a gentle, passive aura, clear in shape but low in magic. Predators and powerful mages gave off a much deeper, more lively aura; as though magic and danger danced together in their souls, setting sparks flying. Her breath caught in her throat as she looked at the thing in the cage.

Its aura was raging, formless and terrifying; a pale but powerful crackling yellow energy which screamed wordless fury in her mind. For a moment, she was utterly overwhelmed. The stark, dangerous laboratory around her disappeared. Thoughts of her mission, her home, everything was washed away by the chaotic energy filling her head. Even the creature itself ceased to matter; it was simply a shell for this gargantuan soul.

Elana was more confused than ever. She sheathed her blade, grateful for the silence which returned. This was no mere creature; and certainly the aura surrounding it was something completely new. She stared into its glazed eyes, her mouth dry, her heart pounding. She'd been anxious before, anxious that it might wake; now she was absolutely terrified. *What are you?* She thought.

The creature's pale yellow eyes opened wide, then swivelled and caught her own. It stared directly at her; not the coincidental eye contact resulting from a lifeless twitch, but a conscious stare. Elana saw pain, and madness, and terror. A sudden wave of excruciating noise filled her mind, forcing her to her knees and drawing a scream from her unfeeling lips.

There were voices spouting gibberish, crashing, thumping, and an intense buzzing which throbbed through her entire body. Her eyes had been screwed shut, and a sharp blade of horror sliced through the cacophony as she realised her guard was down. Forcing her eyes open again, she looked up at the creature. It was still in its cage, but its eyes were boring into her, wide and mad and questioning. Through the unbearable noise, a tiny voice whispered, clear despite the chaos:

What am I?

Mara

Next time she woke, it was the sound of the door closing that pulled her from sleep. The feeling of having something in her head was gone, and she was left feeling alone, confused and terrified. The man who'd entered the room was of indeterminate age and utterly nondescript. The only word that came to her mind looking at him was *normal.* He had the air of a teacher; someone who knew much but didn't use their knowledge to advance in the world, instead simply holding it for those who would. He was impossible to read, his expression totally blank.

He stood in the centre of the room, and watched her. She had no idea what to say, but out of habit she sat upright, legs crossed at the calf, knees together, one hand over the other in her lap. Her left thigh was bandaged where she'd been shot, though the pain was still there, now a dull ache. She realised she was still wearing the dark clothing she'd worn to sneak into the lab, and felt painfully self conscious. He stared at her, unmoving. Finally, just as Mara was about to break into confused and mortified tears, he spoke.

"You're Mara Hayne."

His voice was soft and caring. But the room, and the fact she'd been found outside without a man, and Riffolk... *And dear God, I killed Ermoori soldiers!* No matter how gently this man spoke to her, she knew she was in a huge amount of trouble. Tears slid down her cheeks, and she couldn't bear to look at him any longer. She lowered her head, staring at his boots.

"Yes."

She could barely speak. Silence pressed into her. He didn't move and she was too terrified to look at him.

"My name is Commander Mathys Corby. I'm investigating the incident that occurred yesterday at Overseer Hayne's lab."

He settled once more into silence. Mara didn't know what to say. She was in the centre of the creature's escape, and was seen walking through its path of destruction when she was captured; she couldn't deny her involvement, even though she knew almost nothing.

She tried to think of something to respond with, and opened her mouth before anything real had come to her mind.

"Oh. Am I in trouble?"

He seemed to hesitate; his perfectly still demeanour gave way to an awkward shuffling of feet.

"Not as yet. At least, not for your involvement with the creature's escape and Overseer Hayne's hidden lab. Evidence may surface, but for now we're simply asking some questions. You were wandering the city without an escort though."

The last part he added with a sympathetic tone, gentler than his previous words. She looked up at him then, and found a caring face, the face of someone who wasn't trying to blame or break her, but to understand her. Despite the stark, cold room she sat in, and the fact that she was being held and questioned, she trusted Commander Corby.

"I don't know what it was," she said quietly, "but Riffolk was using it for power, or energy, or something. He was going to kill all of her people... all of Tyra."

Her voice faltered. Pera's face swam into her mind, clear and painful. The ruin of her body was stamped into her memories like a detailed oil painting. Commander Corby shifted again, tense now. The gentle face was gone, and a much more intense expression fell into place.

"What do you know about Tyra?"

"I'm – nothing, only what Pera told me. They've been turning those giant wheels for ages. Riffolk said a thousand years. And then Ermoor uses the power from them for the city. He said he'll kill them all, sir, but that's not true... Is it?"

She couldn't stop the words once they started. The look in Commander Corby's eyes became colder and colder as she spoke, but she still couldn't stop. She knew she was in terrible danger before he replied.

"I see. And what do you think of all this?"

He looked as if he was ready to kill her; the coldness in his eyes was almost as intense as Riffolk's stare.

"I don't know," she said in a rush, "it's not my place. I trust in God and in Ermoor, and I -"

"Enough."

He didn't yell, but she flinched as though he had; his tone was cold enough to chill her heart.

"Did you see where the creature went?"

She shook her head, looking at his boots again.

"Why were you following it?"

She shook her head again, and then realised he hadn't asked a yes or no question.

"I don't know."

"Did it attack you directly?"

"Umm. Yes."

"Show me."

She glanced at him, shocked. It was an oddly personal request, but he'd asked with such casual coldness that she felt exposed already.

"I... It scratched my shoulder, I'd have to take this off..."

Her left hand came up to her right shoulder, rubbing the black cloth gently. The buzzing was still present, and she winced as her hand brushed over the point where the creature had grabbed her.

"Show me," he repeated.

She felt herself blushing, and she was suddenly both terrified and thrilled that a man was asking her to remove her clothing. What if he saw her body, and wanted her the way Riffolk did? Although she didn't want it to happen, she found herself excited by the thought. She imagined herself half naked in front of him in the cold room, and him suddenly taking her as roughly as Riffolk did, and her blush deepened. Her cheeks were hot and tingling as she stood, both hoping and fearing that he would have his way with her. She unbuttoned the dark blouse, her heart fluttering. Unable to look at him, she found herself hoping that his eyes followed her hands as they slowly undid each button. She dropped it to the ground at her feet.

She'd been wearing a coat when she arrived at the lab, but when she woke in Riffolk's restraints it had been taken off her. Under the blouse she wore a camisole, and under that her brassiere. Excited now, and oddly emboldened, she grasped the bottom of the camisole with her arms crossed, and brought it up.

"Stop, that's enough." Commander Corby said.

Her hands were at the height of her chest; she hadn't yet taken the camisole off. She glanced at him, then lowered her hands, letting go of the undergarment. He stared directly into her eyes, unbothered by her partially exposed body. The intensity of her disappointment shocked her. *Do I really want him to want me that badly?* Suddenly she was disgusted with herself, and her body felt shameful. She crossed her arms over her chest, lowering her eyes back to Commander Corby's boots.

"Turn around," he said gently, "I'm going to approach you but I won't touch you."

She turned instantly. Somehow, the ability to follow orders, to have control in the hands of a man with authority, made her feel excited and scared and relieved all at the same time. Even a strange man she didn't know could make her feel these confusing things. Standing, facing the wall, his footsteps approaching, she felt a sickening but exhilarating thrill. *He might still take me,* she thought. She thought of Riffolk, and the way he treated her behind closed doors, and she found herself wet under her skirt.

His steps stopped close. A slight touch of air on her neck raised her skin into goose pimples as he exhaled. He leaned in, and his second breath touched her shoulder, the gentle sensation mixing with the constant buzzing she felt. Gasping slightly, she turned to look at him. His face was so close. She bit her lower lip, looking up into his eyes. He glanced at her, then back to the wound on her shoulder.

She hadn't properly looked at it, or at least couldn't remember doing so, and followed his gaze. Her shoulder was a colourful mess of bruising and scratches, vivid and fascinating to look at. Staring at it at first made the buzzing more intense, and she flinched. But she eventually grew used to the sight. It felt like looking at a painting, like it was separate from her body. But knowing it was her own shoulder, and that she was so damaged and injured, excited her in a dark, indefinable way.

A few times, after Riffolk had used her, she'd been left with bruises. On her neck, her arms, her buttocks. Seeing them made her sick, but she also felt a stinging, fluttering pride in her chest. *I let him do this to me,* she thought to herself each time, *I couldn't stop it, but I took it without too much screaming, and I survived.* And each time, she grew a little less sick and a little more proud. Seeing the mess of deep bruising on her shoulder made her feel sick again; it was so much worse than anything Riffolk could have done. But she felt an even more intense pride. *This time it was a real, actual monster. And I still survived.*

"What did it do to you?" He said, barely even whispering, "how did you survive this?"

She shrugged, then gasped at the pain, her head spinning as the buzzing intensified. Perhaps out of impulse, perhaps out of desire, his hand rose straight to her uninjured shoulder, and he steadied her. Without meaning to, she let out a tiny moan as his hand touched her. For a second he removed his hand, and she felt him tense up behind her. Then his hand fell on her again, gently. No man had ever touched her so gently. She turned, facing him full on, and he handed her the blouse she'd dropped to the floor. He looked her in the eye, ignoring her body again.

"We have medical facilities here, the doctors will examine you properly to make sure there's no internal damage. After that, I have some more questions for you."

His tone was gentle, but firm. Mara faltered. She thought there was something between them; that he desired her the way Riffolk did. She thought he was on her side, that he'd protect her. *Like Riffolk? Like Pera? Like father?* No. She looked into Commander Corby's eyes, ignoring her own wishful thinking with a huge effort, and told herself there was nothing there that would help her. She sat on the bench, dropping almost as if her knees had given way. Memories had begun flooding her mind, now stripped of their previous shiny lustre. Beneath it all was the image of Riffolk shooting Pera right in front of her, of Pera's body laying on the cold lab floor, her head a jagged and broken stump.

A sickness spread through her insides. A kind of cold, twisting weight. Had anyone ever truly cared for her? Did she matter to anyone at all? Her father sold her off to the richest family in Ermoor, her husband only paid attention to her when he needed her body, and Pera... She had been a friend, hadn't she? *She gave me nothing,* Mara thought, *she only wanted to get to the lab. She... She used me. She never cared.* And Commander Corby was using her to find the creature; he didn't care either.

Emotion suddenly felt beyond her. She was numb and cold, her mind a roiling storm. Everything she had believed was either broken, misunderstood, or simply wrong. *Even God.* She closed her eyes, tears running down her face. Commander Corby strode from the room, his heavy boots thumping the ground. In the chaos of her mind, she barely noticed.

God had suddenly become an empty concept, a desire as naively wishful as the love she'd thought she had from those she cared about. His lack of contact, not just with her but with seemingly all of Ermoor, made His absence that much clearer.

Since the creature's escape, however, she'd felt its presence in the back of her mind. She'd heard its voice, and spoken to it with her mind. It was how she'd imagined a relationship with God would be; it was what she thought the Priests experienced, and everyone else who was devout enough. Except her. But now, she could feel this powerful being in her mind, was connected to it, and she felt a thrilling sense of importance.

When she was younger, she had occasionally grown frustrated with never hearing God's voice. She would kneel by her bed, recite as many prayers as she could remember without reading from the scriptures, and then she would wait for a response. Usually, with a terrifying anticipation, she would speak directly to him. "Are you there?" she would whisper, her eyes squeezed shut as she imagined a booming voice replying. Each time she spoke to him, she felt almost certain he would say something back, anything. There would never be a response. After the anticipation melted away, there was only her empty, silent room.

Now she was alone, in the cold, bare room, and the same terrified anticipation seized her. She didn't pray, but she did kneel on the floor in front of the bench, placing her hands together and closing her eyes. In that place in the back of her mind, where she always hoped God's voice would speak, there was usually a horrible void. Now, she could feel its presence. Only faintly, but definitely there. She reached out tentatively, hoping for a reply and dreading one at the same time.

"Hello?" she said, "are you there?"

Nothing happened. The room's silence suffocated her, making her heart thump loudly in her ears. She focused on the presence in her mind, not fully understanding what she was doing. It felt like a hand, on her shoulder, but a little less *there* somehow. Like the feeling of being watched, or the tiny whoosh of air she felt if someone moved close behind her. Or like seeing a faint shadow or the vague shape of a person standing in a distant window. Imagining all of those, she pictured herself facing them, signalling the person in the window; turning to face the person behind her, the person watching her.

"Are you there?" she said again.

This time, she felt a shift. A sudden movement, like the shape in the distant window suddenly coming to life.

I am here.

Mara's breath caught in her throat. For the first time, she'd reached out to another being, asking for acknowledgement, and she'd been answered. She wasn't sure if the creature was God or something like him, but knowing it answered when she asked was enough.

"What are you?"

I am still unsure. Though I am almost certain I am one of the Gods.

One of? The thought terrified her more than she would have believed. How could there possibly be more than one God? It made no sense at all.

I can sense their power. There are four others like me.

"Where are they?"

A pause stretched between them.

They exist on a different plane, a different realm, for now. I cannot reach them. I am not sure what brought me to the physical world, but I know it's what the Others are trying to achieve.

"What for?"

If this creature was telling the truth, four immensely powerful beings were all trying to enter Pandeia, along with the one that had destroyed a large chunk of Ermoor. Mara had a lot of trouble believing they were Gods, but then again this thing could speak directly to her mind, something the scriptures said only God himself could do. And its power was undeniable; she'd seen the aftermath of its escape with her own eyes. No mortal creature held that kind of power.

To continue the war.

The creature didn't elaborate. Mara's entire body shook; her mouth was dry, her mind wiped blank. Ermoor was going to be destroyed. *Pandeia* was going to be destroyed. She couldn't even conceive of a battle between creatures like the one she spoke to now, but she knew it would be devastating. Her shoulder pulsed, and as she glanced down at it she remembered the power she'd felt while being attacked by the soldiers. She'd reduced them to ashes in an instant, and there was a distinct feeling of depth to the energy coursing through her; as though she'd barely even scratched the surface of the deadly magic.

"Can anything be done to stop them?"

I am sorry, child. I do not remember.

Arthor

A *monster is loose in the city. Riffolk Hayne is dead.* The servant's voice echoed in his head, driving all other thought from his mind. Riffolk's terrible project, the thing with the power of a whole city, had escaped and destroyed everything in its path, including Riffolk himself. *Just as I warned the Twelve,* he thought, though it gave him no satisfaction. He wondered if this meant they'd be less likely to kill him, or more so. *The Twelve are the most stubborn and prideful people I've ever had the displeasure to meet; they will definitely still send someone after me.*

Hopefully hunting the creature down and keeping it contained would distract them for long enough to allow Arthor to find some way to escape Ermoor; though he doubted it. Ellie had woken up before the servant broke the news, so she heard the whole thing.

"A *monster?* What monster?" Her voice was shrill, disbelieving but still fearful.

Ellie didn't know any of the work that Arthor did for Ermoor. She knew he was the Lord Commander, of course, and she knew he commanded the military. But any more specific details than that were strictly forbidden to discuss with those outside the highest circles of authority. So when she glanced at him in fear, and found him looking scared, but not shocked, her skin paled and she shrank from him, bunching the blanket in her hands up to her neck. It broke his heart.

He'd always thought of himself as a good man. Anything questionable he did was done in the service of Ermoor. *For the good of all.* He didn't agree with the methods the Twelve Crowns used most of the time, but they were working towards achieving a just and secure society. He didn't like it, but whenever he felt guilt for Ermoor's attacks on Shanaken, he reminded himself that he was serving Ermoor, and God.

What saved his conscience, the one thing that helped bring what little sleep he got, was the knowledge that the Shenza were vicious, tree-dwelling savages. If they'd been a civilised society more like Ermoor, they could have established trade negotiations and spread the wealth and knowledge of Ermoor to Shanaken. Every archived military report Arthor had read about the first contact between Shanaken and Ermoor was devastating; the Shenza began their attack before the Ermoori explorers even realised the country was already inhabited.

Ever since the first landing, the Shenza had been ruthlessly intent on destroying any trace of the Ermoori from their land. The Twelve Crowns maintained that Shanaken held some immensely valuable resource necessary for Ermoor's growth and development. Arthor had no idea what it was or how it was used, but the records didn't lie; the original explorers had found literal tons of it, according to their journals. The only thing redacted was the name and use of the resource.

The original landing had been at least a thousand years ago. Arthor enjoyed learning about history, and knew everything there was to know about the ancient conflict between Ermoor and Shanaken. Over the years of research, Arthor had uncovered a huge number of gaps in recorded events, ranging back to even before Ermoor landed on Shanaken for the first time. There was also almost no recorded history he could find on the other countries in Pandeia other than ancient myths and legends, and only a few minor accounts of Ermoor having landed on them. All of Ermoor's exploration and military history revolved entirely around Shanaken. Their latest preparations were alarming in comparison; a full-scale invasion of Pandeia. This was no exploratory mission; they were setting out to take over.

Arthor returned his attention to Ellie and the servant. He'd taken too long to respond; feigned shock would be as obviously false as waving the "monster" off as nothing. He was stuck. Facing his wife, he took a deep breath, steeling himself for the difficult conversation ahead. He gestured to the servant first, keeping his eyes on Ellie.

"Leave us," he said.

With the door closed, and his wife more terrified than he'd ever seen her, he began to speak. Instead of simply telling her about his choice to shut down Riffolk's lab as he had earlier, he told her everything. There was no reason to hold back any more; either the Twelve would kill them both, or the escaped creature would destroy all of Ermoor. Either way, all he wanted in that moment was for there to be no secrets between him and his wife.

Ellie held him close, and though she hadn't said anything since he stopped talking, her willingness to be this close comforted him more than he could say. Her only reaction to his words had been to steadily grow paler, her mouth shrinking into a thin line. When he finally reached the creature, and its potential power, combined with the fact of its escape, tears began streaming down her ghostly cheeks. Now, it had been at least half an hour since he'd stopped talking. She continued to hold him, silent and trembling.

Finally, he pulled her away, holding her shoulders gently and looking into her eyes. They shone with tears and fear, wide and innocent and trusting. After everything he'd just told her, knowing she trusted him still brought tears to his own eyes, and she sobbed when she saw him crying.

"What can we do?" her voice shook as she asked.

Stay. Fight. The Twelve deserve to die.

"I don't know. I think we need to leave Ermoor, but the Twelve have eyes everywhere."

She nodded. They talked for a little longer, each desperate for ideas. Eventually, Arthor started packing their things into a large chest; it was time to leave.

Mathys

If any man in Ermoor truly deserved to die, it was Riffolk Hayne. Mathys would never have said it out loud, but it rang as true as the blue in the sky nonetheless. Still, hearing the news brought no pleasure to him. He didn't wish death upon anyone; but he refused to mourn for a man such as Riffolk. There was no funeral, at least not yet; no body was found, and Riffolk was revered by the public. They would be devastated to learn that the man who single-handedly brought Ermoor into a new technological era was dead.

Riffolk's wife, Mara, wasn't devastated. The more he thought about her the more it disturbed him. There was something wrong with that girl. Even after the trauma she'd suffered, and after losing her husband, she attempted to seduce him. By all accounts, the girl had been absolutely in love with Riffolk. Why then, would she behave so crudely such a short time after his death?

There were also the reports of her capture. Several soldiers said she'd shot lightning from her hands. A couple of them said she had some secret weapon Riffolk designed for her, which was the most logical possibility; except for the fact that no such device was found after her capture.

One said he saw a glimpse of the creature in her place as she was knocked out, and that it wasn't Mara Hayne at all. Mathys immediately disregarded that as hysterical, although the idea had briefly chilled him. Regardless of his soldier's exaggerations, one thing was certain; three of his men had died trying to bring her in.

He sat at his study desk, the scent of the heavy oiled wood mixing with the candles burning. There were electric lights in his study of course, but they were harsh and gave him headaches. The candlelight helped him relax and brought a cosiness to the study that he greatly enjoyed. An array of documents splayed over the desk; reports of Mara's capture, damage reports from the mysterious creature's rampage through the city, reports from the attack on Dreadhold, and more.

Several of Riffolk's latest inventions, *Photographs*, were spread over his desk as well; he still hadn't gotten used to the idea of capturing such a life-like image on paper. The devastated street where the creature had rampaged loomed up at him. Riffolk's lab, half destroyed, sat eerily flat on another sheet of paper. Sighing, he pushed his reading glasses up with his fingers to rub his eyes; the Lord Commander handled larger issues like warfare and national security. Mathys' job was to administer law and order, which included disasters and strange events like the one he was looking at now.

It didn't make him more equipped to do this particular job; it was baffling. The creature was obviously linked to Riffolk; most likely part of his project, but Mathys had only caught glimpses and snippets from sitting in on meetings. As far as he could tell, the creature was being drained of some kind of power, which was to be used to develop weapons. Mathys had argued endlessly with Arthor about the project, to no avail.

Added to that was a young girl who seemingly had magical powers, a destroyed lab and a dead scientist without a body found so far. He could make assumptions based on the nature of Riffolk's project, which were logical, but Mathys never gave much weight to assumptions until they became facts. Besides, the Twelve wouldn't act on anything without proof, and even that could take a long time.

He'd spoken with Mara several times, and as far as witnesses went, she was almost useless. Her memories were vague at best, she was confused and hysterical, and her moods completely changed from moment to moment. But she seemed to be a genuinely good person, and Mathys found himself wanting to protect her. Protection of individuals wasn't part of his job description at all, but something about her was so naive and vulnerable that he couldn't help it.

At the same time, he recognised the significance of her being at the centre of the mystery; he would only protect her as far as she remained innocent in the eyes of the law. Obviously she'd been found without a male escort, and she would be punished accordingly for that, but her involvement in the mysterious creature's escape and the death of Overseer Hayne was yet to be ascertained.

He felt certain of one thing, however; regardless of how innocent Mara Hayne was, there was something very different about her.

Riffolk

Riffolk woke, confused for the first time in his life. His entire body hurt, but his shoulder and neck pulsed with an intensity that made his eyes water. Then he remembered where he was; in his secret lab, on the cold ground. It was dark for the first time since he'd had it built. *No power. It's escaped.* Both thoughts were immensely unsettling. His plans had never gone so wrong before. The worst part about it was that he'd allowed the Tyran girl to surprise him into firing at the tank, setting the creature loose and destroying his project; it was his own fault.

At least she was dead now. How satisfying it had been to obliterate her head as she made her last defiant attack. Though now he'd never get away with wiping out the rest of the Tyrans; without the creature and its power, Ermoor was once more completely reliant on the giant wheels under the city. And with his project shut down, he wouldn't be able to continue his work without the separate source of power. And what good was his vast fortune if he couldn't use it to fund his work? He would have to plan and build another secret laboratory somehow... But power still remained an issue.

He paced the room, noting all of the undamaged equipment. He kept prototypes and final projects in a secure hidden safe-room, so he knew they were all still in perfect condition. He entered the safe-room, gazing over the designs he'd made in secret. His mind was always working, always creating. The safe-room was another level of security in an already secret lab; the door was a seamless section of the wall, and it contained not only his prototypes and blueprints, but a workstation and a self-sustained living space.

The first thing he had to do was protect the secrecy of the lab. With the Tyran dead his secrecy would be relatively safe, and if people assumed his death they'd have no reason to look too closely at the lab. Mara would be an unreliable witness; she would be confused about her feelings for him, and traumatised by the other girl's death. But there would of course be at least a cursory investigation at the lab; there was no way to hide the fact that the creature had originated there.

He inspected the storeroom entrance; the doorway was mangled, the room full of scorch marks. There was no way to seal it up again. When he stepped out of the storeroom, the creature's passage through his lab was clear as day; scorch marks covered every surface, as though the building had been set on fire. There was a curious energy in the air, and his shoulder throbbed as he walked through the destroyed building. He felt something peculiar.

Could it be? He thought, his mind racing, *a transference of energy? I theorised I may be able to do it... Even hoped. But it couldn't be as simple as a touch from the creature, could it?* The tingling in his shoulder grew again as he touched one of the scorch marks on the wall. A tiny spark of lightning jumped from the blackened wall to his finger. Where the spark touched he felt a tingling, but no pain.

Through his travels, he'd encountered magic before, and even used magical artefacts and devices. He'd accepted a long time ago that magic and science could coexist, that the existence of one didn't rule out the other. And he knew that magic could be bestowed upon someone, even if they'd been born without the ability to use it.

Focusing, he brought his hand up, staring at it as he pictured it crackle with lightning. A buzz emanated from his body, and an arc of pulsing energy leapt from his hand, slamming into the wall. He smiled. Magic, although wildly out of the bounds of conventional science, still followed rules. He'd read all he could find, and the knowledge finally paid off. He understood magic in a way that the vast majority of living beings never could, and now the ability itself was under his control.

He wandered further down the corridor, and saw that the creature made a more or less direct path straight to the main lab on the street side of the building before crashing straight through the wall. Its path led straight from the hole in the wall to the storeroom that housed the secret entrance. It was no good; he needed confusion, misdirection. Looking again at his hands, then at the perfectly clean walls around the lab that the creature hadn't touched, he lashed out with crackling energy, covering everything he saw. He laughed as the lab smoked and burned.

Elana

It was her one shot. There was no way of knowing when the secret laboratory would be unattended again. She told herself it was her only option. It was her mission. It would save lives. None of it helped; she would never forget those terrible eyes.

She couldn't kill it. It would stop Riffolk in his tracks, but it would cost an innocent life. She couldn't free it either; it had nowhere to go, and would only be recaptured or killed. Besides, Elana had no idea if it could even survive outside of the cage.

Her only option was to try to alter the outcome of Hayne's inhumane experiment. She examined the consoles surrounding the creature closely, and the wires leading into and out of the cage even more closely. She realised some of the wires were providing the creature with food and water, and some of them were draining something out of it. After carefully observing all of the components of the experiment, Elana unsheathed her sword. Squinting her eyes and bearing through the pain of the creature's insane thoughts, she began her work.

Don't kill it, she thought as she sliced into one of the outgoing wires, *Please don't kill it.* If she was right in her assumption, Riffolk had discovered how to use this mysterious creature's magical power as energy for whatever weapons he was building. If she could stop, or at least slow down, the energy being siphoned out of the poor creature... Maybe it would be enough. In the short term, at least. Until she found a way to eliminate Hayne.

She made a few small cuts, then worried at the wires with her blade, trying to make it look naturally frayed. If it looked natural enough, Hayne might think some vermin snuck in and chewed at the wires. She damaged as many as she could, and was satisfied when needles in several of the unlabelled gauges turned down almost to zero. As she sheathed her sword, she heard thumping footsteps beyond the metal door; Hayne already knew something was wrong.

Delving into the clear, slow focus that Shadow Magic bestowed, she traced the tattoos lining her fingers, first one hand, then the other. They tingled and glowed purple as the spell took effect. She squatted low, traced the symbols on her calves, and as soon as she felt the tingle of magic, leapt straight up to the high ceiling. Her fingers, now imbued with a binding spell, stuck to the smooth metal as though it was a part of her skin. She pulled herself into an upside down squatting position and settled into the roof, tracing the invisibility spell just as the door opened.

The lab was brightly lit, so Elana had no chance of complete invisibility, but the ceiling was high and she was banking on Riffolk's concern about the creature to distract him; he would be staring at the cage and the "chewed" wires long enough for her to escape.

But Hayne was unlike anyone Elana had ever seen. Despite the stakes, despite potentially losing his project, he entered the room slowly; he held a weapon in his hand, and his eyes scanned the entire room before glancing at the cage. Taking a few careful steps, weapon poised, Hayne looked ready for anything.

"I know you're in here," he said. His voice was conversational, but flat. There was no emotion whatsoever.

"I have many security measures in place. Whoever you are, you will not escape with your life. You've just – Ah. Hello."

His eyes, which hadn't stopped scanning the room, finally settled on the blurred, shadowy shape of Elana.

"One of the Shenza assassins, I presume?" His voice remained steady, his eyes cold and measuring. The weapon was pointed directly at her. Elana had seen the damage those weapons could do; they could be held and fired with one hand, but exploded like cannons, shredding and tearing the target to pieces in an instant. Elana stayed where she was, keeping the invisibility spell up.

"I'm no assassin," she said, trying to keep her own voice as steady and emotionless as Hayne's.

"But I will kill you if I have to."

A subtle smile tugged at the scientist's lips, never quite reaching his eyes.

"Feel free to try."

Sometimes, Shanaken's isolation from the rest of Pandeia was more a burden than a blessing. The *Duulshen* held to their traditions though, and most of the time, Elana heartily agreed. But sometimes it was infuriating. Not a single Shenza warrior would have challenged her the way Hayne had, not even her fellow *Kaizeluun*. If Shanaken was better known, better understood by Pandeia, Hayne would be terrified to be in the same room as a *Kaizeluun*.

She was caught. There was no use trying to hide from him. But she may still be able to get out of the lab. Hayne wouldn't tell anyone about her presence; admitting someone broke through his security to the Lord Commander would injure his reputation, perhaps stall or even stop the project. Besides, Hayne's arrogance new no bounds. In Elana's experience, arrogance was only a few steps from defeat.

She launched from the ceiling just as Hayne fired his weapon. She shot straight down, landing coiled on the floor. The ceiling above her exploded into a mess of shredded metal. By the time Hayne's eyes and weapon were trained on her again, her sword was in her hand and she was standing, ready. His eyes widened slightly at her speed, then narrowed into focused slits. Even that small amount of surprise was immensely satisfying.

Hayne's aura was almost as shocking as the creature's, though obviously nowhere near as powerful. There were layers to his energy, almost as though she was looking at several people standing in a row and seeing all of their energies on top of each other. Each layer was slightly different, not quite aligning with the others. He had no magical ability, she could see that at a glance. But there was *something* there. A kind of energy she'd never seen before.

"What... *are* you?" she couldn't stop herself from asking. He ignored her.

Even considering the speed and power of Hayne's weapon, Elana felt relatively confident. She'd fought the Ermoori before, after all. The only difference this time was the intelligence of the man before her. She'd never come across anyone who could design and build machines. Despite her confidence and skill, she would have to play this carefully. Other than her initial jump from the ceiling back to the floor, Elana moved as slowly and steadily as she could, keeping eye contact, her sword lowered. Riffolk was just as slow, just as careful.

"I will kill you if I have to," she repeated, "but murder is not the mission."

He seemed genuinely surprised.

"What else would you be here for?"

She gestured at the creature with her sword, careful not to move the blade too fast. The hand holding his weapon twitched the instant she moved, but he didn't fire; his reflexes were sharp. He smiled.

"Do you know what it is? What it will do to your people?"

She just stared. He knew the answer already; how could she know? Riffolk sighed.

"No, of course you don't. Well, it seems we have a decision to make."

His eyes were so, so cold. Elana tried to imagine Hayne being a loving husband to the young wife she knew was waiting for him at his mansion; she found it impossible. His marriage was either a fraud which the young girl was in on, or he was an incredible manipulator and the girl was genuinely in love with a monster. As much as it saddened Elana, she found the latter option much easier to believe.

"I have no reason to trust you, of course," he said, "but as it stands we are both equally in danger from each other. While I don't cherish the idea of letting you live, I'll make no move to kill you if it means you leave this place tonight."

He waved at the creature with his free hand, "you've clearly already done whatever damage you came here to do. It'll either slow me down, or it won't, but that's out of your hands now."

A small tattoo on the inside of her palm, two parallel lines in the centre, held a vital combat spell. On intuition, she balled her left hand into a fist, ready to draw her two middle fingers along the lines. Hayne kept talking.

"So the decision is this: leave, and we both live. Or attack, and one or both of us die. I warn you though; I have far more weapons at my disposal than this-" he lifted the weapon slightly, pointing at her face instead of her chest, "-and even if you kill me, it's unlikely you'll escape with your life."

Elana almost laughed.

"I got through your defences, Hayne," she said, noting his discomfort at her using his name, "I've been here for weeks."

"And I've been monitoring you the entire time."

No. He couldn't have known.

"Nothing happens in this lab without my knowledge."

She stared again, a sliver of doubt weaving through her thoughts. Had he really known she was here? Simply letting her explore the lab while watching? A cold fear stabbed her heart; was the information she'd found even true? The meeting with the Lord Commander couldn't have been an act... could it?

A smirk spread over Hayne's lips as he watched her doubt grow. His arrogance was infuriating. He watched her chase her thoughts the way he might watch a baby animal play with an insect; idle amusement mixed with smug superiority. It looked almost as if he pitied her. If a monster like Hayne was even capable of pity.

"So?"

The sharpness in his voice snapped her out of her thoughts.

"Fight or flight?"

She balanced her sword in her hand. It was a purely habitual gesture; the *Kaizuun* was perfectly balanced to her, and she'd trained extensively with it. Hayne noticed, widened his stance and brought his weapon up. Her weight was balanced perfectly on the balls of her feet, her centre of gravity low. Her body was relaxed but prepared for sudden movement. She dipped into the magic within the *Kaizuun*, feeling the energy and strength it held flow into her.

Hayne reached into a pocket with his free hand, and Elana moved before his hand had touched whatever it was reaching for. Her fingers dragged up her palm and a black circle bloomed around her forearm. He fired his weapon, the noise deafening. Her shield took the brunt of the attack, but ragged pain seared her thigh as she ran at him. She kept her shield raised and cannoned into him, throwing all of her weight into the attack. He flew backwards, smashing into the metal door on the opposite side of the room and spilling into a heap on the ground.

His left hand held a small device, and although he was no longer conscious, a red light blinked on its face, painting his hand and face a sickly shade of orange. Clanking and whirring echoed from somewhere in the building, growing louder. Elana sheathed her sword and leapt for the ceiling in one move, crawling along the smooth surface as quickly and easily as running on the ground.

As she reached the vent in the ceiling, she realised too late she'd forgotten to reactivate the invisibility spell; the device Hayne had planted screamed and exploded right next to her head.

Riffolk

It was time to take control. He'd tried working under the Twelve Crowns, making himself indispensable and providing Ermoor with a new technological era. He'd tried working in secret, continuing the project without the involvement of the Crowns so that he could work without the bureaucratic nonsense they imposed.

There was one path of action left to him, if he wanted to finally finish his work. He needed access to the power and resources of Ermoor, without the approval of the Twelve Crowns. Nobody in Ermoor knew who the Twelve Crowns were. Nobody knew where they lived or where they met. They governed from the shadows. Unfortunately for them, Riffolk had decided years ago that he wasn't willing to work for people he couldn't meet or keep track of. Finding them had been difficult, but well within his capabilities.

Some of their identities had surprised him; his own father, for example. But regardless of the names attached to the Crowns, they were in his way. A plan formed in his mind. He set to work with a smile on his face.

The underground lab was lit again. There was nowhere near as much power as he'd had before, with the creature, but enough to use the scaled down equipment in his safe-room. Once he covered up the creature's tracks and built a makeshift door in the storeroom out of shelves and a section of the lab wall, he'd filled one of his energy orbs with lightning. The first one exploded, but after some tinkering, he was able to charge them directly in his hands.

The image transmitting device, which for want of a better term he'd dubbed the television, sat on one of the small benches in the small space. He set up two transmitters, one in the underground lab and one in the corridor outside the safe-room entrance, which sent images to the television. He could flick between them using a switch, but for now it was set on the corridor; if anyone approached, he needed to see them before they potentially found the secret entrance.

He kept the main underground lab dark and empty, just in case. No light escaped from the safe-room, he'd tested it when he first set it up. The false shelf acting as a door looked heavy, but could be moved easily; so he had fast access to and from the lab. Fog would have helped a lot, but the weather was turning warm; so he only left the lab and returned under cover of darkness.

Five of the Twelve were dead, including his father. He'd set each one up to look like an accident. The look on Sir Isaac Hayne's face as he died brought a shiver of pleasure down Riffolk's spine. His father had ever been a damper on his work. Despite all the public comments he made about being proud of his son, his actions told another tale. As useless a Crown as he was a father, Riffolk was not at all sad to see him die. Planning the act had been a joy in and of itself; he had to make sure there were no witnesses, no evidence, and nothing to shed a suspicious light on the man's death. It had been a puzzle he'd greatly enjoyed solving.

Since no one knew the identities of the Twelve but themselves and Riffolk, having all twelve of them die in a short time wasn't going to be suspicious beyond the fact of a spate of sudden accidents. There would be investigations, possibly, but Ermoor would go on without realising their leaders were dead. Their layers of secrecy made his work relatively easy. It was almost laughable; in staying so well hidden, they'd guaranteed their deaths would go unnoticed.

The one thing he couldn't be sure of was Symonds' reaction; he didn't know if the Lord Commander knew any of the Twelve's identities, or if he would recognise their absence for what it was. He knew it was fairly common for only one or a few of the Twelve to meet with him at a time, and he'd be able to take advantage of that in the short term. But beyond that his knowledge of what Symond knew was severely lacking.

He would overcome that obstacle when he came to it; in the meantime, his focus was the complete destruction of the highest levels of Ermoori Government, to be replaced by himself. His research had uncovered far more information than just their names; he knew how they accessed the city's treasury, where their records and archives were kept, the contacts they held both internally and in other countries... He had enough to effectively take over with little to no negative effect on Ermoor itself.

Returning his attention to the present moment, he looked down at his father's corpse. With the other four so far deceased, he'd arranged things so that they died while he was elsewhere. He couldn't be seen now that he was assumed dead, and it was an unnecessary risk to bother killing them all in person. But he'd wanted to be present when his father died; he'd wanted to look into the man's eyes as his life fled his body. Sir Isaac Hayne had been a great man, despite

Riffolk's dislike of him; he couldn't deny that. But he was still a lousy father and a bore.

Smiling, he left the guest house in the Hayne Mansion's garden, closing the door behind him. Moonlight shone on the vibrant green grass, turning it a serene silver-blue, and Riffolk found himself in a pleasant mood as he returned to the secret lab. It took almost two full days for his father's body to be found.

The funeral, just like the man for which it was held, bored Riffolk almost to tears. Held at Rookfell Square, where he'd been named Overseer for Scientific Advancement, the memorial service was long and pointless. Sir Isaac Hayne was only well known by virtue of being born into the Hayne family, and for fathering a genius. Other than that he could boast no public accomplishments of his own. Riffolk barely listened to the words being spoken.

The only interesting part of the funeral was the presence of the remaining five Crowns; he'd been able to eliminate two more before the service. They must have attended funerals for the others he'd killed too; he wondered if they were scared yet. He watched them closely from a window in a nearby Government building overlooking the square, hidden from their view; they looked weary, and he could have sworn their eyes wandered through the crowd, paranoid. It made the long service bearable. He already had everything set up for the next Crown. They would die today.

The Spectre

The armour felt good. He stood on the corner of a building rooftop, his cloak flowing in the breeze. It had been a long, long time. Dozens of weapons and tools lay hidden within the armour, the fabric sleeves and the folds of his cloak. He knew the placement of each one, and could snatch them out ready to use in the blink of an eye.

The Twelve were after him. If he wasn't careful, they would succeed in their quest to have him killed. He cursed them for being so well hidden; if they slipped up at all, he would have killed them already. He loved Ermoor, and he was willing to do whatever it took to make sure it was a safe and beautiful city.

The Twelve Crowns, for all their talk of building a secure society, were no longer acting in Ermoor's best interests. He had to stop them. Not just from the invasion, but from themselves; they were corrupt. The Twelve had been ruling from the shadows for almost two thousand years, never changing, never growing. Their only redeeming quality now was that they'd held onto God and remained devout.

On the street below, he saw two cloaked figures emerge from an abandoned building. Ivorstorm was home to at least a dozen abandoned factories, putting more of the lower class out of work than ever before in Ermoor's history. The two figures he watched walked together down the street, eyes forward. They moved purposefully, their steps strong and certain.

If they'd been careful, they would have moved slower, wandering and talking, as the workers of Ivorstorm did. It was the first time he'd seen members of the Twelve slip up.

He'd long suspected the abandoned factories as potential meeting places, but so far had never seen anything to back that up; until tonight. Something was happening; something serious enough that the Twelve were losing their focus. It was finally his time.

They walked straight towards Ironhaven; another mistake. He followed for a while, finally close enough to hear their hushed voices.

"I don't understand, how is this possible?"

"I know everything you do, brother. It shouldn't be possible at all."

"We've remained in the shadows, completely undetected, for close to two thousand years!"

"Maybe what the Lord Commander was saying is -"

"Shut up! Not out here, not outside the chamber. There could be listeners anywhere."

The figures both looked around, and he stopped moving, crouching on top of the street light where he stood. In broad daylight, he would have been as obvious as a cartwheeling clown, but the nights in Ermoor were foggy, and the street lights were bright and colourful, creating a visual barrier between the ground and everything above.

"Anyway, we must focus on protection, as brother Dreadhold said. There aren't many of us left."

"Shh!"

They scurried on, oblivious to him. He followed, but nothing more was said between them.

Elana

She woke with a start. Her body was stuck, bound by something that felt like a metal clamp. The brightly lit room slowly came back into focus, and Elana found herself staring into a large red triangle of light. She was hanging half a metre from the ground. As her vision finally returned, the light in front of her became a terrifying machine's eye, trained intently on her. It bristled with weapons, each one aimed precisely. She strained against her bonds; she couldn't move at all.

"I did warn you."

Hayne's voice carried gently through the silent room. He stepped from behind the machine, watching her with that same amused, condescending expression.

"I may not have a magical sword, but I can assure you the weapons I've designed are far more deadly."

Elana let him talk. She couldn't hope to escape the metal device holding her, not with physical strength. If she could reach her sword, she had no doubt it was sharp enough to slice through the metal. Shadow magic was far stronger than the metal used in Ermoor. But her sword was in Hayne's hand, and her arms couldn't move at all; it may as well have been back in Shanaken. She could move her hands though. Not much, but she could make a fist. It was enough.

"You have no idea how deadly Shadow Magic is, Hayne."

As he started laughing, she activated the shield spell with both hands. The shields spread instantly, rending through the thick metal binds with a loud grating sound. She dropped to the ground, rolled, and sprinted past Hayne, snatching her *Kaizuun* as she went, keeping him between her and the machine. It sidestepped its master, and a high pitched whine started as its weapons prepared to fire.

She brought her right hand back and shot it forward, hurling the shield with all her strength at the machine. Her shield hit it directly in the bright red eye at its centre just as it started firing. Her left shield was already up, but only a few shots from its weapons hit before the machine was thrown off balance by her attack.

She moved instantly, sliding her sword from its sheath and launching herself in a high arc at the machine before it could recover. It kept firing blindly, aiming at where Elana had been. Her shield, buried in the machine's eye, disintegrated after a few seconds; but the damage was done, and the red triangle was dull and cracked. Her leap carried her over the thing's head. She dropped the left shield spell, took her *Kaizuun* in both hands, and swept the blade down hard.

Her Shadow Blade sheared through the metal as though it was the tender meat of an animal, and the machine crumpled to the floor as she landed in a ready stance facing Hayne. He still didn't look scared. Instead, her skill and refusal to be captured appeared to enrage him. A tight snarl pulled at his lips, though his eyes were as cold and dispassionate as ever. He aimed his weapon at her and fired, again and again. She leapt straight up, drawing as much strength as she could from her Kaizuun. She spun, landed feet first on the ceiling and kicked as hard as she could at an angle, shooting over Hayne and behind him.

He kept firing, reloading after every second shot, trying to keep up with her speed and failing despite his reflexes. His weapon boomed over and over, filling the room with explosions that left Elana's ears ringing. A sharp pain flared in her left arm, and too late she activated the left shield again. Landing behind Hayne, she shoved her shield savagely into his back before he could turn to engage her. He sprawled onto the cold metal floor. He didn't lose his grip on the weapon, and snapped around to face her faster than she would have believed. She brought her shield up and braced for more explosions, but a dull click came from the weapon instead.

Elana lowered her shield just enough to look Hayne in the eyes. He threw his weapon away, staring at her. This time his expression spread further than his lips; a tiny spark of fury danced in his eyes.

"What you do here today will make no real difference," he said, "Shanaken will fall."

The fury in his eyes vanished almost as quickly as it appeared.

"All of Pandeia will fall."

Mara

The doctors were cold, clinical and uncaring, looking at her as though she were simply an object with no thoughts or feelings. There were three of them, in a room as barren and sterile as the room she was being kept in. Wordlessly, they passed her between each other, staring, prodding and groping. Not just her shoulder wound, but her entire body. They'd stripped her the moment she was lead to the examination room, with even less passion than Commander Corby. Each of the doctors carried a pad of paper and a pencil, and each made constant notes as they moved her around and stared and probed at her body.

Afterwards, they simply left the room, leaving her to pick her clothes off the floor and get dressed alone. Not a single word had been said between any of them, and Mara had been too terrified and uncomfortable to ask any questions. For a brief moment before they left, she'd felt the energy within her swell as her anger grew, and a small flash of light coloured the room a pale yellow. The doctors stopped scribbling for a moment, before each rushing to take notes even faster than before. Inside her, a mindless hunger told her to destroy them all, destroy the building, destroy Ermoor.

No. Your moment will come. For now, you must hide your power.

The creature's voice brought her back from the insane hunger she'd felt, and her fear of the doctors seeing her power stopped it from coming back. The examination, though simple, was already uncomfortable enough; she couldn't imagine the kinds of tests they'd do if they realised she had magic powers.

The thought made her pause. *Magic isn't real,* she thought, as images flashed through her mind of what she'd done to the soldiers trying to take her. There was no easy answer. She'd been told her entire life that there was no magic but for the miracles performed by God himself.

Now, not only had she found a being who seemed as powerful as God, but she was also able to wield magic herself. None of it made sense. Maybe the entire thing was a test from God. Maybe she'd already died, and this was the journey towards heaven, the weighing of her soul to determine how she lived for eternity. Or maybe she'd been hit in the head too hard by an Ermoori soldier, or by Riffolk himself, and everything that was happening was some awful nightmare.

After the examination, she'd dressed in a numb haze, feeling helpless despite the incredible power she felt inside herself. When she opened the door to leave, a guard standing just outside grabbed her, forcing her down the corridor and back into the room she was kept in. He left without saying a word, and she sat on the bench and stared at the floor. She'd always been helpless, she knew that now. The difference was that now she finally had power, but couldn't use it.

In a distant echo, coming from a small, dark corner of her mind, the creature's voice emerged again.

Your moment will come.

Commander Corby entered her room as she was waking up, her eyes still blurry. She'd been given a plain white slip to sleep in, and didn't bother changing into regular clothes during the day. She would either be examined by the scientists, or would spend another day alone in the bare room; there was no reason to be dressed up. Other than her horrible memories and nightmares, the one thing that bothered her was not having access to make-up; her face felt naked and exposed, and it was the first time anyone but her parents or Riffolk had seen her without make-up on.

He closed the door behind him, standing with his hand on the door knob until she sat up. It had been four days. She still didn't remember much of what had happened, and what she did know, she wasn't sure she wanted to tell them. Too much had happened lately to shake her faith, and now she had no idea who or what to believe. The only thing that seemed real was the energy flowing through her body and the constant buzzing of the wound in her shoulder.

"We've run every test we can. Your shoulder doesn't make sense from a medical perspective, but we need to keep you here to monitor its healing."

His eyes bored into her own, piercing and relentless. *How much longer?* She wanted to ask, but she was too afraid of the answer. Surely they weren't allowed to keep her here too long... there had to be rules against it.

"We also need to talk about what you remember, Mara. Ermoor needs to know."

Lowering her eyes to his boots again, she waited for the questions.

"You told me there was a girl from Tyra who spoke to you. A girl called Pera. Where is she?"

Tears sprang into her eyes without warning. The image of her corpse on the cold ground of the lab was still vivid, her destroyed head jutting up from her shoulders like some horrible, jagged crown.

"She's... He killed her."

"Oh, Mara. I'm sorry. Where did it happen?"

"He shot her in the lab, just before the thing escaped."

"Do you remember which room?"

"What? There was only one room."

He paused, genuinely confused.

"Riffolk's lab is the largest scientific facility in Ermoor. There are dozens of rooms, including several separate laboratory rooms. Do you remember which one she was killed in?"

Mara couldn't stop the sobbing; her chest and shoulders heaved as she gasped for breath.

"No, it was in the secret lab, under – underneath. The thing – it smashed out of – of the door... didn't you see it?"

Commander Corby stared at her as though she had suddenly grown an extra arm.

"We searched the entire lab after collecting you from the street. It was already empty from the shut down. There were signs of severe damage from the creature's rampage, and some remains of Riffolk's clothing, but nothing like what you're describing."

She shook her head violently, her heart thumping. He wasn't listening!

"There's a secret entrance, the thing was under his lab in a huge tank! He took us and kept us down there, and then he shot her and then it escaped and I shot him but the thing grabbed him and threw him and then it grabbed me and threw me too but I survived, and then I walked out of the lab and soldiers found me but the secret entrance was still open!"

She fell silent, and he went back to simply staring at her. It was simple enough in her mind, but the words kept getting jumbled and she was close to panic. Everything she said seemed to go right past him.

"You shot Riffolk?"

"Yes... Yes. I'm sorry. He killed her and I thought he set the thing loose and I was so scared and he hurt me so badly."

Catching herself before she went into detail, she lowered her eyes and forced herself into silence. He shifted, his eyes narrowing.

"He hurt you? What did he do?"

"Nothing! He was my husband, it's not my place to complain. He loved me, I know he did. I loved him."

"So it was you who killed him, not the creature?"

"No! No, I shot him with the sleeping dart gun, the monster grabbed him and threw him across the lab. I never wanted to kill him!"

"If I brought you back to the lab, could you show me the secret entrance?"

She froze. To make him believe her, she would have gladly gone back there. But if they hadn't seen it, that meant someone sealed the door and covered it up again, immediately after she left. It meant Riffolk was still alive.

Riffolk

Riffolk smiled, waiting in the dark chamber. Over the last week, each of the remaining Twelve had died, one by one. Now, the 'Crowns' were scheduled to meet with the Lord Commander to discuss how the invasion could proceed with the project cancelled. He'd already informed Symond that only one Crown would be attending. As far as Symond knew, the Crowns were still at odds with him for cancelling the project against their wishes. He had no plans to dissuade the Lord Commander of that notion.

Riffolk waited in place of the Crown, the dark cowl they wore in their secret meetings stuffy and irritating. But nothing could damper the satisfaction he felt now; the last Crown lay in a pool of his own blood, less than twenty feet from the chamber. He'd died only minutes before, babbling about how Riffolk had no idea what he was doing, how Pandeia would be unbalanced and destroyed now that the Crowns were dead. He'd said it with no trace of irony, as if he genuinely didn't realise how utterly useless the Twelve Crowns had become.

There were two entrances; one, reserved solely for the actual Twelve, and the second, a private and hidden entrance only revealed to those who had business with them. With the Twelve dead, their secret entrance was now a complete secret, known only to Riffolk. From what he could determine, there were fewer than a dozen people in all of Ermoor who knew about the second entrance. He had no fear of any of them revealing it; as far as they knew, the Twelve were alive and well, and just as dangerous as ever.

Under the black robe he wore, his two guns sat in their holsters, one on each side of his belt. He wasn't sure what to expect of Symond in his desperation, especially now that he knew he'd be meeting with a single Crown; he needed to be ready for anything. By this point, Symond would be willing to do almost anything to get himself and his wife to safety. Riffolk was aware of the order for Symonds' retirement, of course; it had been given a day after he'd killed the first Crown.

Almost two weeks later, with all the Crowns dead, it was almost time for Symond to be removed from office. Riffolk still didn't have a suitable replacement, which worried him. Perhaps the Commander, Mathys Corby? All of his information indicated a man as morally upright as Symond himself; if that was correct, replacing Symond with Corby would only create the same problems he was dealing with now.

The command structure in Ermoor was odd, to say the least. It was designed to keep those who had money and connections in power, without regard to intelligence, skill, or any other merit. He understood it from their perspective, of course; but it was an objectively terrible way to rule a massive city. The brilliance of it, however, was that the Twelve Crowns had almost complete power. They could do anything in Ermoor, regardless of the law, because they created the law.

And now that power was his. The one aspect of Ermoor's administration he didn't have complete control of was military matters. And since his project was military based, he was still stuck. As he waited for Symond to show up, he realised he might need the Lord Commander after all. The thought irked him more than it should have, and his mood darkened. By the time footsteps began echoing through the chamber, announcing Symonds' entrance, he was as certain about his plan as he was furious.

Arthor

Arthor's boots thumped against the cold, black stone, echoing as he approached the Twelve. He'd been called to an emergency meeting at the last moment; there was no way to refuse. Ellie had begged him not to go, but to decline a meeting with them at this stage would invite an immediate retaliation. It was only one more day until his 'retirement'. If he could smooth things over with them, or at least make them believe he was going to cooperate, it may just assist him to escape.

He'd tried to leave Ermoor earlier, but to no avail. He was too easily recognised; the problem with being the public face of the Ermoori Government. If he'd been one of the Twelve there would be no such trouble; he'd have almost limitless resources as well as anonymity. But every time he tried to leave the country, he was seen, confronted, asked questions. He had, at the least, sent Ellie away, and was glad for that much; she'd be safe.

Now there was just the matter at hand; he found himself shaking as he walked through the dark corridor, certain he was walking to his death. The coded letter he received said they wanted to discuss how to proceed with the project after he'd cancelled the production of energy and weapons; asking him how to get around the obstacle he himself had put up for them. It was an insult and they knew it. He assumed they were trying to provoke him into attacking or at least putting himself in contempt again to justify killing him now.

The chamber was deathly silent when he entered, and full of shadows. As he was forewarned, only a single member of the Twelve was present. He could have taken it as an insult, but he was too scared to be angry about it. Besides, just like with everything the Twelve did, it was most likely either a game or a trap or both; they were simply seeing if he would take the opportunity to attack one solitary person. The other eleven members were probably hiding in the chamber somewhere, watching and waiting.

He moved to the centre of the room, surrounded by the twelve seats where the Crowns usually sat. The one Crown who'd showed up sat in one of the two middle seats, sitting proper and tense. Arthor was immediately alarmed; they usually sat in arrogant hunches, their posture as bad as their attitude. There was something eerily different about the Crown sitting before him, and yet horribly familiar. It felt as though a monster sat in place of the person, a monster he'd seen in his nightmares. For a second, he thought it might be the shadowy being that spoke into his mind; but he didn't say anything in case he was simply imagining things. He stood silently, waiting for the Crown to address him. He was determined to do everything right. For a moment, the Crown simply sat, watching.

"Lord Commander Arthor Symond. You were previously found to be in contempt of the Twelve Crowns, and given the order to submit for retirement one day from today. This meeting is to discuss Ermoor's future plans for Pandeia, and how they might be realised. You have made it clear that you don't believe Overseer Hayne's methods were sound."

His voice remained level, emotionless, and Arthor struggled to keep calm. *Of course his methods weren't sound!* He thought. *He captured some creature and set it loose on the city!*

"You now have a chance to redeem yourself. Do you see any alternate pathway to the same goal?"

The words struck him like a bucket full of cold water. *A chance to redeem myself?* He thought immediately of Ellie; he'd sent her away already, but if he could salvage the situation with the Twelve and remove his retirement order, he could call her back.

"There are always other paths. I can achieve the same goal as Riffolk, I promise."

Even to himself, his voice sounded oddly calm and confident. The man in front of him didn't react at all; it felt like staring at a statue.

"That remains to be seen, Lord Commander. We wish to discuss *how* you will deliver your promise. Without a plan, your promises are meaningless."

Arthor didn't have an easy answer. The truth was he could deliver what they wanted, but it would take much, much longer than the timeline Riffolk's project made possible. It felt far too early to give them such bad news, however, and he got the uneasy feeling of walking on thin, cracking ice above a deathly cold lake.

"We still have the energy coming from the Tyrans," he said quietly, "that's on top of the factories in Darkpoint, and using blueprints Riffolk already drew up, we will be able to begin manufacturing units almost immediately, though they will need to be projectile weapons instead of energy based. Without the systems he designed and the automation process, it may take a little longer. But we will get to the same result."

The Crown stared again. They were usually easier to read, and he found himself again filled with the odd feeling that the person in front of him was someone else. *Something* else.

"I see," the Crown finally said. "How much longer?"

He hesitated, but there was no point dancing around the bottom line; the Twelve would find out eventually.

"Years. The original timeline, before Riffolk's project started, was twenty years. As you know. Now, with the recent setbacks our scientific district and resources have suffered, it may even be longer."

The Crown finally reacted, with an audible scoff. "We simply cannot wait that long, Lord Commander. You're not fighting very hard to avoid your retirement."

"You're forgetting one thing, your honour; without Riffolk, you have no choice. I am your only way to achieve Ermoor's goals."

It was a risky move, a bold statement. He had to force himself to stand still, maintaining eye contact. Another silence filled the chamber, pressing in on Arthor until he heard his heartbeat in his ears.

"Very well. The order for your retirement is hereby retracted. You will oversee this project, though we urge you to use any means necessary to expedite the timeline. This project is paramount. You have one last chance."

Arthor's mind was whirling as he stepped out from the secret entrance into the tunnels that lead to the Chamber of the Twelve. *Another chance!* He'd desperately hoped for exactly that, and it seemed almost too good to be true. He knew he had to be careful; it could be a trap, a way to lull him into feeling safe so they could more easily 'retire' him. He decided to let Ellie go for now, to continue her journey to Tarsium in safety; just in case. He would write to her every chance he got, and would call her back as soon as he could be certain of their safety in Ermoor.

In the meantime, he had to find a way to continue work on the invasion, without Riffolk's help. The creature had already escaped, so he knew it wouldn't be used again. With that moral qualm silenced, he could work on the project without the heavy sense of guilt he'd felt before. Invasion always meant death, there was no way around that; but moving things along using honest work and fighting with honest weapons was something he could feel okay with.

Besides, the Shenza seemed to relish in warfare; they were the most effective warriors he'd ever seen, and he'd read reports of the Thearan desert tribes and their savagery. The Shenza approached battle with a sort of dignity he begrudgingly admired. They didn't take pleasure from killing like his own soldiers did, but their skill was unrivalled. Ermoor had landed on their shores many times over his career, and never made it beyond the sand into the forests.

So for the moment, his guilt was gone. He had spent his career leading the attacks on Shanaken, so warfare was not something that troubled him. What had bothered him so much about Riffolk's methods was the sheer brutality of it. He stripped every chance their enemies had away, effectively turning war into slaughter. Arthor could lead men into battle, could order the deaths of thousands, but condoning weapons that rendered their enemies completely helpless? It was akin to invading and destroying a village full of children. It wasn't *right.*

War must be won at all costs. Right or wrong is irrelevant.

Still, he had a second chance now, if the Crown wasn't simply playing with him. He could try to steer Ermoor back onto the right path. If it didn't work, at least he could say he tried. When he got back to his office, he sent a servant to fetch Mathys. Commander Corby was a reliable source of objective moral guidance. When he walked into Arthor's office, he was more animated than usual. Arthor raised his eyebrows.

"How goes the babysitting?"

Mathys laughed, shaking his head. People who didn't know him assumed he was a perpetually serious man, but around Arthor at least, he was quick to smile and laugh.

"How do you think? A sixteen year old girl after a trauma; not fun."

"At least it's an interesting investigation, if nothing else. I've read the reports of her capture. Your men have some impressive imaginations."

Mathys laughed again, though with less real humour.

"Yes... It's proving to be more puzzling than I thought."

"How do you think those men died?"

"I really don't know, Arthor. Regardless of the stories, the girl was clearly involved somehow. As little sense as it makes, she's the one common thread."

He shook his head, and Arthor saw how many hours Mathys had already spent thinking about the issue in the darkness under his eyes. He dropped it and moved on; Mathys had a habit of fixating on problems until they were solved, to his own detriment, and Arthor didn't want to contribute to his stress.

"I'm sure you'll get there in the end. You've got a great team of investigators, the mystery will become clearer with each day."

"We can certainly hope so. But I've never seen anything like this, Arthor. The creature. I received written orders from the Twelve, you know. To commission a task force to track down and recapture it."

That jarred him, and he couldn't stop his reaction. Wordless for a moment, he simply stared at Mathys with his mouth slightly open. It would have been comical were it not for the circumstances.

"They want the creature back in the city?"

"The orders stated they could contain it once captured. If it's allowed to roam loose, it could come back to the city anyway and destroy even more."

"You know they'll just attempt to use it for power again."

"Orders are orders, Lord Commander. You know that better than most. My duty is to the Twelve Crowns, and more importantly to Ermoor itself. I will do whatever it takes to keep this city safe."

He is working with the Twelve. They are keeping secrets from you.

"But the creature... The simple fact of its escape shows it won't be safe here."

"Do you think the Twelve would have ordered its capture without a plan in place to hold it?"

"I think they believe they can hold it. But if Riffolk himself couldn't, how could they?"

Mathys thought about it, then shook his head.

"You know I haven't always agreed with the Twelve, Arthor; or with you for that matter. But if we don't have faith in our own Government, how can we live in peace? They've given me orders, and unless I have a real reason not to, I intend to follow them."

Arthor sighed. As moral as Mathys was, he was also stubborn and ruthless; his previous life attested to that. He'd been strongly against the project Riffolk had designed, but still argued the same way whenever the issue had come up between them; orders were orders, and he would protect Ermoor no matter what. He was a great Commander, but the same traits that made him so also made him difficult to talk to when it came to moral issues.

Arthor had expected this kind of conversation, but he hadn't even raised the topic he'd meant to raise.

"We're still planning the invasion," he said.

Mathys didn't react at all for a moment. He had an uncanny ability to keep his face utterly emotionless.

"I see. And the weapons you were going to use?"

"Won't work without the creature's power. We'll be using projectile weapons."

He gave a slow nod.

"And you called me here to ease your conscience now that the creature isn't being harvested to create weapons of mass murder?"

He doesn't understand.

There was no judgement in his tone, but the words still cut right to his core; Mathys could always tell exactly what lay in his heart. He was an eerily accurate judge of character, even with people he didn't know as well as he knew Arthor.

"Well you have what you desired, Arthor. I'm pleased that horrible project is done. The war to come won't be pleasant, but at least it will be fought honestly. It's the least we can hope for."

He strode from the room before Arthor could respond, then stopped at the door and turned back.

"I just pray you're wrong about the Twelve. If they decide to use the creature again, even if we win the war, we'll lose our souls."

Elana

Elana sat on her bedroll on the rooftop she'd claimed as her camp-site, thinking about Hayne and Ermoor. In many ways, he embodied Ermoor itself; advanced, intelligent, and headstrong, but also violent and cruel. It was a toxic place. Her connection to Shadow Magic was growing weaker. If her fight with Hayne had occurred in the forests, he could have thrown dozens of his machines at her, and she would have walked away without a scratch.

Her injuries were worse than she originally realised. The focus of combat had died down now, leaving her tired, shaking, and sore.

Her right thigh, her left bicep, and her left calf had been torn by whatever projectile Hayne's weapons shot out. From the mangled look of her injuries, it seemed as though the hand cannons spewed chunks of jagged metal.

She was grateful the weapons could only carry a finite number of projectiles. Once unarmed, Hayne had been easy to take down. She hadn't killed him, though perhaps she should have. But at the moment her chance came, he'd thrown his weapon away, and lay helpless on the ground. Regardless of his intentions, she was honour-bound to let him live. She adhered strictly to the three tenets of the Shenza;

Peace without weakness;
Strength without aggression;
Growth without forgetting.

The second tenet, *Strength without aggression*, held that unprovoked aggression was a terrible crime. Murder of an unarmed victim, regardless of the situation, was seen by the *Duulshen* as one of the worst possible things a Shenza could do. So she'd knocked the scientist unconscious, damaged as much of the lab's equipment as she dared, and escaped through the air ducts.

It left her doubting the *Duulshen* just a little for the first time. She knew there were other lives at stake, Shenza lives, but this was the first time she'd been asked to eliminate people for a mission. *They must have meant eliminate without killing, surely,* she thought. There had to be a way to eliminate them without murder.

Her mission was drawing close to an end; she could feel it. For one thing, she'd already been discovered, albeit by a man who wouldn't admit what had happened to anyone else. For another, she knew as much as it was possible to know. If the information she'd found was somehow faked, she would never be able to find the real information now that Hayne was onto her. If it was real, she had more than enough to bring back to the Duulshen. She knew the meeting between Hayne and Symond wasn't faked. Symond was insane, but he wasn't the type to play games, especially not with Hayne; his dislike for the man was evident from a distance.

All she had left to do was find a way to eliminate the Lord Commander without killing him. Now that she knew how unstable he was, she just had to think of a way to exploit it.

Drawing her *Kaizuun*, she rose and settled into the *Zuunshai*, the blade dance, which also served as meditation. Despite her torn flesh, the dance gave her energy and relieved the soreness of her muscles.

After the dance she meditated, activating a healing spell with the tattoo over her heart. The injuries weren't completely healed; she didn't have enough magic, but the pain shrank to a dull ache. When she was finished, she dressed the wounds as best she could, ate some stolen food, and fell into a troubled sleep.

The Lord Commander's mansion was in Ironhaven, one district over from the military base that contained his office. It was luxurious, but sparsely furnished, making it feel to Elana like one of the training platforms in Shanaken. Symond was married, his wife young and beautiful just like Hayne's. But unlike Hayne's marriage, Symond and his wife seemed genuinely in love. They shared a meal every night, talking and laughing as they ate. He was caring and attentive with her, and it was clear she had no idea that he was insane.

While in the mansion, he never lapsed into the mad rambling she'd seen so often from him. In fact, he hid his madness from everyone perfectly. It made Elana uncomfortable; how could someone control their own insanity? It didn't make sense. She had to find out more about his mental state; it was the key to eliminating him without resorting to murder. If she could reveal him to his wife, to Ermoor, his command would be called into question. Ermoori politics were a mystery to her, but they seemed to have complex processes for everything; approval, voting, meetings, and so on, even to get something simple done. Something as important as the role of Lord Commander would surely take a long time to resolve.

She watched them eat and talk, staring into each other's eyes. The young woman's love and admiration for her husband were strong and unquestioning. Seeing him smile, confident and charming, Elana couldn't blame her; if this had been her first impression of him, she may not have believed he was insane after all.

After their meal, the two made love in their bed, passionate and intense. They fell asleep curled into each other's embrace shortly after, and Elana slipped down from her perch on a nearby rooftop and slipped into Symond's mansion.

Symond didn't keep a journal, nor any written records, in his home. There was nothing she could use against him. Briefly, her hopes had begun to rise when she'd found a folder marked *Medical Records* in his study, but the documents within were disappointingly generic; heart tests, general check-ups, and eye tests mostly.

Not only was there no trace of Symond's insanity in the mansion; there was barely any trace of his military career. The only evidence she could find that he was Lord Commander was the rich, immaculate uniform he wore hanging in his closet, and a glass case full of military medals. With her eyes boosted by shadow magic, the metal trinkets glinted at her in the darkness, as though in sunlight. More than a dozen medals sat behind the spotless glass. Medals won by mass murdering her people.

Before she realised, her *Kaizuun* was in her hand. She swept into the bedroom, the clean, beautiful medals shining in her mind's eye. Symond slept, oblivious, within reach. Her breathing came ragged into her lungs, fast and painful. *It would be so easy.* Her blade swept down, glittering pure black, in her mind. She saw the blood, the eyes opening too late, gasping and struggling weaker until silence returned. The temptation pulled at her. She'd never felt the urge to commit murder before, not even with Hayne. She'd seen Hayne as a genuine threat whom she would kill in combat if necessary, but it had been relatively easy to walk away when he'd been disarmed. This time, with the image of all those war medals burned into her mind, sheathing her *Kaizuun* was one of the hardest things she'd ever done. She let out a sigh, closed her eyes, and put her blade away.

She thought about the man sleeping in his wife's arms, and what she'd seen tonight. It didn't add up. How could such a loving, gentle man spend his career ordering the deaths of thousands? There had to be a way to discredit him. There had to be a way to eliminate him and stop Ermoor's invasion of Pandeia without shedding more blood.

Riffolk

Pretending to be a Crown was far more satisfying than he'd anticipated, and his mood was far brighter once Symond left the chamber. It may take a while to turn the Lord Commander to his will, but it could be done. He'd certainly been desperate enough to avoid his retirement. Through the channels available to the Twelve, he knew Arthor had sent his wife away. She was an easy target, and he would do anything to protect her. But Riffolk wouldn't go that far unless he absolutely had to. Too much hatred would make for an inadequate servant.

For now, he had the Lord Commander under pressure and indebted to him; that was more than enough for the short term. Even better, Symond didn't suspect that the Twelve were compromised at all. He'd be able to go about his business, at least for a little while, without worrying about that. Eventually Symond would grow suspicious, of course; meeting with only one member of the Twelve was fairly inconspicuous if it happened once, even a few times, but not indefinitely. He would just have to manipulate Symond into place before his time ran out.

It wouldn't be difficult. The Twelve were keeping tabs on Symond; his erratic behaviour had been noticed. They held extensive notes, records and copies of his personal documents dating back years. Reading through it, Riffolk discovered much about Symond he'd never known. He'd noticed a lot of the behaviour, of course, but the Twelve had been watching and recording his movements and actions for a long time.

Their plan had been so small. Ruling over a few countries, as though that made one all-powerful. He couldn't believe their naivety. Then again, they hadn't seen the things he'd seen. Whole worlds mere steps away, magic and technology working together, myths and Gods and vehicles that soared through space. They had no idea.

Riffolk was going to bring a new age to Pandeia, even more incredible than the technological revolution he'd started in Ermoor after his first travels. He would be on the same level as the Gods themselves, and the creature would help him get there. He looked again at the chest in his safe-room. It was small for a chest, but incredibly well protected; almost indestructible.

Acquiring it had cost Riffolk substantially, both financially and in other ways. But its contents were worth more than he could say. He hadn't dared touch the large book with his bare hands, as it was bound in pure electricity. But when he first brought it back to his lab, he'd managed to move it into a protective glass enclosure without touching it; the same glass enclosure which ended up holding the creature.

He obtained the book years ago now, but the memory still flooded him with triumph. It contained everything he needed to know to become as powerful as a God. He closed his eyes and remembered opening the book for the very first time, sparks flying from the tome as though it was as impatient as Riffolk himself. Underneath the magical cover, it seemed to be made from normal paper, and the sparks had immediately quieted. Riffolk felt a momentary disappointment, until he saw the words on the page:

Taranos: God of Power

His mind had reeled; despite the things he'd seen even back then, and despite the rumours that had surrounded the chest before he acquired it, seeing the words for himself was something he wasn't prepared for.

The book was fascinating; not only did it give him a full understanding of Gods in general and a detailed break down of Taranos itself, but it taught him everything he needed to find and capture the God of Power. He'd set to work immediately, and within a few years held a God in the palm of his hands.

Returning his mind to the present, he glanced at his hands and set a small cascade of sparks spilling to the floor. He made them weak, just dancing light; his control was growing every day. The book contained some information about Power Magic, and Riffolk had read it over and over again the first time he'd opened it.

He looked again at the chest. Walking over to it, he completed the series of puzzle locks on its surface one at a time until a satisfying thunk sounded within its depths. Carefully, he pulled the lid open. The book's cover swam in pure electricity, constantly moving like a waterfall. Bringing a surge of power to his hand, he reached in quickly and grasped the book.

Mara

Riffolk's lab was silent, a large hole ripped into one of the walls. Earlier, when Mara and Pera stood before it in the late night fog, it looked like a hunched beast ready to devour her; it now looked like a corpse, dead and empty. Stepping gingerly through the gaping hole in the wall, Mara stared around the large room. She hadn't seen it properly on the way in, and couldn't remember walking through it when she left.

Commander Corby walked next to her. His presence was confusing; his confidence and authoritative nature comforted her, but his coldness left her feeling strangely alone. Deep scratches and black scorch marks covered most of the interior of the lab, as though the creature wasn't just escaping, but trying to destroy the whole building. Looking at the destruction, Mara's shoulder throbbed. She felt close to the creature here, as though being near its energy made the connection between them stronger.

They reached the opposite side of the lab together, and Commander Corby looked at her with his eyebrows raised. She moved through the destroyed doorway and down the corridor she thought led to the hidden lab. Glancing down another corridor as they passed, she saw more scorching and scratches. The damage lined every corridor. They approached the end of the corridor she took them down, but there was no storeroom at the end. Face flushing, she turned quickly and started back the way they'd come.

"What are you doing? Where's this secret lab?"

"Umm, I thought it was... Pera found it, I don't know how. There's a storeroom at the end on the left, so we just have to find the right corridor."

He shook his head, but didn't say anything, and waited for her to lead the way again. Even with Pera's help, finding the lab took a while. Without her, Mara had no idea how to find it. She wandered the lab, second guessing every corridor and every storeroom. Every minute that passed, she became more terrified and more certain Riffolk would appear, his cold blue eyes boring into her own.

Hours passed in the silent, dead lab. Hours of walking up and down identical corridors. She'd thought the storeroom at the end of the corridor would make it easy to spot. She thought she'd be able to remember which one was the entrance to the lab just by seeing it again. But there were so many storerooms, and so many corridors, and Mara became overwhelmed.

Soon enough she broke down, crying and trembling. *Pera found it so easily!* She thought. *Why can't I see it when I've been there before?* She felt like she'd walked up and down every corridor in the building by now, probably more than once. Commander Corby simply stood, impassively watching her cry.

"You know," he said, his voice firm but quiet, "you won't get in trouble if you tell me you're confused."

"What do you mean?"

"Well, your memories are broken and unclear at best. If you tell me now that there was no secret underground lab, you won't get in trouble. I won't be angry. All I want is the truth."

She was back on her feet before she realised, and his stance changed even faster than her own; suddenly he looked less like an unassuming middle-aged teacher and more like a deadly, experienced warrior. But the intimidation that should have stopped her fell flat against the power of her sudden rage.

No!

A flash arced from her, without conscious effort, and crackled against the wall to her side. Commander Corby flinched, then his eyes flew wide open and he stared at her in shock.

"I'm not making this up! I was held down there, I saw the huge tank with the creature in it, I saw the horrible inventions he built! I saw – I saw him... Kill her. That thing... it changed me."

Stop!

Her hands, which had balled into fists, slowly unclenched. Her rage dissipated again as Pera's face swam into her mind. They stood still like that for a moment, Mara lost in thought and Commander Corby waiting for an attack. When she looked up at him again, he relaxed slightly, but remained in a ready stance. She moved past him, determined again to find the entrance.

Commander Corby followed, and together they turned down yet another corridor. Mara felt his unease as they walked; he knew how dangerous she could be now. She cursed herself inwardly, for showing her powers to someone when the creature had told her to wait. He hadn't said anything, but she knew he was going to tell those horrible scientists, and they would do even more tests.

They turned again; the lab was a maze, or so it felt to Mara. At the end of the corridor they just turned onto, there was a dead end.

Quite a few of the hallways ended that way, including the entrance into the secret lab. As they approached the end, her hopes grew. By the time they were a few steps away, her heart was hammering in her chest; there was a storeroom door which had been destroyed.

Many of the doors in the lab had been destroyed, mostly storeroom doors, but seeing it still made her pulse speed up. Especially seeing it at the end of a corridor. Commander Corby glanced at her, and she returned his look with a wide eyed look of her own. But the storeroom beyond looked totally different to the one Pera found.

Not knowing how to tell Commander Corby, she instead walked slowly into the small room. But as she go closer to the back wall, she felt a tingling in her shoulder. There was a *pulling* feeling, coming from below the floor somewhere. She didn't understand how magnets worked, but it felt to her like the same thing.

The memory of Riffolk being grabbed and thrown surfaced in her mind again. If he had survived, he was touched in the same way as her, which meant he had powers too. She felt an intense, almost physical pull towards the shelves at the back of the room. Looking back at Commander Corby, she gestured back.

"Stand back," she said, "this might get messy."

She focused on the shelves, almost certain they were just a cover for the entrance. Reaching within herself, embracing the buzzing in her shoulder, she touched the energy that flowed through her body, preparing to unleash it on the shelves.

No.

In an instant, the power was gone to her. Even the buzzing in her shoulder faded, and the sudden lack of feeling there made her cry out; it felt like an absence from her body, as though a limb had suddenly been removed.

She fell to her knees, and dimly heard Commander Corby yelling if she was alright. After an aching, empty moment, the buzzing returned to her shoulder, and she could breathe again. Energy returned, the power flowing once more through her body in tingling waves, and she felt well enough to stand again.

"What just happened?"

"I... I don't know. I think we need to leave."

Elana

Her heart was still beating fast. Not from the dash over rooftops back to her camp; that was as easy as breathing. It was the conversation she'd had with Symond. Elana had never taken such an unplanned risk in her life. There was so much she didn't understand about Symond and his state of mind. So many ways it could have gone wrong. *Should* have gone wrong. But somehow, he'd believed her. He really did hear voices in his head. The idea was terrifying to her.

Hopefully Symond could get the project stalled or stopped soon, otherwise the voices he heard might change his mind again. She didn't think they would; relief had painted his features the moment she told him to stop Hayne. He wanted the project stopped as much as she did.

Lord Commander Arthor Symond suddenly made a lot more sense to Elana. He *was* a good man, or at least had been once. But the voice in his head corrupted his thoughts, made him do awful things. It might have even been responsible for all of his military career, though she doubted it.

She decided to leave Symond for now, and simply keep an eye on his actions. Knowing that she could appear before him later on put her mind at ease.

Arthor

The conversation with Mathys troubled him. His remark about their souls being lost affected him more than he would have believed. He'd always struggled with his faith, but Mathys had a certainty about God that radiated from him, like the priests themselves. It was hard not to get caught up in it.

He just wanted to do what was right. Regardless of what the Twelve said, or the voices in his head, or even Mathys. He just wanted to do the right thing.

I will lead you down the right path.

He closed his eyes tightly, willing the voice away. It had never worked; in the years since it started, the voice kept coming to him no matter what he did to avoid it. Usually, he could ignore it. Lately, he'd been successfully pushing it to the background, but it was starting to creep into his mind when he was talking to people, and that was dangerous; It was only a matter of time before he reacted to the voice in front of someone.

And what then? He would be locked away in Ravenmire Asylum, in a padded cell, stripped of the title of Lord Commander. He couldn't even imagine what would happen to Ellie.

Rain tapped against the windows of Arthor's office, chaotic and soothing. He sat silent in the big chair behind his desk, trying to find peace. His mind had been a battlefield lately, and he'd been losing the fight. Whatever spoke to him had been speaking more often, more insistently. He couldn't drown it out any more. It was becoming impossible to tell what were his own thoughts and what were the suggestions of the voice.

Ellie had been gone almost a week by now, and he was struggling; though he knew she was safe, he still hated being without her.

You don't deserve her.

Gritting his teeth, Arthor shook his head. That was the voice, the Other. Wasn't it? It didn't mean anything. Of course he deserved Ellie. He'd been nothing but loyal and loving to her.

You don't deserve this office, or the title of Lord Commander.

His hands turned into fists; trying to breathe evenly, he sat still and forced himself to ignore it. He'd sent everyone away. Servants, Officers, soldiers, anyone who had any business near his office. He couldn't afford for anyone to see him like this, not until he got the voice under control again.

You were never in control.

Yes I am, he thought, *you're not real, just a voice. I can get rid of you.*

You have no idea what I am, mortal.

Screaming wordlessly, he brought his fists up over his head, then slammed them into the desk. A throbbing pain started in his hands immediately, and he pulled them to his chest, his head hanging.

You are pathetic. I will not leave until your purpose has been fulfilled.

Everything stopped. Arthor opened his eyes. *My purpose?*
"What's my purpose?"

You will see, soon enough.

"When will you tell me what you are?"
He'd asked the voice many times when it first started talking to him. It never gave him an answer. He knew how insane it was to listen to a disembodied voice in his head, but there was a deep, dreadful certainty about it. The voice had told him to do many things over the years, and although Arthor hated hearing it, it had always been right.

When your mind can handle it. For now, all you need concern yourself with is doing as I tell you.

Without warning, tears streamed down his cheeks as he sat in the shadows. For the first time, the voice made him feel utterly helpless. He was beginning to doubt that he was merely insane. It was so convincing. Too convincing. For a while, he'd known the voice was something else; as much as he tried to convince himself otherwise, there was always that knowledge laying underneath.

"What do you want?"

He knew there was no hope. The voice wouldn't leave him. Even if it wasn't real, he would be tortured endlessly by invisible words if he didn't do as he was told.

The invasion must happen as soon as possible.

"But... I stopped it, like you said. Riffolk; the creature he was using... You told me to-"

I told you no such thing. You have been tricked.

"But how? You appeared on my ceiling, no person can do that."

A pulse shot through his mind, bright and hot, and for a moment all he could feel was inhuman rage. Consumed, the office around him utterly disappeared behind the burning light in his mind. He'd never felt anything like it; he wouldn't have believed it possible.

I do not know who is responsible. You will find out for me. I do not appear in your world unless I am summoned, and even then only in a limited form for a short time.

The blinding rage slowly calmed, and his office gradually appeared again, though it didn't look solid until the light in his head was completely gone. *Something else spoke to me,* he thought. *Whatever that voice is, there's more of them.*

Mathys

Mathys returned to the lab the day after Mara tried to show him the alleged secret underground lab. He'd taken note of the corridor she went down when she found the storeroom she suspected. Finding it again wasn't particularly difficult; unlike Mara, Mathys spent a lot of his time around secrets and in unfamiliar areas, so navigating a lab he'd been to once before was achievable.

He reached the storeroom at the end of the corridor, moving slowly and carefully. Despite his cynicism regarding the lab's existence, he didn't take chances; and if the lab was where Mara said, and still hidden, it was likely Riffolk was still alive. If so, the fact that he'd remained in hiding after the creature's escape told Mathys that he didn't want to be found, which meant Mathys needed to be on guard.

The door to the storeroom was destroyed, as with most of the others. But Mathys spent a lot of time around crime scenes, and he'd seen every kind of property damage. The marks here were directional, all pointing from the back of the room to the door, and then down the corridor. He'd catalogued the marks in each corridor, noting them each separately and closely. Almost all the marks throughout the rest of the lab were directionless; almost as if they'd been placed one by one, with no goal.

When he looked closely, a clear path had emerged; from the storeroom Mara led him to, all the way out to the destroyed wall where the creature escaped into the street. This told him two things; firstly, the creature had definitely escaped from behind the back wall of the storeroom, and something or someone wielded the same kind of destructive energy as the creature itself.

Mara shot lightning from her bare hand, he thought, *and killed three of my men.* If Riffolk was still alive, could he be using her as a weapon? Was his own wife the result of one of his evil experiments? *Her confusion and fear is genuine.* He didn't believe she would be in on whatever Riffolk was doing, but Mathys wouldn't have been surprised if Riffolk was somehow using her without her knowledge.

The shelves at the back of the storeroom hid a secret entrance; he was certain. He looked closely, and there were signs not only that the back wall had been partially destroyed, but that the shelves could move. In that moment, he cursed himself for being so dismissive of Mara's claims of a secret lab.

He unholstered his gun, made sure it was loaded, and gave the shelves a hard shove to the side. Nothing happened. He pushed, pulled, tried everything to move them; nothing. On a whim, he lifted, just to see if they'd budge at all.

A low creaking split the silence, and the shelves gave way slightly. Mathys almost let go in shock, but managed to hold its weight. He kept pulling up, and when its movement stopped, he pulled outwards; the shelves, as one unit, swung out to reveal a blackened hole in the wall and a flight of stairs leading down into darkness.

"Is there anyone down there?" Mathys called.

No one answered. *Idiot,* he thought, *Riffolk is down there and now he's ready for me.* He started walking slowly down into the dark, his gun trained evenly in the centre of his field of vision. Mathys had seen battle many times, had even been on the front lines on the north shore of Shanaken during one of their crusades. He knew all too well the sense of fear, anticipation and certainty that followed every soldier into battle. *I will die today,* he thought, every time, *this is it.*

At the bottom of the stairs, the lab opened out to him through yet another destroyed doorway. Completely dead, empty and dark. Mathys felt his spirits drop slightly; after the intense flood of emotion leading up to battle, the anticlimax of an empty room hit him hard.

Nothing stirred in the massive room. In the centre, he saw the hulking remains of a giant glass tank, exploded from the inside. A few metres from that, a headless corpse lay in a pool of blood, the darkness making the blood as black as midnight. *Riffolk?* He thought, *or the Tyran girl?* Then he remembered Mara had said she'd shot Riffolk with a dart gun.

When he reached the body it was confirmed; a skinny female in dark clothing that matched Mara's. *She was telling the truth.* He spent a while in the underground lab, inspecting everything, finding nothing. There was no equipment, no lighting or power, no sign of recent activity other than the dead body and the exploded tank.

Suddenly paranoid, he stood still for a moment, eyes closed, straining to hear anything in the silence. It was a heavy, dead silence, the kind Mathys had experienced at dawn on the battlefield in Shanaken, when the fighting stopped and the dead lay piled on the sand.

A small sound made his eyes fly open; a tiny sound, as though it was muffled by walls, in a different room. Immediately dropping into a crouch with his gun level, he scanned the room, trying to find the source of the sound.

Bright light bloomed from one side of the lab as a low rumble echoed. Mathys heard the slight grunt of a male's voice followed by a few heavy metallic thunks. Decades of training and habit forced his eyes shut and the heels of his hands over his ears, his gun momentarily pointing uselessly towards the ceiling. He felt the explosions and saw the bright flash of light through his eyelids, and despite his hands his ears split into high pitched ringing.

He moved as soon as the explosion was over, heading straight for the door and aiming towards the source of the light, shooting as he ran. He didn't bother reloading after the first shot; unless the attacker had closed in on him, guns were much less effective from across a room of this size.

Even so, as he neared the door two shots rang out, each within seconds of each other. Clangs echoed from the ball bearings hitting the metal walls, but Mathys wasn't hit. He bolted up the stairs, reloading only when he was sure he couldn't be hit. *Two shots, that fast?* He though wildly, *no one can reload these guns that quickly!* He was sure of two things as he escaped the lab; Riffolk Hayne was alive, and he was working with someone else.

Riffolk

Riffolk let out a slow breath. He held the book in front of him, its power mingling with his own. A feeling he couldn't describe filled his entire body; a feeling of pure energy and peace at the same time. It felt like the book had been made for him, and it was finally where it belonged.

A red flash suddenly filled the room, and he looked straight at the glass screen on his bench. *Corby,* he thought, *I should have known he wouldn't be able to let the mystery go.* They'd shown up the day before, snooping around the lab, and Mara had been unable to find the entrance, as he expected. He'd relaxed too soon; he knew exactly the kind of person Mathys was, and should have known he would come back alone.

Cursing, he placed the book back in its chest and closed the lid, grabbed his gun and a handful of flash grenades, and waited to see what Mathys would do. The Commander managed to find his way down into the underground lab, and spent far too long inspecting the area. If given any more time, he would find Riffolk's safe-room; it was time for him to die. He put the dart gun down and unholstered the real one.

Riffolk opened the safe-room door and tossed out the flash grenades without hesitation; Mathys was an experienced soldier, and wouldn't go down easy. After the explosion, he ducked back out of the safe-room, his gun raised, but Mathys was already moving, and aimed back at Riffolk as he moved. Riffolk stepped behind the wall, but not fast enough. The boom of Mathys' gun was as deafening as the flash grenades, and Riffolk felt a thump on his thigh followed by searing pain.

He ducked out and fired twice at the running Commander, but it looked as though he missed. He swore, loudly, after he was sure Mathys was gone. There was no point giving chase now; his leg throbbed, and Mathys already had too much distance on him. *At least he hasn't seen my face*, he thought; though it was little comfort. Mathys was no fool, he'd know Riffolk was alive now.

He closed the safe-room door again, and began packing everything. He felt remarkably out of control. He'd never been this far on the defensive before; usually he was the one making moves and forcing others into corners. Sighing, he prepared for his next step; it was time to move again.

Mara

The bench she lay on was always cold. She was still being kept, and though they hadn't run any more tests on her, she figured it was only a matter of time before Commander Corby told the scientists about her power. He hadn't visited her in at least a day, maybe two; her sense of time was warped.

She spent the time making little sparks in her hands, making them dance and flash. Aside from the excitement of magic, there was an indescribable joy she found in the lightning. Watching it arc from her fingertips, knowing she was controlling it, made her happier than she'd ever been.

The sparks never burned her, nor her clothes, they were just fun to watch. She made a cascade of them flow from her hands onto the floor, and gasped as they bounced and winked out. They made such a beautiful whooshing sound, like a river of pale yellow fire.

The creature hadn't spoken to her again either; she was totally alone. *Why won't you speak to me?* She thought it as loudly as she could, trying to send the words out to wherever the creature may be. At least the magic was still hers.

I have been busy, child.

Mara jumped off the bench. She hadn't been prepared for an actual answer.

"What have you been doing?"

Thinking, and exploring. And learning. My memory is coming back.

Her eyes went wide, and her skin erupted in cold bumps.

"Does that mean you know... what you are?"

I am Taranos, the God of Power.

"God? You're really a God?"

One of the five, yes.

"So the others... the ones trying to get to Pandeia... they're as powerful as you?"

Three of them, yes. Only one is far more powerful than the rest of us.

One thing still didn't make sense to her.

"How did you end up here? If you're a God, how did Riffolk have you in a cage?"

He knows my weaknesses, my strengths; his intelligence is beyond human.

Elana

One discovery left her as unsettled as she was confused. Without the magic of the *Kaizuun*, she never would have known. She was prowling through the military district, trying to locate anything that might afford her some extra knowledge of the Ermoori before she left, when she kicked a loose stone on the pavement. It skidded across the ground and clanged into a bin. A shout broke the eerie, lifeless silence.

"What was that?"

She dove silently into an alleyway, drawing her sword as she swept into a crouch. The man who'd shouted appeared as a bright aura through the thick fog, craning his neck to see. He was looking in a different direction to where Elana had been; towards where the rock hit the bin. She relaxed her guard slightly, lowering her gaze and breathing a quiet sigh of relief. Then she stopped, her breath cut off mid sigh. She was staring at the ground; solid pavement. And yet there were hundreds of people down there... thousands, toiling and moving in organised lines and circles. They moved the way colonies of ants moved along the forest floor, and up tree trunks; in formation, never stopping, never losing rhythm.

Something about it made Elana's stomach churn. She knew at once that these people were slaves, working for the Ermoori somehow. Her mission was supposed to be over; but she couldn't abandon thousands of underground slaves. Something had to be done. They had to be saved, helped.

She wondered if the *Duulshen* knew. They couldn't possibly... could they? But she suddenly realised that as well as saving lives, helping the slaves would strike a blow against Ermoor that they may never recover from. Her attention returned to the guard; but after a brief search of the alley around the bin, he was satisfied there were no people around. He wandered off, leaving Elana to herself again.

Her gaze kept being drawn to the thousands of people working under her feet. Ermoor was a truly terrible place; every time she looked, she found something horrible lurking within the city. Omatus used slavery, but at least their slaves worked outside in farms, tending to orchards and more or less surrounded by life. The slaves of Ermoor worked underground; no natural sunlight, no trees, just the shadows of a dead city.

Mathys

A lot of pieces had fallen into place. Riffolk was alive, and he'd been holding the creature in a secret lab underneath the lab that had been shut down. After his death, he'd hidden the lab once again, but he apparently had yet *another* secret lab, another layer of secrets. The creature escaped, destroying everything in its path. Riffolk used its energy to damage the rest of the lab to disguise his secret.

His working theory was that the creature's energy had transferred to both Riffolk and Mara in its escape; from examining

Mara's wound, and from her assertion that the creature had attacked them both, it seemed to be the only conclusion. It made no sense to him, but there was no other explanation for what Mara could do. The lightning she shot from her hand was inescapable proof.

He'd only heard bits and pieces of the project, just what Riffolk and Arthor had spoken about whenever Arthor let him sit in on their meetings. Enough to know it was wrong. Enough to fear for their souls. Seeing the cage it was held in had made him feel sick.

He was back at his desk, and as always happened with complex cases, a notepad covered in hand written words, phrases and names sat before him on the rich wood. Staring at it, he felt as though he understood a lot of what had happened, but much was still a mystery. What was Riffolk up to that he wanted to remain 'dead'? What exactly was the creature, and how did Riffolk come by it? Why was Mara in the lab when the creature escaped?

Added to the pressure from the Twelve to locate and capture the creature, Mathys was beginning to feel overwhelmed. It would have been difficult enough to sort out the problems within Ermoor itself, but the creature had headed straight to the west once it left the lab; to the swamps and wastelands outside the city.

Ermoor itself only took up a fraction of the country's land mass. Of the rest of it, the eastern half was foggy swampland, and the rest to the west was brutal desert just like Theara and Omatus across the sea. Searching that massive wasteland would have been difficult even for the entire Ermoori military; for the small forces at Mathys' disposal, it was impossible.

He rubbed his eyes again, and one of the candles flickered as it neared the end of its life. Almost out of wax, the tiny flame guttered, steadied, and guttered again. The puddle of melted wax below it grew until it finally engulfed the brave little flame.

Riffolk was a bigger threat now than he'd been before he 'died'. Mathys had written to the Twelve advising them, but they were unwilling to consider the possibility that he was still alive at all. Each day, he was beginning to lose his faith in the Twelve more. They'd never been so blind before, and the events of the last few weeks were far more troubling than the Twelve's reactions implied.

It would have to be handled outside of the law. Mathys was a very moral person, he always did what he knew was right. He tried as best he could to abide by the Twelve's laws. But sometimes what was right conflicted directly with what the Twelve wanted to do. He'd done what needed to be done in the past. He'd gone against the Twelve, in secret. He'd even done terrible things in the name of justice.

No one knew but him. Even the Twelve Crowns themselves didn't know the things he'd done, and they kept a close eye on everything. Now that Riffolk was such a threat, and the Twelve were intent on being blind to it, Mathys had to once again resort to terrible actions to bring peace to his great city.

He knew the consequences. He'd never been caught, of course, but that didn't bother him anyway; the consequences on his soul, however... The things he'd done were terrible, and deserved an eternity in hell. But he was doing them in the name of peace, and justice, and all he could do was pray that God would forgive him.

Breathing slowly, preparing for the days and nights ahead, Mathys prayed again. No matter what happened, people were going to die soon.

"Let my actions lead to peace," he said, "let my hand be guided by your will. Let no innocents be harmed, and let the world know the love of God. For the good of all."

Mara

Mara hadn't slept well since the conversation with Taranos. She was already scared of Riffolk; but to know he was feared by an actual God, if that's really what the creature was... She almost couldn't bear the thought.

Commander Corby still hadn't come to see her again, and she was beginning to feel like she'd just be kept in the small bare room until she died. She was still being fed, of course, and had regular general examinations by the scientists; but no words were spoken, and the Commander was nowhere to be seen.

She hated the silence of the scientists; she would have preferred to never see them at all, even if they weren't poking and examining her every day. Their emotionless, wordless observation unnerved her and made her feel more lonely than when she was completely alone.

Finally, one day as she was throwing little handfuls of sparks at the wall, Commander Corby entered her room. He walked in just as the sparks collided with the wall, making a thud and a high pitched buzz. His gun appeared in the blink of an eye, his stance low and balanced, his eyes alert.

When he saw her sitting cross legged on the floor, staring up at him with shock, he put the gun away and straightened.

"You need to be careful with that stuff," he grumbled.

"Sorry, sir," she said, though she couldn't help smiling.

"Don't call me – just call me Mathys," he said.

She nodded, and moved to the bench when he gestured to it.

"I'm sorry I was so dismissive earlier. I believe you."

He seemed to really struggle saying it, as though he'd never used those words before. But his tone was genuine, and softer.

"You believe me?"

"I do now, yes. It shouldn't be possible... Magic. If that's what it is. So it took me a while to accept things as they are, despite the evidence."

Mara found herself grinning, staring up at Mathys as though he'd told her she was free to go.

"I went to the lab. I found the entrance, the girl's body, and the tank where the creature was kept."

She was shocked, and delighted, and terrified. Emotions rushed through her head faster than she could process them. *He believes me!* But Mathys was still talking; she tried to listen as her mind whirled.

"There's more, Mara. Riffolk attacked me from some other hidden room. He's alive."

Knowing Riffolk was alive terrified her. She'd suspected it, of course, after feeling the energy pulling her towards the hidden lab; but knowing for sure was different. The first thing that came to her mind was the power she'd gained after being touched by Taranos. *Does he have it too?* She couldn't imagine what a monster like him would do with that kind of power.

Mathys told her everything he'd seen, and was finally willing to listen to her account of events again without dismissal. She didn't tell him anything more about Taranos, nor the other Gods; she still wasn't sure what to believe about that. After they talked, he'd left her room again, promising he would stop Riffolk at all costs. Mara believed him.

Wake, child.

Her eyes flew open. Taranos hadn't spoken in a while. She sat up, completely awake.

The scientist is incredibly powerful. His mind contains secrets even I am unaware of. He has the potential to destroy Pandeia.

"No, no. No! Stop, please, stop talking!"

Mara hugged her knees to her chest, crying and shaking her head. She was already scared enough by Riffolk; why was Taranos saying these things to her now? She simply couldn't believe it. *Wouldn't* believe it. It wasn't fair. How did someone so evil have so much power?

"Can't you stop him?"

Not directly. Being in the physical world greatly reduces my power and strength. It is one of the reasons he summoned me in the first place. I will need your help, and the help of anyone you trust. He is simply too great a threat to be ignored. War is coming, and if he is allowed to become any more powerful, he will turn the tide.

Elana

Ermoor was a massive city. It twisted and turned into itself, never leading anywhere final, never offering a break from the lifeless paved streets. It was a never ending dead forest made from stone, metal, and false lights twinkling through the gloom. The people all looked the same, the streets all looked the same.

Observing the city from the rooftops, Elana could stare for hours without a single flicker of movement other than the artificial lights twinkling. The city was dead. Shanaken, on the other hand, was constantly alive, never a moment of stillness. And yet, the constant movement, the chaotic sense of life, gave her peace; and the utter stillness of Ermoor left her hollow and unsettled.

She'd explored the city extensively from the rooftops, and still hadn't spotted an obvious way down to where the slaves were. It was clearly somewhere in Dreadhold; the highest concentration of slaves were underneath the military district, and the fact that there were already soldiers patrolling day and night meant they could guard without raising suspicion.

Elana crouched behind a low wall skirting the roof of a building. Only a few stories above ground, she could see the street clearly. The soldiers stood guard in seemingly random places. Civilians weren't allowed in Dreadhold, and the difference between the military district and the rest of the city was jarring. Most noticeable, other than the sheer number of soldiers present, was the technology and weaponry on display.

In every other district, technology was purely for comfort and convenience; self-driving carts, street lights, heating. In Dreadhold, every piece of technology was designed to kill. There were weapons stations on every street corner. Slim beams of green light scanned every wall slowly like tiny spotlights. Every soldier carried several deadly looking gadgets on his belt, the functions of which Elana didn't want to know.

Getting to the slaves was one thing, and daunting enough. Getting them out, past all of the security measures in Dreadhold, would be almost impossible. She didn't understand most of the technology in Ermoor, and was no match for it on her own. Plus, her connection to Shadow Magic was the weakest she'd ever felt it; she could still use it, but it required intense concentration. Still, she had surprise on her side, and magic coupled with stealth would make a huge difference. Hopefully.

Soldiers walked constantly, in overlapping patterns, though when she looked closely and for a while, she noticed there were spots where they couldn't be seen by their fellows. Side alleys, building entrances, adjacent streets. The longer she watched, the more she realised it may be possible to take the soldiers out one by one. Drawing her *Kaizuun*, she summoned as much strength and magic as she could; it was going to be a long night.

Mara

The scientists still hadn't done any more invasive tests, nor treated her any differently. It meant Mathys wasn't telling them about her powers. He was leaving her alone far more though, and she found herself spiralling into the same depression she'd been in while living alone in Riffolk's mansion. Only now there was no wine to help her escape, and she was stuck with the horrible nightmares of Pera's death and Riffolk's abuse. She had the magic, at least, but even then she had to be incredibly careful about using it.

Days went by; how many she couldn't tell, but other than the regular silent examinations, she didn't see or interact with anyone. She slept a lot, despite her nightmares; horrible images of Pera plagued her even when she was awake, so it made no difference. She'd also given up trying to ask the scientists questions when they escorted her into the examination room.

After a while, she considered trying to sneak out; but the idea didn't last long. She had no idea where she was, how big the area was, and how many soldiers might be in the building. And even if she could sneak out, there was nowhere to go.

Other than sleeping, Mara spent a lot of time conjuring sparks and small bolts of lightning, to stave off boredom if nothing else. But she felt that energy inside her growing every day, and every time she created a spark she felt an intense rush of power.

Not knowing what else to do with the energy, she simply stuck with cascades of sparks and small arcs of electricity, always aimed at the roof so the scorch marks wouldn't be as easily spotted.

Finally, after what could have been days or weeks, Mathys walked into her room. He looked exhausted, but his voice was gentle.

"You can go, Mara. Go home. I'm assigning a small squad to you for protection, they'll stay with you until Riffolk is found."

Her mouth dropped open. *I'm free.* Then the thought of Riffolk coming for her wiped the joy from her mind.

"Do you really think they can protect me?"

He sighed, and a cold fear bloomed in her chest.

"I hope so, Mara," he said, "but the Twelve Crowns won't allow any more men on such a minor task. They have other priorities."

As soon as he said it, a terrible certainty filled her; she was going to die soon. *What do I do?* She thought, somehow numb and terrified at the same time.

"Oh," she said.

I will protect you as best I can.

She must have jumped; Mathys frowned, looking at her more intently. But it passed, and she stood.

"There's more," Mathys said, "with Riffolk being dead - publicly, anyway – his wealth goes to you as his widow."

Mara froze, not quite daring to believe what she'd heard. Riffolk was the wealthiest man not just in Ermoor, but likely all of Pandeia. She couldn't even imagine the amount of money he had. *And now it's mine,* she thought, her excitement rising.

"All of it?"

"Legally, yes. If he reveals that he's not dead, of course, it will all go back to him. And I'm not sure what secret plans he has in place which might stop it from going to you. There's simply no way to know with Riffolk."

Mara shook her head, marvelling. The Watson family had been struggling financially for several generations, despite remaining one of the most respected houses in Ermoor. If Riffolk's money went to her, their family would become the wealthiest overnight. She could just imagine the look on her father's face when he found out; he might finally be proud of her.

Mathys cleared his throat, bringing her back to the room.

"Of course, Riffolk will know that his money is going to be bequeathed to you. You may be in more danger now than ever."

Nodding, she thought about Riffolk's power now that he could most likely use the same magic as her. *Can I tell Mathys about the magic?* She thought, focusing on the image of Taranos in her mind.

If you trust him. Be careful, child.

"Mathys... there's something I need to tell you."

After she'd told him everything, he looked stricken. As though he'd seen a ghost. At first, he'd just shaken his head, frowning as though he was simply disappointed. Now, he sat as still as a statue, staring at her like she was a wild animal he'd never seen before.

"So it's real? Real, actual magic?" He finally said.

"Yes. And Riffolk most likely has it too."

"And it came from a God? Not *the* God, but *a* God?"

"Yes. Taranos."

"Why didn't the scientists see it in their tests?" He asked, but Mara could tell from his tone he was talking to himself.

"The soldiers weren't lying then. They said they saw the creature in your place... Maybe they just saw the lightning and their minds did the rest."

Mara shrugged and shook her head; it was the first she'd heard about what his soldiers reported to him. She thought it sounded logical though.

"I didn't believe any of them," he said.

"Well nobody will believe you either."

He glanced at her and flinched as though she'd threatened him with a handful of lightning.

"Well," he said, "this makes Riffolk even more dangerous. I have to send you back home, there's no way around that. My hands are tied with the amount of soldiers I can spare to guard you too. But I'm running my operations from the city, so I can stay nearby."

She blushed; she couldn't help it. Her cheeks flushed and grew warm, and she couldn't look at him directly. The offer was so unexpected and kind that she had no idea how to respond. Mathys looked uncomfortable, so she tried to move on, her cheeks flushing even more.

"What can I do if he attacks?"

"Run," Mathys said. He didn't even hesitate. "He's simply too dangerous."

She nodded. She pictured his cold eyes, his cruel smile. Running from that monster was something she would gladly do.

When Mathys dropped her back to the mansion, the guards accompanied her inside; except for one, who stood by the door servant to keep watch. Four guards were assigned to her, and the three who came inside with her followed her through the entire building until she reached the master bedroom.

Though she'd spent enough time there before to call the room her own, it now felt cold and unfamiliar. There was a quiet sort of threat she felt, sitting on the silk bedsheets; almost like Riffolk was hiding somewhere nearby.

One of the guards stood directly outside the door, and the other two entered the room with her. Their presence gave her no comfort at all. They didn't care the way Mathys did; they were just doing their job.

She asked them to leave while she had a shower and changed into new clothes. She hadn't worn real clothes since the night Pera was killed, and she'd forgotten what it felt like. Pulling a beautiful blue dress from her wardrobe, she sighed as she slipped it on and tied the bodice in place. It was tight and restrictive, but so elegant and beautiful that she finally felt herself again.

After putting on some make-up and fixing her hair, she finally let the guards back in. Both of them raised their eyebrows and looked her up and down, and although it made her feel a little less protected, a small rush of excitement filled her belly and her cheeks flushed again.

The rest of that day was spent in almost complete silence, except for the occasional curt small talk from the guards. Just after sundown, a visitor arrived. The guard outside the door brought him in, holding him by the arm, but when she recognised him he was let go immediately.

"Uncle Lewis!"

"Mara, I was so worried about you."

"What are you doing here?"

"I have some great news!"

Uncle Lewis' smile was always brilliant. He beamed through his bushy moustache, and behind his small round glasses, his eyes twinkled as though they were made from the stars in the night sky.

"The money has come through," he said, beaming.

"I did the paperwork myself!"

Mara giggled at her uncle's smile, as she always did. He looked at her with nothing but warmth, as though the guards weren't even there.

"Would you like to know how much money you own, Marmar?"

She paused, trying to think if she'd ever heard Riffolk's fortune spelled out. Even when she was little, he'd been a very private and withdrawn person. For her at the time, that had simply added to his mystery and made him more attractive, but now she realised how silly she'd been to fall in love with someone she knew nothing about. Rumours of his wealth were repeated constantly among Mara's friends, with increasingly more ridiculous numbers each time.

Remembering the girls shouting "ten thousand!" "a hundred thousand!", "a million!", before running out of numbers, she grew suddenly quiet; not only could she finally get an answer to those rumours, but the money would actually belong to her.

"Umm. Yes?"

Uncle Lewis beamed even wider, his bushy eyebrows jumping up and down. Despite everything, she giggled again. He looked expectantly at the guards in the room, who grumbled and left to wait just outside the door. Once they were gone, his eyebrows resumed their bouncing.

"Mara, you are now in possession of the single largest fortune in the entire world; twenty million crowns."

Twenty million. It was almost unthinkable. She wasn't even sure how many zeros that was. One thing she did know was that, as long as Riffolk didn't get to her, she would never have to worry about money for the rest of her life. Her family could move into a proper mansion. They could afford to go to the lavish parties and balls that were held every week. The possibilities were endless.

Mara felt like the luckiest girl in the world; it almost made marrying Riffolk worth it... almost. One thing she could do was use Riffolk's money to fix all the damage he'd caused. Rushing to Uncle Lewis with tears in her eyes, she hugged him and thought about all the good that could be done with that much money.

Elana

Breathing heavy, Elana crouched behind a large rubbish bin in a side alley. *Four down,* she thought, *a thousand to go.* She had no idea how many soldiers were actually nearby, but she had to assume the worst. So far she hadn't been seen, but it was only a matter of time before the soldiers realised their colleagues were disappearing. Footsteps echoed down the alley; another patrol. Two soldiers, by the sound of their feet. Crouched and waiting, she brought two throwing blades up from the tattoos on her palm. Her Kaizuun was still in her hand, and glancing back through the rubbish bin revealed the auras of three soldiers, instead of two. Cursing silently, she brought up another throwing blade and readied herself to attack.

Ermoori soldiers barely spoke to each other as they patrolled, only making cursory small talk at each stopping point before focusing their attention on security; to a man, they were diligently professional. Elana had to be utterly silent in everything she did. Which meant multiple enemies were a problem. She waited for them to pass the bin, hoping they wouldn't cast their eyes around too early. Her position made it easy to kill them the second they became visible to her, but noise was a problem if they saw her too soon.

There was a spell which created a cushion of shadow on the ground, dampening noise and providing protection against falls. It was designed for jumping out of trees safely without alerting the dangerous predators of Shanaken to a warrior's presence, but Elana thought it was perfect for her situation. She briefly dropped the throwing blade spell, and readied the cushion spell instead. She could only dedicate one hand to magic; she needed her Kaizuun ready at all times, not only to fight, but to bolster her connection to Shadow Magic as much as possible.

The first soldier stepped past her cover less than a metre from her, staring ahead into the alley. She was wrapped in Shadow, of course, but she could still be seen this close, if he gave her any more than a cursory glance. He kept staring ahead, though, and she was immediately relieved; they weren't actively looking for an enemy, which meant her previous kills hadn't been spotted. She'd hidden the bodies, of course, up on rooftops mostly, but there may have been some evidence she'd overlooked in her rush to remain unseen and unheard.

The second and third soldiers entered her sight at the same time, the one furthest from her scanning the alley with a bored but dutiful look. His eyes passed over her, and a momentary frown creased his face, but there was no recognition or alert, and they kept walking. The second their backs were to her, she moved to the centre of the alley. She cast the shadow cushioning spell just in front of them, and immediately drew three throwing knives from her wrist tattoo.

All three soldiers noticed the shadow bloom in front of them immediately. Assuming the obvious, they looked straight up, expecting some large object blocking the light of the moon and the small, single street light in the alley. Their confusion gave her ample time. Her left hand flashed forward, and the throwing knives found their targets, as they always did. Guided by magic, the knives thumped home in the base of each man's skull, buried to the hilt instantly. She rushed at them, ready to catch them if they fell in the wrong direction. Two of the men fell straight onto her spell, making absolutely no sound. The third crumpled almost straight down as his knees gave way, and she dropped to her own knees and half caught him before he made too much noise.

Not silent, she thought, *but hopefully not loud enough to get caught.* Standing with the soldier in her arms, she struggled over to the large bin, lifting the lid and dumping the corpse in. Luck finally touched her; the bin was mostly empty. Once the other two soldiers were hidden inside, she shuffled the rubbish around to cover them, then closed the lid again. *Seven down, a thousand to go.*

Half the night had gone by, and Elana was still no closer to finding a way down to the slaves. She'd taken down another fourteen soldiers, though, and still hadn't been caught or raised any alarms. She kept moving constantly, watching every soldier's movements to find any patterns. Surely they would be guarding any entrances to their slave workforce even more diligently than the streets and alleys they patrolled? There was no area that seemed to draw their attention, however, and Elana found herself wandering around in circles trying to spot something she wasn't even sure would be there.

Then, all at once, the pattern became clear. After hours of watching, she saw what had been right in front of her. She thought they'd been patrolling at random, picking odd spots to stand watch based on nothing but habit or routine. But as she crouched on a low rooftop, staring at the soldiers as they moved in neat patterns, she finally saw it. Their patrols weren't based on what was happening on the surface; they stopped at points where they could clearly see the heavy metal plates which covered holes running up every street.

They must have had a proper entrance, but these holes apparently joined to tunnels that accessed the slaves. Immediately, she felt a huge wave of relief. *They can escape after all,* she thought, *or they would have no reason to guard the holes like this.*

She'd seen the metal plates all through the city. Maybe there were extensive tunnels underneath all of Ermoor, all joining each other. Escape in that case would be much easier than she first thought; she could get in through the military district, free the slaves, and escape through the tunnels to a safe distance before coming back up to the surface. With a target now, Elana focused on getting into one of the holes in the street without being seen.

She ducked behind a bin, squeezing her eyes shut. *Dammit, they're watching every single one.* In her search for a way down, she'd taken down a few more soldiers, but she was getting dangerously close to being discovered. A few of the soldier's absences had been noticed, and the ones who were still alive were beginning to get nervous. Every point of entry that lead underneath the city was being watched. She would simply go to any one of the other districts, where the military presence was almost nil, but she would get lost before she found the slaves.

Ermoor was already difficult enough to navigate; every building looked more or less the same, and was organised neatly row by row so that every street looked the same too. Elana was used to navigating by the sun, and by landmarks in the forest. The shapes of certain trees, certain Shenza buildings that were shaped differently depending on their purpose. If she had to go underground, she would be at a total loss. No sunlight or moonlight, no landmarks, no map. If she at least found the slaves first, she could just move in any direction for as long as possible and emerge when it felt like she'd put enough distance between them and Dreadhold.

A metal plate sat in the centre of an alley; almost all the rest were right in the street. Behind her bin, she waited until two soldiers crossed paths over the plate, one heading away and the other heading towards her. Her back to the bin, she was facing the street, and if it wasn't for the fog she would have been spotted for certain. With her magic active and her *Kaizuun* drawn, she saw three soldiers in her line of sight. Every now and then, a soft breeze rippled the fog, and the street opposite briefly melted into view. Wrapped in Shadow, she waited.

Steps echoed next to her, and she swept up, slashing her blade through the soldier's neck faster than he could react. A dry clicking sound escaped his mouth as he tried to swallow. She grabbed him, opened the bin with one hand, and threw him in. As she closed the bin, he started gurgling and choking. When the lid was closed, almost no sound escaped.

She sprinted to the metal plate, activating a strength spell in her left arm. More steps approached around the alley's corner, where the other soldier had gone. Close. She reached the plate, wrenched it out of the ground with a short metallic scrape, and dove in, shoving it back into place with magic. As the total darkness enfolded her, she heard the heavy clang of a soldier's boot hitting the metal plate as he continued his patrol.

Mara

Shortly after her fortune was revealed, the guards had come back in, and Uncle Lewis sat with her for the rest of the night as they stood watching in silence. They talked about everything, like they always did. Uncle Lewis was full of interesting facts, things she'd never even think to think about.

Halfway through a rant about the stars and the shapes they made when linked together, a scuffle sounded from somewhere in the mansion. Mara saw the guards glance at each other. When Uncle Lewis stopped talking, Mara knew for certain that something was wrong. Still smiling, he placed a hand on Mara's shoulder, but looked at the guards and cleared his throat. One of them immediately left the room, and the one who stayed pulled his gun out of its holster.

Her breath became ragged, and tears leapt into her eyes without warning. *He's here*, she thought, her chest tightening. *He's going to kill us all*. Taranos spoke at almost the same time.

He is here. You need to run.

A crash echoed through the mansion, and screams followed. Mara felt a surge of the energy flowing through her; the pulling feeling again, pulling her towards the door. Towards Riffolk. She felt it shift, pushing instead of pulling for a brief moment, and she was suddenly certain that he could feel her presence.

Outside the bedroom, the two guards shouted something. There were gunshots, deafening despite the closed door, then an even louder buzzing sound. It filled her ears, drowned her thoughts, and shook the floor beneath her feet. The air itself became electric, her skin buzzing almost as much as the wound on her shoulder.

He'd used her so many times, and she could never fight back. She belonged to him, legally and emotionally. In the hallway beyond the door, footsteps approached, and Mara's mind swirled with a chaos of panic and horrible memories. She couldn't move, she couldn't think, and all that existed in that moment was Riffolk. The loving man he'd been during her courtship and the wedding. The iconic genius who changed Ermoor for the better. The abusive husband who discarded her after he'd taken his pleasure. The evil scientist who killed an innocent girl.

He was on the other side of the door, and Mara's heart beat so fast she thought she might die. His face swam into her mind's eye, the cold eyes boring into her soul. Pera's destroyed corpse appeared again. The room blurred, and she tried to disappear, screwing her eyes shut and trying to blot out the world.

The door exploded inward, shattering into a cloud of dark wooden pieces and filling the room with scratchy dust. Her eyes flew open again, of their own accord. The guard in the bedroom with them exploded too, into a sudden drift of ash. Mara couldn't tell if she was screaming.

"What the bloody hell is happening?" Uncle Lewis shouted through the din.

Riffolk stepped into the room, saw them, and she felt the shift again. The power, Taranos' energy, swirled around them like a storm, and she felt it move with his mind. Panicking, reaching out with her own mind, she grabbed hold of the energy too; that magic was the only true comfort left to her, other than Uncle Lewis. She wasn't in control, couldn't think at all; but reaching for the power was automatic now. A look of horrified confusion splashed across Riffolk's face.

"You... You don't deserve this power!" He screamed.

She felt the arc of lightning before she saw it; felt it before it started towards her. They were connected now, both using the same magic. Connected to Taranos. It told her what to do, but not with words; with feelings. It reached beyond her terror, through her panic and touched her with the same feeling of completeness she'd felt in the street when she used magic for the first time. A slight nudge pushed her left side, and the arc of lightning was there a second later, but she met it with her own, throwing her left hand up and forcing an explosion of pure power.

Riffolk's lightning scattered like fog in the wind, and she brought her right hand up and unleashed an avalanche of sparks directly at his face. He grunted, bringing his hands to his eyes, and in that moment she felt the change; all the magic in the room flowed to her mind, under her control.

She pushed, with everything she had, and the magic around her reacted. Riffolk was thrown backwards, slamming into the wall behind him. She pushed again, this time gathering as much magic as she could and focusing it into a single bolt of lightning.

It hit Riffolk so hard that Mara heard a physical thump, then a crack, and then the entire wall behind him exploded out into the night. His presence was weak, but still there, and she knew it wouldn't be long before he recovered and came back for her. She felt him retreating, and dropped to her knees, exhausted. Her own energy was weak too.

After a while, she wasn't sure how long exactly, the silence pressed a little too heavily down on her. Looking around, she realised the room was empty.

"Uncle Lewis?"

She looked at the foot of the bed, where they'd been sitting. A pile of ashes lay there, half on the bed and half on the floor. It was messy and spread around from the magical hurricane her and Riffolk had caused. Sitting on the bed upside down was a pair of small round glasses, the lenses shattered.

Footsteps pounded down the hallway, getting louder. Mara didn't care; barely heard them. It could have been Riffolk coming back, and she wouldn't have moved. Uncle Lewis was dead. He'd died while he was right next to her, and she hadn't even noticed. Even worse, he'd died because of her magic. It might have even been the lightning she'd thrown that did it.

His glasses were in her hands. They felt so small, so fragile; she hadn't held them since she was a baby. When she last held them, they were far too big for her face, and slipped down constantly. In her mind it replayed, but what was previously a beautiful memory now felt sharp and cold. Vaguely, she heard the footsteps reach the destroyed bedroom door.

"Mara... you're okay."

Mathys. She couldn't look at him. If he'd been around, or if he'd allowed more soldiers to guard her, Uncle Lewis might still be alive. A heavy, painful silence stretched between them; Mara didn't take her eyes off the ruined glasses.

"Mara, we need to go," Mathys said, "this place isn't safe any more."

"Nowhere is safe." Her voice sounded strange even to herself, flat and dead.

"I can get us to safety Mara, you just need to come with me."

Still not looking up from the glasses, she stood and followed Mathys out of the mansion.

Elana

The darkness was complete. Elana crouched low, ready for anything. A few moments passed before she remembered herself and traced the spell at her eye; shadows became as transparent as daylight, and a long, slightly curved tunnel materialised in front of her. It stretched out in both directions, and she saw points where intersecting tunnels joined it on both sides. She froze for a moment; as well as she could navigate the forests of Shanaken, her sense of direction wasn't great. There were absolutely no markers to indicate where she was or where anything else was. Every tunnel looked identical.

Then she drew her *Kaizuun*, and a faint mess of auras bloomed in the distance. She strode through the tunnel, gathering as much magic as she could. The darkness helped; naturally dark places, even those without much life, were a source of Shadow Magic. It was much more difficult taking energy from pure darkness than from a life-filled forest at night, but it still felt good to embrace the utter blackness underneath the city. Above ground, Ermoor was not only devoid of natural life, but was constantly lit by colourful street lights, which made drawing Shadow Magic almost impossible.

Silence filled the tunnels. Surrounded by black stone and metal, with no light but the auras of thousands of slaves and no life other than the slaves themselves, Elana grew suddenly weary. She had found nothing but pain in Ermoor, and she found herself wishing the *Duulshen* had sent someone else on this mission. She wasn't even sure she'd made enough of a difference to be able to report back to the *Duulshen*. She'd never failed them before, but being in Ermoor was like trying to run underwater. Not only did she feel as though her potential couldn't be reached, she also felt like she was slowly drowning, deprived of air and with no view of the surface.

Eventually, she reached a dead end. The tunnel simply stopped, and she was still several hundred metres from the closest of the slaves. As she watched the figures moving, exhausted and faint, she noticed several dozen much stronger auras patrolling. *So the slaves are guarded from below too*, she thought. None of the slaves reacted to the soldiers. She didn't think much of it, until it occurred to her that the soldiers weren't reacting to the slaves either; there was literally no interaction between them.

They're in the walls. It hit her suddenly, and she took a closer look at the wall in front of her. The tunnel lead straight here, with nowhere else to go; *hidden doors*. The soldiers could guard entrances without having to manage the slaves directly. But if that was the case, what kept the slaves working in the first place? If no one was there, cracking a whip or punishing those who slacked in their work, why did they continue working so efficiently?

After half an hour of examining the wall, she finally found a trigger, and the wall slid open to reveal a brightly lit, warm tunnel, which resembled the corridors in the scientific laboratory she'd sabotaged. Dropping the Shadow Eye spell and sheathing her blade, she stepped into the corridor as the wall slid closed again behind her.

Elana sprinted through the brightly lit tunnels under Ermoor. Her Shadow spell wouldn't do much to hide her in the relentless light; there were no shadows at all. She'd counted at least thirty soldiers patrolling through the halls before she'd sheathed her *Kaizuun*. She sprinted around a corner and came face to face with a soldier. He wore red and orange armour, a kind she'd never seen before. It had a full-faced helmet in the shape of a demonic face. Taken aback, she paused for a few seconds, staring at the odd armour. The soldier was just as shocked as she was, and paused too. They both stared, transfixed, until the shock wore off and the soldier reached for his gun. Elana swept her blade straight from its sheath through his neck before his hand touched the gun's handle.

Cursing at herself, she glanced around as her *Kaizuun* made the auras of dozens of soldiers and thousands of slaves reappear before her. *Why did I sheath it in the first place?* She thought as she kept moving. The soldier behind her fell to the floor, his armour making a heavy clack as it connected with the smooth surface. She wouldn't remain unnoticed for long. With the soldier's auras showing their locations, she was able to take them down before they could see her, but it was only a matter of time before a patrolling soldier saw one of his fellows dead on the floor.

She moved as quickly as possible. She'd killed over a dozen soldiers by the time an alarm rang; it clanged through the corridors along with a yellow flashing light, making her wince as she approached another target. He turned as the alarm rang out, and his eyes went wide as she sliced his throat. Another soldier ran into the corridor ahead, too far for her to get to. He drew his gun, but she'd drawn and thrown a blade first. It hit him in the face as his arm brought up the gun, and it fired as his hand twitched. An explosion echoed through the small space from the soldier's gun, overtaking the alarm for a brief moment and making her ears ring. The actual projectile went nowhere near her; his arm had twitched to the side, and the gun fired straight into the wall next to him. But the sound was more than enough to pinpoint her location to the others.

Soon enough, under the constant wailing of the alarm, footsteps started thudding towards her. She sprinted for the corner where the soldier who'd fired his gun had come from. Auras were moving either side of her, rushing to the source of the sound along the adjacent corridors. They'd already drawn their weapons.

Mattias

Mattias ran alongside his fellow guards, heart pounding. He'd passed three corpses already, either decapitated or close to it. The shot fired a minute ago was the first gunshot any of the guards had heard; whoever they were about to face, he was either very fast, very stealthy, or both. Mattias had never seen actual combat before, let alone corpses. The Tyrans had never revolted, never found any of the secret exits into Ermoor. They didn't even know they were slaves. Guarding Tyra was every Ermoori soldier's dream job; they were essentially paid to walk up and down empty corridors.

But now, he was terrified. Bright red blood had spilled and pooled along the entire corridor from each corpse they passed, reflecting a sickening pink light through the walkways. He couldn't avoid stepping in it as they rushed toward the sound of the gunshot; it made the same splashing sound shallow puddles of water made when running in the rain. He'd looked back after the first corpse. That had been a mistake; his footsteps followed him, a trail of blood chasing him towards whatever killed its owner. His stomach churned, was still churning, but still he ran next to his fellow soldiers.

They reached the corner as a group. Mattias stepped around to see the body of the soldier who'd fired his gun; a clean slice opened his face just next to his nose, and thick black smoke curled up from the wound. The wall to his right was pockmarked and blackened from the gunshot; he hadn't managed to hit his attacker. Further down the hall, another headless corpse lay in a pool of blood. There were no enemies to be seen, but somehow that scared him more.

"Where is he?" one of the others said.

"Split into groups and search the corridors, now!" Captain Barclay shouted.

Mattias went with the group to the right, into the corridor with the two dead soldiers. There was nowhere for the enemy to hide, and more soldiers turned the corner ahead of him into the corridor. It seemed impossible; the gunshot and alarm had only gone off a moment ago and they'd sprinted here as fast as they possibly could.

The enemy simply *had* to be here somewhere. Mattias and the others slowed down as soon as their fellow soldiers appeared at the opposite end of the corridor. He stared at every inch of the empty hallway, feeling sweat run down the back of his neck. The corridors were kept fairly warm, but this was the first time he'd ever sweated, even in full armour. A horrible thought snuck into his head as he walked slowly; *what if it's the Spectre? What if he's returned?* The Spectre was known for killing those he deemed unjust, and Mattias had a feeling Tyra wouldn't exactly impress him.

The alarm was still raging; a yellow alarm. Each soldier had a hand-held pad with different coloured buttons on it which sent signals back to the command rooms. Yellow was a local alarm, just for Tyra; it told all soldiers on duty to get to one spot quickly. It was used usually only if the Tyrans found a way out or stopped turning the wheels. Red went to the barracks, and was for more serious situations, ordering reinforcements. The red alarm was silent in the barracks, simply setting off flashing red lights so as not to alarm the citizens. The black button was a city-wide alarm, and had never been used.

Through the sound of the wailing in his ears, he almost didn't hear a low scuffling sound behind him. When he glanced around, a blurred shadow streaked into the small group of soldiers, and a spray of blood swept along the wall. Gunshots thundered, overwhelming the alarm. One soldier aimed at the shadow and fired, only to hit the soldier behind it. Mattias tripped backwards trying to get away from the thing attacking them. Four soldiers had died in the few seconds since he'd turned around.

Across the corridor, the second group were shouting, their footsteps thumping the ground as they rushed to join the fight. Panicking, and with no idea what else to do, Mattias fumbled the alarm pad out of its holster on his belt, and mashed his thumb into the red button again and again. The yellow flashes turned to red and a different alarm started wailing through the corridors. It could take reinforcements as much as twenty minutes to arrive, but at least they were on their way.

Gunshots boomed almost constantly, coming from the few survivors in front of him as well as the group rushing to join behind. Mattias saw another soldier get hit by Ermoori rounds. The shadow was in constant motion, blurred and untouchable. He scrambled backwards, still on the ground, waiting for it to notice him and attack. As he scooted backwards on his hands and ankles, the second group of soldiers sprinted past him.

It was like something out of a nightmare. There had been a dozen soldiers in his group and there were another dozen in the group that just rushed in. Now, excluding himself, there was only one soldier from his group left. Finally, he pushed himself onto his feet, and ran down the corridor, away from the massacre. Gunshots continued to echo after him, and screams drowned out the alarm. He reached the decapitated soldier, his blood mixing with the flashing red light to create a corridor straight out of the depths of Hell itself. As he reached the corner, he glanced back to see three soldiers left, trying desperately to kill the shadow and failing. It couldn't be human.

Flashing red lights, deep red blood, soldier's screams, the piercing and wailing sound of the alarm; it was just too much. As another soldier fell with his head cut off, Mattias vomited. The last two soldiers were still fighting, but he couldn't watch any more, and he ran as fast as he could.

Riffolk

The Twelve Crowns had many secrets. Most, if not all of them, were known to Riffolk. He'd managed to move most of the safe-room contents into one of the Twelve's secret chambers under the city straight after the confrontation with Mathys. It had only been so easy because the safe-room contained very little in the first place.

Ermoor contained two separate tunnel networks underneath the surface; one was for the slaves and the soldiers guarding them, and the other was for the Twelve. Within the Twelve's network of tunnels, there were a dozen secret chambers with personalised lock systems; one for each Crown.

Riffolk moved into one of these chambers. He'd designed the custom locking mechanisms himself, though at the time the Twelve hadn't told him what they were for.

The chamber he moved into was large, and though it was dark and a little damp, it was luxurious. Riffolk ignored the decorations and the rich furniture, and set to work building another lab.

The creature wasn't going to be found again; he accepted that. But he could still use its power, and it had entered his mind several times. Riffolk hated the sensation of another being seeing into his mind. It took some concentration, but he was able to block it from completely connecting with him. He couldn't shut it out totally, but it was better than nothing.

With the power at his disposal, he was able to charge dozens of orbs a day, and use them to power his lab. He installed them into the machines he was building, used them as fuel for weapons, and had spares in a storeroom, adding to them each day. He used the Twelve's influence to reopen the factories, and put Arthor in charge of overseeing production. Of course, he couldn't use the energy he created without revealing himself as alive, and it was too early for that.

So, for now, he had to accept the longer time frame Arthor gave for the invasion. It was definitely going ahead; Riffolk wanted it perhaps more than the Crowns themselves had. He could afford to wait. Other than Mathys coming after him, no one suspected a thing, and even Mathys wouldn't be able to find the secret chambers he lived in now.

Arthor was slowly coming around. Riffolk kept in touch through written instructions as the Twelve did with most of their underlings. The Lord Commander played his part very well, and there was still enough instability in his actions that Riffolk knew he wasn't feigning loyalty.

Riffolk watched him a lot; most days. He always spoke to himself when alone; had been for quite a while based on the Twelve's observations. But lately he'd been reacting oddly during conversations, and in the presence of others. He needed to know more before he could properly exploit Arthor's insanity, but it was definitely a weakness open for exploitation.

Avoiding meetings was difficult, but necessary until he was ready to reveal himself to Symond. Before that happened, he had to be certain Arthor wouldn't attack him on sight. It took careful manipulation and time, so Riffolk used the written instructions for as long as he could.

He gave instructions to Mathys to send Mara home, with the smallest possible guard detail. Mathys fought to either give her greater protection, or keep her in the facility where she'd been held. He rejected all of it, and Mathys finally gave in.

When he saw Mara leave the military compound for home, he prepared to act. Soon, she would be granted his fortune, and when that happened he had to be sure she would be too terrified to spend it or give it away.

He sat in the chamber where he'd set up his new lab, fuming; so furious that sparks of lightning were crackling around him, throwing the dark room into harsh clarity. *How is she so strong?* His command and knowledge of Power Magic should have easily won out over sheer power; but the girl had some edge he couldn't quite grasp.

It shouldn't have happened the way it did. The attack was meant to terrify her, drain her of magic and injure her badly enough to make sure she'd never act against him. Instead, he'd been thrown out of his own house and his energy was drained, other than the sparks his fury generated. She'd pushed him too far. Scaring her obviously wasn't enough; he needed to kill her.

Her energy still pulled at him; he could feel her, the magic within her, and he knew she felt him too. He hoped she felt his rage. Fear was the last tool he had against her, and he knew she was afraid.

Arthor

He was on the Twelve's good side now. He followed orders, always in the form of written instructions now, and stayed out of public as much as possible to avoid reacting to the voice's increased activity. At night, he shut himself in his office and let the voice speak to him. Without Ellie to go home to, he stayed there most nights, sitting in the dark, sweating and clenching his hands into tight fists as the voice spoke.

Since the voice revealed that he'd been tricked, Arthor began obsessing over the thing that spoke to him from the ceiling of his bedroom. Now that he'd thought about it for a while, there was only one possibility, and once it occurred to him it seemed painfully obvious: The Spectre of Ermoor.

Mathys. Arthor was perhaps the only person in Ermoor who knew the identity of the Spectre. Of course, Mathys hadn't been active as the Spectre in over fifteen years; so why would he choose now, and why would he speak to Arthor when Arthor knew who he really was?

He never wanted the war in the first place, he thought, *and he was always against the creature.* Mathys' stern, judgemental face appeared in his mind, staring in silent accusation. Arthor couldn't bear it. He paced the dark office, stuck and helpless.

He is a powerful foe.

"Yes, but he is just one man. He can't stop the invasion."

Do not be so quick to disregard your enemies. I can only help you so much.

My enemy? The word echoed in his mind, feeling heavy. Mathys wasn't his enemy; they'd served together for decades. They were brothers.

Then why is he undermining you? Why is he trying to ruin your plans?

"He's always been strict in his morals... It's why he became the Spectre in the first place. It suited his need for justice. But an enemy... I can't see him that way."

And that might be exactly what he is counting on to beat you.

The voice knew everything. It always had an answer. Every time it spoke, Arthor felt less and less sure of the world around him. Could Mathys really be his enemy?

Are his the actions of a friend? No.

Another flash of rage, this time dull enough that the office stayed where it was. His heart thumped so hard it turned his breathing into a rhythm. Vaguely, he felt his hands throb in pain.

He will not stop. You know him. You know what he can do.

"Then I'll just kill him!"

You live in a world with rules. Outright murder will not help my cause; yet.

Mathys walked into Arthor's office just as the voice stopped talking. He paused, seeing the emotion on Arthor's face.

"Arthor, what's wrong?"

He didn't respond at first, trying to settle himself; his first reaction to seeing Mathys was to tense up for an attack, and he knew he couldn't win that fight.

"Nothing. Everything. I don't know."

Mathys moved towards him, and though he looked genuinely concerned, Arthor couldn't help feeling vulnerable. If Mathys really was his enemy, he didn't stand a chance alone in his office at night. But his Commander sat in one of the chairs to the side of the room, as he always did, and stared at the ground, looking as lost as Arthor felt.

"I know exactly what you mean, old friend."

A horrible gap stretched between them; Arthor felt it, and he was sure Mathys felt it too. It felt as though they were watching each other from opposite sides of a battlefield; a dangerous tension, unwanted by both but unavoidable. If Mathys was truly trying to stop his work, the Twelve would seek his death sooner or later. And if they didn't take him down, he would take Arthor down, and possibly even the Twelve themselves. He'd never once felt threatened by the man sitting across from him, in all their years of friendship; until tonight.

"Do you think we can be redeemed, Mathys?"

He raised his eyebrows, but didn't answer.

"What you were saying before, about our souls... If we're lost, can we be saved?"

Mathys sighed, his eyes remaining on the floor in front of his feet. It was a heavy sound, full of sadness and regret. Arthor knew in that moment that Mathys would kill him if he had to, despite their friendship. Under the heavy desk he sat behind, his hand moved to rest gently on the butt of his gun. He doubted he could draw and fire in time if Mathys truly wanted him dead, but the feel of it under his hand was reassuring nonetheless.

"I don't know how to answer that, Arthor. I hope so. But you know the scriptures as well as I do. God is not forgiving."

He nodded. It was the answer he'd expected. Mathys never budged when it came to morals or God. There was no way around it. Arthor took a deep breath, his exhale ragged; Mathys looked up at him.

"I saw something a little while ago," he said carefully, "something I hadn't seen for fifteen years."

"Oh?"

"At least I think I saw it. The Spectre."

"Surely not. Wasn't the Spectre confirmed as a myth by the Twelve Crowns?"

"Mathys..."

"You must have seen something else, Arthor. The Spectre has not been active for a long time."

"Can you promise that?"

"What's this about, Arthor? Really?"

He stopped, hand still on his gun, and really stared at Mathys for the first time that night. He looked tired. Exhausted. He'd been dealing with the girl, Arthor knew that. The Twelve knew too. They were keeping an eye on his activity, suspicious that he might be helping her in some way, hiding her involvement in the creature's escape.

"If the Spectre is active again, it won't be long before the Twelve hunt him down. I saw him. But it might—it might have been something else. Mathys, I'm not sure how to say it. I'm beginning to think there's something wrong with me."

The words tumbled out of his mouth before he could stop them. He was almost convinced Mathys was going to kill him, and yet he still turned to the Commander in his time of need. There was simply no one else he could tell. Mathys watched him, a spark deep in his eyes that Arthor could have sworn was predatory.

"What's happening, Arthor? What have you seen?"

"I've... I can't say. I've already said too much. If I know you as well as I think I do, Mathys, nothing I say will make a difference. But I need to say it anyway, for my own conscience; please, don't do whatever you're planning to do. The Twelve will get their way, they always do. Please don't stand against them."

"Even if they destroy Ermoor? Are you so eager to follow orders that you follow them straight to hell?"

Arthor felt his words hit harder than any punch Mathys could have thrown.

You see? He is an enemy. Turning you against the people you serve, against Ermoor itself.

"And what are you doing, Mathys? Saving the city by planning to slaughter its leaders? Waging a one man war against Ermoor?"

"What are you talking about?" Mathys' voice was low, quiet and utterly lethal. "I'm not the one killing the Crowns, Arthor."

A moment of unbearable tension stretched between the two men, and Arthor felt their friendship stretching with it.

"But you're planning it."

"I never planned that. Listen to what you're saying, Arthor. The Spectre is Ermoor's saviour. Do you really think he would be murdering the Twelve?"

He lies, and talks about the Spectre as though it is separate from him. It is an insult to your intelligence. The Spectre has become a danger to Ermoor.

The shadow on his roof had to be Mathys; there was no other possibility.

"The Spectre is not welcome in Ermoor any more. Mathys, I know you. I know the Spectre won't stop if he's decided to return. But don't make me choose between you and the Twelve."

Mathys stood so quickly that Arthor drew his gun. He stopped himself from pulling the trigger just in time, but the barrel pointed squarely at Mathys' chest.

"You've made your choice already, old friend."

Elana

Elana ran towards the slaves, hoping desperately for an easy way to get to them. One of the Ermoori had survived, running off to get more soldiers. She let him go; the alarm had been going a while now, there was nothing to be gained by wasting time chasing him down when more soldiers were most likely on their way already. She had to get the slaves out before they arrived.

Her breathing was ragged, her steps forced; one of the soldiers had hit her in the side and leg. A glancing blow, but their guns were powerful, and she was bleeding. She'd survive, but she didn't have the time or the magic to heal it now. Besides, her *Kaizuun* filled her with energy and strength; that would have to carry her through. Her older wounds, from the fight with Riffolk, still hadn't healed completely either.

She got as close to the auras of the slaves as she could, and found a small room with a control console remarkably like the ones in the laboratory. Next to the console, a section of the wall stood blank and waiting, clearly designed to be a door.

Among the controls and switches, a large red button took up the centre of the console. She put her hand gently on it, preparing to push down. Just as she put a little pressure on the button, she faltered; she realised she would have to take the slaves above ground at some point.

She stopped, and ran from the room, a half-thought plan burning in her mind. She sprinted through the corridors, keeping track of the turns she made, until she found one of the dead soldiers. She grabbed his corpse, and his severed head, and ran to the nearest room. It was a storeroom filled with bags and boxes of foodstuff, but she ignored the contents and focused her attention on getting the soldier's armour off his body.

A minute later, she sprinted back to the control room, dressed in blood-splattered demonic armour. Luckily the red and orange mostly hid the blood, but she was beyond caring about that. She brought her fist down on the red button, and the door rumbled open faster than she anticipated. Stepping over to the entrance, she paused, transfixed by the sight in front of her.

Over a hundred people filled the room in front of her, most of them turning a gigantic horizontal wheel around endlessly. As she stepped into the dark, candlelit space, all eyes snapped to her. Two things happened almost immediately; the people turning the wheel sped up noticeably, and anyone not pushing it started sprinting for the doors. She had expected a panic, even maybe the beginning of a fight, when she revealed herself in the Ermoori armour; but for the slaves pushing the wheel to work even harder... It took her a few moments to gather herself.

"STOP!" Her voice echoed through the cavernous room.

They stopped, staring at her with weak, pale faces. A tense silence filled the room. Behind her, the light in the small control room switched off suddenly. The slaves stared at her as though they'd never heard a person talk before. She didn't have time for their shock; the alarm was bound to bring more soldiers at any moment.

"I am here to help you," she said, "you are slaves, and I'm here to set you free!"

A moment of silence filled her with doubt. Did the slaves even want to leave? In the silence, an idea came to her, and she removed the helmet. Gasps and cries filled the huge room.

"They're not monsters!" A voice shouted over the shocked gasps of the crowd.

"It's just a girl!"

"What does she mean, slaves?"

She raised her arms, and the crowd stilled.

"We must move quickly if we're going to get out of here, there were dozens of soldiers guarding this place, and there are many more on their way!"

The room filled with intense murmuring, every slave trying to have their say, most talking to each other but many shouting at her. She couldn't understand a word of it; there was far too much noise. Several of the slaves started moving towards her, and once they stood before her without getting killed, others followed. There were still questions being asked, but the crowd milled at the entrance into the guard's corridors. Elana turned to lead them out, but one of the slaves nearby called for her to stop.

"Wait." he said, "what about the others?"

"What others?" Elana said.

"This is just one wheel room. There are ten, with over a hundred workers in each one. Then there are a hundred sleeping halls, for all the Tyrans who are in between shifts." Without waiting for Elana to reply, the old man turned and shouted to the people at the back of the crowd.

"Go and get everyone, now!"

She hadn't realised how many of them there were. This place must have been the size of a town at least. Panicking now, she nodded and waited for the slaves to run off and gather the others. The wounds in her side and her leg pulsed, and she felt blood slowly dribbling down her leg. It had started warm, but was now cold and sticky. She replaced the helmet on her head, closing her eyes and trying to collect herself. She was losing strength, magic, and time.

Mara

They sat in the study of a modest home in Dawnton. Though lovely, it was even smaller than the Watson mansion. Mathys must have been making good money; why did he live in such a tiny home? A comfortable chair stood in the corner, and a straight-backed working chair faced it.

Mathys, sitting as straight-backed as the chair itself, looked at her with an expression of genuine concern. If her father had ever worn it, she would have thought of it as a fatherly expression.

"We need to be very careful," he said, "Riffolk is the most dangerous man in Ermoor, and he wants us both dead."

"You said you could take me to safety."

He nodded.

"And I can, but we need to sort some things out first. With Riffolk being publicly dead, his finances belong to you now. It puts you at both an advantage and a disadvantage. You can use his money to achieve things both him and the Twelve wouldn't have wanted, but it also means you'll be the target of anyone who wants that money for themselves."

"You mean not just Riffolk?"

"Not just Riffolk," he agreed, "there are dangerous people in Ermoor, Mara. Thieves, spies, assassins, criminals. And the Twelve Crowns themselves."

His voice had dropped to barely a whisper. When they first entered the room, Mathys lit a candle, and its small flickering glow was the room's only light. It was scented, and the smell was sweet and heavy, like nothing she'd smelled before. There was a weight to it, and it seemed to settle in her lungs, slowing her breathing. Her eyelids drooped, and despite her fear, she couldn't concentrate on Mathys' words.

She couldn't remember feeling this exhausted in her life. He cleared his throat, and though she heard it, she was too far gone. His hand closed around her wrist, gently but firmly, and he pulled her to her feet. She followed him, her eyes still drooping, until she stumbled and he picked her up. After a long walk, he laid her gently on a soft mattress. She fell asleep before she felt a pillow under her head.

She woke in flickering light, and the smell of Mathys' candles clung to her nostrils, making her dizzy. She was in a cosy bedroom, in perhaps the most comfortable bed she'd ever slept in. After the incident with Riffolk at his mansion, she'd been utterly drained. But now, sitting up and stretching, she felt brand new. Knowing there would be no more examinations, no more cold scientific stares, made everything sweeter.

She left the room, looking around the cramped hallways for signs of Mathys. For such a small house, the hallways were quite long, and the ceiling high; Mara found herself walking down one hallway for what felt like an entire street.

She wasn't in the house Mathys brought her to. It looked similar, but at the same time very different. For one thing, the walls and roof were lined with shiny black metal plates. Richly polished wooden beams ran up and down the hallway roof, and a soft carpet covered the floor. For another, there were no windows at all.

As she walked, she stared at everything. The black plates were covered in strange runes, carved into the metal. They were beautiful, but somehow scary. A strange, uncomfortable energy seemed to emanate from them, as if they followed a rhythm her body couldn't match. She jumped as soft music floated down the hall, from a candlelit room ahead.

Mathys stood before a cabinet with his back to the door, hunched over something in his hands she couldn't see. A slow, sad melody played from the teleradio in the corner. Hanging from the walls, filling every available space, were countless weapons. Things she'd never seen nor even imagined hung from hooks on the wall.

Blades, guns, coiled ropes, and things she couldn't even describe. A cabinet next to the one Mathys stood before held a mannequin dressed in black plated armour with a dark grey hooded cloak. Under the hood of the cloak, a mask she recognised instantly stared at her. *The Spectre of Ermoor!* She looked at Mathys again, beyond words. As gently as she could, she stepped back, moving back out into the corridor a bit at a time.

"Don't leave."

She froze. Her heart completely stopped for a long, painful moment. *How do I keep getting in these situations?* She thought as Mathys turned to look at her.

He held a gauntlet, armoured and covered in what looked like machinery. It was the kind of thing that could only have been made by Riffolk. Screaming, she fled down the hallway, running as quickly as she could. She managed less than half a dozen steps before a strong hand grabbed her arm, pulling her to a stop.

"Mara, I know how this looks," he said, "but you need to trust me."

Gathering her energy, she conjured a bolt of lightning, focusing it around her fist, and punched him as hard as she could. He grunted and flew backwards into the wall, and she ran again. She couldn't think, couldn't tell where she was. *Mathys is the Spectre of Ermoor.*

The stories she'd grown up hearing as a child flooded her mind, all at once, melding and overlapping. One fact underlaid them all; there was a spectre in Ermoor, and had been since the city was built. A protector, a ghoul that sought vengeance against those who did wrong.

It couldn't be a person. It couldn't be Mathys. The Spectre had been around for almost two thousand years; there was a chapter devoted to him in the history textbook she'd seen when she was at school. Of course she hadn't read it herself, but there was an illustration that had given her nightmares when she was little.

"Mara!"

The voice wasn't human. Ahead of her, a sudden cloud of fog exploded into the hallway, completely obscuring the way ahead. She kept running, and cannoned into something unmoving. Her momentum completely halted, she fell to the floor, and through the fog the Spectre loomed above her.

Riffolk was terrifying, but she understood his magic and his guns. The Spectre, Mathys, had taken a lightning fueled punch and still managed to appear before her in a puff of fog like something out of a nightmare. Faster than human. Stronger. She wasn't sure she could win this fight, and that was even with the powerful magic at her command.

"Mara," the voice was gentler now, though no more human, "I need you to trust me. I'm not going to hurt you, but you can't leave. You're not safe."

Arthor

If he was going to survive, he needed to have the Twelve on his side. He had to go all-in. Total loyalty. As soon as Mathys left his office, he sent a signal to them. A button under his desk was linked to some kind of alert which was monitored by the Twelve; it told them when he had something worth reporting. He didn't understand how it worked, but they were always able to meet him within an hour of the button being pushed.

He left as quickly as he could, heading straight to the secret entrance into the meeting chamber. The walk took a little while, and he strolled through alleys and streets, cycling back sometimes, going at a leisurely pace despite his chaotic heartbeat. He wore a dark cloak, his military uniform folded neatly in a draw in his office. All important protocols to keep from revealing any of the Twelve's secrets.

The entire time, all he could think about was Mathys. If he was truly moving against the Twelve, it would mean a lot of deaths. Possibly Arthor's, possibly Mathys', but certainly many more before that. He'd seen the Spectre in person once, back before he knew who wore the mask. It had been terrifying.

It was no less terrifying now that he knew who the Spectre was; if anything, knowing Mathys was capable of such brutal and seemingly impossible things made it even more terrifying. Now, as he walked carefully through the city towards the Twelve, he couldn't help suspecting that Mathys was nearby, watching and following.

A deep shadow filled the chamber, almost as deep as the silence. Arthor stood in front of one of the Crowns, trying his hardest not to fidget. *Again,* he thought, *only one of them bothered to show up.* Finally, the Crown spoke.

"The Spectre... interesting. Very interesting. You're quite certain?"

"Yes. He is going to move against you soon, possibly has already started."

"Thank you for your concern, Lord Commander. We are safe, but if he is a threat he must be eliminated."

It is for the best. Mathys will not stop until you and the Twelve are dead.

Arthor's chest tightened, a weight growing in his stomach. They knew he was loyal now, he had to hold on to that. But to prove it, he'd given Mathys' life. *It was him or me,* he thought, *and Mathys has no wife or children, no family to protect or continue his name.* The thought was meant to comfort himself, but instead the weight in his stomach twisted and burned.

Mathys was perhaps the best person he knew; strong, dedicated, loyal, intelligent, and devout. He'd worked all his life, tirelessly, for the betterment of Ermoor and its people.

No. He is plotting against you. He is going to destroy what you have worked so long for. He already sabotaged you, lied to you by pretending to be me.

"I know!" Arthor shouted. He couldn't help it. The Crown recoiled a little.

"I'm sorry. My emotions are running high lately."

"Ah, yes. You and Mathys are close, aren't you?"

"We've known each other a long time."

"I see. I'm sorry, Lord Commander."

"So am I."

A short pause followed, and Arthor could have sworn he saw the Crown give a slight nod before continuing.

"I'm sorry," he repeated, "but the Commander made his choice. Call for an announcement at Rookfell Square as soon as possible, and announce to the public that Commander Mathys Corby is hereby sentenced to death."

The stage at Rookfell Square was massive. An open area, backed by a wall of navy blue banners with the symbol of the Twelve Crowns in blazing white on each. In front of him, thousands of people watched and listened as he told them of Mathys' crimes. Some were invented in his meeting with the Twelve the night before, some were real.

Printed photographs of Mathys were plastered everywhere. A reward had been set, an outrageous amount, for information leading to his capture. An even larger sum would go to whoever captured and brought him to the Lord Commander; dead or alive.

The entire time he spoke, he felt exposed. Mathys had nothing to lose now; no reason not to attack. But no attack came. The crowd reacted to his accusations the way the Twelve knew they would; anger and outrage and demands for justice. Mathys wouldn't be able to set foot on the street without a mob coming after him.

He is trying to destroy everything we are working towards.

Hearing the voice inside his head while standing in front of thousands of people was a uniquely terrifying experience. *Stop,* he thought, panicking, *if I react I'll be branded a lunatic in front of all of Ermoor.*

Everything will be okay.

It was the first genuinely reassuring thing the voice had ever said to him. He could breathe again, and the crowd seemed far less dangerous than it did just a moment before. He gave the stage to Commander Barton, and left as the new Commander addressed the crowd. As he stepped off the stage, out of view of the people, the voice started again.

Mathys

Mathys reeled, his stomach twisting and burning. A public order for his death; he expected that from the Twelve eventually, if they found enough evidence; but coming from Arthor himself? *Nowhere is safe.* He ran over rooftops, back to the safe house; though calling it that felt wrong now. The Twelve, to his knowledge, had never known the real identity of the Spectre. But no one had ever known the real identity of the Twelve before, either; Mathys couldn't rely on secrets any more.

He had no idea what Riffolk was truly capable of. Before the mess he found himself in, he'd never have thought the scientist capable of murder or assassination. He'd long suspected some foul play on the part of the Overseer, but the methodical brutality he'd witnessed was beyond anything he could have imagined.

With so much cruelty, so much intelligence, and now unlimited power, both as the 'Twelve Crowns' and as a wielder of magic, Riffolk had become an unstoppable force. And now Arthor was allied with him too. Mathys' training would make no difference against such a threat. Mara was barely a month into her training; there was no way she would be ready to fight if they stayed in Ermoor. His only choice was to disappear, and make a plan.

Tarsium was the obvious choice, but they had to disappear for a while first. His task force had begun searching the swamplands, but were called back after the Twelve—no, Riffolk—finally realised how useless the search would be. It didn't take long; Ermoor, or at least the continent outside of the city, was the size of Shanaken and Tarsium combined. With at least half of that gigantic land mass being swampland that was difficult to cross at the best of times, there was no way Mathys and his men could have found the creature. It was the perfect place to hide.

Elana

Finally, the room had filled with every slave in the underground city they called Tyra. There were so many that they filled the tunnels leading into the rest of the city. Elana gestured, and strode into the now dark corridors. The slaves could see perfectly, and their footsteps behind her gave her strength; she was moving with purpose again, in front of a veritable army.

She sprinted through the dark corridors, thousands of footsteps rushing behind her. The entire place was as dark as the stone tunnels leading out from the room where she'd saved the slaves from. *They're here,* she thought as she ran, *they've arrived and they've shut off the lights to scare us.* But even as she thought it, Shadow Magic showed her the corridors, and there were no Ermoori soldiers; at least not too close. She looked above and saw thousands of them milling around certain areas, trickling downwards one at a time, into the underground corridors.

Elana led the slaves as quickly as she could, not paying attention to the direction, only to the soldiers above. They drew closer every second. She looked in every direction as she ran, and every direction seemed hopeless; the soldiers were everywhere.

"We're going to have to fight!" she shouted back to the slaves, "be ready to attack!"

Her voice sounded too quiet in her own ears, barely audible above the deep rumble of thousands of sprinting slaves; but she heard them pick up the call, shouting it down the tunnel so everyone would hear. They had no weapons, or armour. But there were so many of them, and the tunnels were dark, and there would only be so many soldiers that could face them at one time in the limited space below Ermoor.

The tunnel kept going straight, but in a corridor that branched off to the right, she saw a group of bright, strong auras gathered. The group was growing every few seconds as more soldiers lowered themselves into the tunnel. She saw them looking around, uncertain and confused at the immense sound of the running Tyrans. Echoes made it impossible for the soldiers to tell where Elana and the slaves were coming from. She rushed around the corner, feeling the ground quake as the Tyrans followed. It took a few seconds for the soldiers to see them in the darkness.

"Halt, slaves!" one soldier said. Disgust was plain in his voice. "Get back to your work, or die."

Then Elana was on top of them. She slashed the head off the closest Ermoori, the one who'd spoken, then leapt over them and into the small group. She heard the slaves reach their captors and the sounds of battle raged through the darkness. Gunshots exploded. There were screams, and cries, and grunts. Glancing over at the slaves, she saw them fighting more brutally than any Shenza warrior she'd seen.

They were bloodthirsty, ripping soldier's throats out with their bare hands, biting, clawing and scratching like wild animals. She killed another three soldiers, then heard gunshots booming deeper in the tunnels. She glanced over where she'd come from, and saw the slaves milling there looking towards the back of the crowd; Ermoori soldiers had surrounded and closed in on them. As she looked, soldiers rushed in from the other side of the same corridor they'd come from; the direction she would have led them in if not for the group they were fighting now.

They crashed into the slaves, firing their guns as quickly as they could and bashing with their armoured fists when they could reach. Just in time, she glanced around and saw more soldiers come from the other side of the corridor they'd turned into.

"You cannot stand against the might of Ermoor!" a voice boomed through the tunnels, seemingly from everywhere, "Surrender now or die!"

The slaves reacted to the voice the same way they'd reacted when she spoke. Their hesitation was devastating; the Ermoori soldiers didn't stop attacking, and in those few seconds Elana saw the battle turn. One soldier threw what looked like a fist-sized stone into the crowded tunnel where the slaves were tightly packed. A massive explosion rippled through the crowd, ripping dozens of Tyrans to pieces in an instant and spreading flames through dozens more.

Elana had seen the devices before, and knew all too well how deadly they could be. On the north shore of Shanaken, in the open air of the beach, they were brutal. But in a tightly packed tunnel, the death and destruction it caused was nothing short of terrifying. Another explosion went off further down the tunnel, and the slaves broke. They stopped fighting and raised their hands, even the ones close to the soldiers.

They stayed that way while the soldiers kept killing them, until finally orders were shouted down the tunnels to cease fire. An eerie, awful silence settled into the dark. The smell of blood, smoke and death filled the tunnels. Elana couldn't surrender; regardless of what they did with the slaves from this point, if they captured her they'd torture any information they could out of her and then kill her. She had done all she could. Hopefully it would be enough to slow Ermoor down.

She was surrounded, from above as well as within the tunnels. Tracing the spell to wrap herself in Shadow, she rushed through the crowd of soldiers, sheathing her sword and hoping no one would notice her.

Bustled but otherwise unbothered by the soldiers, she kept a fast pace. She heard grunts, confused shouts and insults follow her as a blurred orange shape shoved Ermoori guards who were simply trying to join the action up ahead. They barely noticed her, assuming one of their brethren had accidentally shoved them. Her wrist was grabbed briefly and her run stopped short, a confused and outraged Ermoori attempting to take revenge for being shoved; but she twisted free and pushed through the crowd again, until the soldier who'd caught her couldn't possibly have followed.

As she'd hoped, with the slaves escaped, Tyra itself was almost empty. She ran into a pair of soldiers and killed them before they realised she wasn't one of their own. One of them managed to fire his weapon before he died, missing her but announcing her presence to any other soldiers that might be nearby. She cursed. She'd had an idea when it occurred to her to come back to the guard corridors; if it was empty, she may be able to sabotage the wheels before all the slaves were herded back to Tyra. That way even with their slaves back under control, they wouldn't be able to use them for whatever the wheels did.

If she rushed, she might make it. If even just one or two of the wheels could be sabotaged, she'd be slowing Ermoor down. She sprinted down the corridors, and just as she approached the control room into Tyra, another slave crept out of the doorway, terrified and confused. A woman, though she couldn't tell how old.

"No! You're too late!" she screamed, as her heart fell; saving this slave meant she wouldn't have time to enter Tyra at all.

But she had to save the woman. She had to save at least one, even if the rest of them had surrendered. She snatched the slave up without breaking stride, and bolted down the corridor. She ran for the nearest entrance to the surface, but the woman suddenly screamed and kicked, and Elana lost her grip.

As soon as the woman landed on the floor she was back up on her feet, sprinting away. A door opened and a group of soldiers spilled into the corridor, seeing the slave almost immediately and running at her. The Tyran tripped and smashed to the floor, screaming as the guards descended upon her, kicking and hitting her.

"Please, save me!" She choked as she was beaten.

Elana leapt at the soldiers, slicing through skin, bone and armour with renewed fury; her chance to save one Tyran slave would not be wasted. They died in seconds, and it took the woman a moment to realise she was safe again. She glanced around herself, baffled at the sudden death that filled the corridor. Then her eyes found Elana, and her terror came back.

"No," she said. "No, no, no!" and ran away from Elana again.

She gave chase, catching up to the woman quickly. She grabbed the slave again, now prepared for any fight she might get.

"Please," The woman said again, "please save me!"

"I am," Elana said.

She sprinted back into the tunnels under Ermoor, now past the guard's corridors. She ran as far as she could, away from the massive crowd of Tyrans and soldiers, until she couldn't possibly be underneath Dreadhold any more. When she reached one of the upwards tunnels that led to the surface, she grabbed the ladder and climbed as quickly as she could, pulling strength and speed from the *Kaizuun* in her hand. The woman was draped over her shoulder now, and had stopped putting up a fight.

She launched out of the hole, punching the metal covering away with a wave of Shadow Magic. She landed, painfully, but kept her focus on saving the Tyran. She glanced around, not sure where to go, where to leave the slave that would be safe. The street above Then she saw a familiar aura; gentle, kind and innocent, hunched against a wall a couple streets over; the girl, the one who was married to Riffolk Hayne. She was perhaps the only truly good person in all of Ermoor. Unable to believe her luck, she rushed towards the young girl. The slave might be safe after all.

Mara

Mathys spoke to her gently, the terrifying face mask of the Spectre sitting in his lap and his voice back to normal. He told her everything. The history of the Spectre, or as much of it as he knew. His own role in the security of Ermoor, beyond the obvious responsibilities as Commander. He showed her the armour, the weapons, the mask. Then, shocking her most of all, he offered to train her.

"Train me?"

"I'm not old, Mara. But I will be before too long. The Spectre must live on. There are more important things than stopping street thugs at stake here. The Twelve Crowns are dead, and Riffolk has taken their place. I think the time is coming when Ermoor will need the Spectre to fight for justice again."

She sat in silence for a moment, staring uneasily at the face mask.

"The Twelve are dead?"

"Yes. He killed them all."

The events of the past few days, or weeks, she couldn't tell, blurred in her mind until nothing made any sense. The only thing that felt real to her was the magic she felt in her body, and even that didn't totally make sense to her.

"So you'll train me to do... what you can do?"

"Yes."

He'd appeared in front of her. The hallway was tiny, cramped, and he'd been behind her, *way* behind. It had to be magic, simply had to be.

"Why didn't you believe me about anything I said when you can use magic too?"

Mathys recoiled as though she'd suddenly shouted, his brows furrowed.

"Magic? I don't use magic, Mara. Only training, and the right tools."

She shook her head.

"No, that's impossible. There's no way you could have gotten past me in that hallway without some kind of magic."

"I'll show you what I know, and eventually you'll understand. But from now on, you have to stay down here."

Down here. She thought she was in Mathys' home. Suddenly the too-long, too-high hallways made sense. *Underground.*

"Where are we?"

"It's best if you don't know. When you're ready, I'll tell you. But for now, you'll stay down here, and you'll train."

Mara was far stronger than when she'd started training, even if that was only a few weeks ago. Mathys was incredible; he knew everything there was to know about combat, stealth, and the massive assortment of gadgets and weapons he kept.

The training was brutal, but she kept up as best she could, the image of Riffolk walking through the exploded bedroom door pushing her to work harder. The image of Pera's mangled corpse still haunted her dreams every night, and she often woke up screaming. Pushing herself to the absolute limit and beyond meant that when she slept, she was exhausted enough that no dreams came. Feeling her strength grow helped her feel like she wasn't so helpless.

Every day Mathys showed her new things; a new fighting technique, a new weapon, a new defensive move. He wasn't gentle, but he was careful; she went to bed covered in bruises, but with no lasting damage. At his instruction, she never used her magic during their training, but she did practice on her own each night, in a safe room he'd set up for her.

The training was so intense, she'd been sick several times. She didn't tell Mathys, just pushed on. He left their safe-house every night, disappearing for a while wearing the armour of the Spectre. Other than that, they spent all their time together training.

The Spectre of Ermoor held so much less fear for her after Mathys showed her how everything worked. Her fear of it never totally vanished, however; stories of it had been told for as far back as she could remember, and it was difficult to let go of a lifetime of pent up fear and nightmares. Every time she saw Mathys in the suit, her heart skipped a beat, and a cold wave of uneasy fear rolled down her spine.

He was fitting a second set of armour and a new cloak for her. It was taking a while; he hadn't built the original suit of course, and he was no Riffolk Hayne when it came to designing and building things. In the meantime, she wore simple, comfortable clothes made from a lightweight fabric. Pants, and a long sleeved tunic. *Pants.* The idea had horrified her at first; no lady in Ermoor would ever wear pants. But after the first few training sessions, she settled into them. After a while, she forgot what it felt like to wear a dress.

Every morning, still, she was sick. She realised it wasn't the training when her stomach became rounder and she felt a heaviness there. Mathys noticed too, when she was late to training after a particularly bad bout of sickness.

"You're late."

"Yes, I'm sorry."

"Where were you?"

"I'm – I wasn't..."

Her stomach had cramped again, she winced, and he rushed to her side. Out of concern, or habit, he placed his hand next to hers on her stomach. He pulled away as soon as he felt the bump, making a low strangled sound.

"You're... Mara, you're pregnant!"

She looked up at him, tears in her eyes.

"We can't let him find out."

Mathys

Through his career, Mathys had built a network of trustworthy contacts, who could each provide him with either information or resources that were otherwise completely unavailable to Ermoor. Most of them lived in the poor districts, though they were anything but poor. After donning a black coat and a fake beard, Mathys ventured into the depths of the city's filth.

The Copper Dragon was a pub on the southern edge of the southernmost district, Ravenmire, almost right on the water's edge. It was the oldest pub in Ermoor, built in 712, over a thousand years ago.

While it was being built, the workers had allegedly seen an actual dragon in the distance, shining with flame and flying above the sea. With the sun beating down on them, reflecting off the mythical beast's back, it took on a copper glow, and the pub was named that day.

Isobel Bennett, the owner, spent most of her time in the office at the back of the building. Women were not permitted to own businesses or property in Ermoor, but no one would have dared take the Copper Dragon from Isobel. She was the eldest surviving child in the Bennett family, and her ancestors had built the pub themselves; it had never been owned by another family. When her older brother, Silas, was killed in a brawl a few years before, Isobel took over.

The first thing she'd done as the new owner was track down the men who'd murdered her brother. She maintained that she'd never touched them herself; but they were never seen again. Mathys had been friends with the Bennett family for twenty years. Isobel's father, Jothan, was a military man, and served with Mathys for five years after they first met. He would have risen to Commander himself if he hadn't been badly wounded in Shanaken and honourably discharged with a medal of bravery. Instead, he retired early and took over the Dragon from his younger brother Alden.

Jothan died a few years after retiring from the military; his wounds were more serious than he'd thought. His younger brother Alden left Ermoor shortly after, leaving Silas and Isobel to run the Dragon. Mathys had never liked Silas, though he'd never admitted it to Isobel, and would take it to his grave now that the man was dead.

He walked through the Dragon's door, flinching from the squeal of the hinges as he always did. This time of night, there were enough people that he could visit unnoticed, and he moved through the crowded main room to a booth at the back. As he passed the bar, he winked to the barman, who'd been working there almost as long as Mathys had been a customer; his usual order would be on the booth's table within moments.

As he sat, the back door opened, and Isobel sat in the booth facing him. She was always watching, always aware of what was happening in her pub.

"'Lo, old man," she said.

"Isobel."

"Don't suppose you took care of business?"

"You know I never keep you waiting."

She smiled, sliding a bag of coin to his side of the table. He shook his head and slid it back.

"Not this time."

"Ah," she said, her eyes dancing, "time for a favour?"

"Yes."

She sighed heavily, but her eyes kept dancing, and a smirk twisted her lips as she leaned back in the comfortable booth. The barman brought Mathys' drink, a bright blue Tarsi liquor called the Jewel of Tarsium. It was sweet and refreshing, with an exotic flavour unique to ingredients grown in Tarsium.

"What could a man like you possibly need from me?" Isobel said.

"I need to leave the city. As soon as possible."

"Mm, I heard the news. Lord Commander's not a fan of you, eh? How much cargo are you bringing with you?"

"All of it—everything you can manage. This is long-term."

The good humour vanished from her face as though he'd slapped her.

"What's happening?"

"It's... not something I can talk about. Listen. There's one more thing, Isobel."

"This isn't a small favour, old man," she said.

"I know."

"What's this one more thing then?"

He swirled the tumbler in his hand, watching the ice cubes and small lime wedge spin as the light caught the bright liquid. The blue glowed under any light source, glinting and sparkling as though it were an actual jewel. Finally, after another long sip, he raised his eyes to Isobel's again.

"There's a girl. I need to bring her with me."

"Oh, so it's a honeymoon, eh? Why didn't you say?"

"No, no. It's not like that. She's young, she's in danger, and she's... pregnant."

"Shit, Mathys!"

"Shh!"

"Damn, old man, what've you got yourself into?"

"It's not like that, Isobel. And don't say that name here, you know that."

"Sorry, I just—I mean, how'd you expect me to react?"

"I didn't think you'd immediately assume the child was mine!" he gestured as if thoughtlessly shooing a fly and moved on. "Can you help me?"

"Of course."

"we'll need to disappear for a while before we actually leave. We're going to be pursued, and if the pursuers think we've already left and leave before us, that gives us time to plan and think."

Her smile finally returned.

"The Cubby-house?"

"The Cubby-house."

Elana

It took a while for her to get her bearings again. After leaving the Tyran with Hayne's wife, she wrapped herself in shadow again and leapt silently onto a nearby light pole. It felt like an incredible effort, the wounds she'd suffered screaming at her to rest. The excitement and energy of battle was draining away quickly, and she felt the damage to her body taking its toll. It was time to leave Ermoor.

As she rushed along rooftops and light poles, her Shadow spell faltered. For the first time since she'd become *Kaizeluun*, she felt the magic completely leave her. Suddenly, even with her *Kaizuun* drawn, she was out of strength. She tripped mid-step halfway along a light pole, and crashed down into the street. It was a long fall; she felt a bone snap in her leg. She'd run far enough that she was out of the military district, but guards were still patrolling randomly; no doubt to search for slaves who might have escaped. *Or for me,* she thought. Pushing herself to her feet, she limped on. The docks were three districts away from Dreadhold, in Ivorstorm, and she was close by. Still, every step was agony, and she had no idea what she'd do if soldiers found her.

As she thought it, five soldiers turned into the street she was limping down. Though there was still fog, she had no magic to hide with and it wasn't long before one of the Ermoori saw her.

"Who's that? You there, stop!"

They ran, their weapons already drawn. She still held her *Kaizuun*, and angled it behind her body as they approached. As they drew closer they faltered, and the tone of the soldiers who spoke changed.

"It's one of us!" One said.

"You're injured!" The one who'd first seen her said.

They reached her, concern on their faces; they wore the standard Ermoori guard armour, much less decorative than the demonic armour they wore to guard Tyra. It was dark, a mix of deep blue fabric and grey armour plates. And no helmets. She waited for them to get close. Two of them stayed back, watching the street. *Damn it,* she thought. The three close to her could be taken out fairly easily, but she was out of magic and badly injured.

She'd never felt this weak in her life. With the Shadow Magic depleted, her strength and stamina were utterly drained. Her wounds pulsed viciously, and her leg was going numb. She brought her hand to her side, hissing at the pain; definitely a bad injury. As she moved her hand to the leg wound, it caught on something half way down; a round shape on her belt.

Smiling grimly, she grabbed it, pressed the button, and threw it at the two soldiers further down the street. As shouting started and the soldiers close to her watched the explosive device fly through the air, she brought her sword up. One of them died instantly, a deep cut slicing from his groin to the top of his head. He didn't even make a sound. Twirling, she severed the head of the second soldier just as the last turned back to her. He brought his gun up, and might have killed her had her momentum not spun her out of the way.

He fired, missing her by a hair, and she brought her *Kaizuun* down through his wrist. Another gunshot boomed, and the soldier grunted as his blood sprayed into the cold night air; the explosive hadn't triggered properly, and the two soldiers had the advantage now. Cursing her luck, she leapt behind the corpses in front of her, hoping their bodies would be enough to shield her. They fired again, and she heard a wet thumping sound as the dead man in front of her convulsed. His gun lay on the ground in front of him, right next to her.

Footsteps, a gunshot and another wet thump followed while she struggled to grab the gun and remain hidden. Several loud clacks filled the silence; the soldiers had reloaded their guns. She waited, their footsteps getting louder, wishing she could see their auras through the dead soldier she hid behind. *I've become reliant on magic,* she thought, furious with herself.

The footsteps suddenly halted, and she knew they were close. Making a guess, she jumped up, her side and leg screaming, took aim, and before she could pull the trigger, a massive explosion rocked the street, throwing her and the closest soldier to the ground. The other soldier had stayed back, ready to fire at her if she killed the one who came close. He would have succeeded in killing her, if not for the delayed explosion of the device she'd thrown. It reduced him to pieces instantly in a flash of light and fire. She'd never used one before, just pressed the first button she saw; but it had been enough to save her life.

Crying out as she hit the ground, Elana rolled onto her feet much slower than she would have without injury. *Too slow. This is it; this is how I die.* But as she scanned the street, she saw the last living soldier moving even slower than herself, groaning and dazed. She raised the gun and fired just as he began rising. He grunted as her shot hit him in the stomach. The gun dropped from his fingers and he slumped back to the ground. She heard his ragged breathing, and limped over to him.

Her *Kaizuun* sliced through his throat as easily as it did through the fog in the air. He died quickly, and Elana moved on.

The docks were busy even at night, but only a small guard crew were stationed there; either the rest had been pulled away to reinforce the others in Dreadhold, or the Ermoori were far too arrogant about the shipments coming to and from their dock. Elana didn't mind. She was done with fighting for now. All that remained was getting herself onto a ship bound for Tarsium.

Without magic, it was going to be tricky. She'd taken off the demonic armour in an alley near the docks, and felt much lighter without the heavy armour weighing her down. It did wonders for her energy, but she was still at the end of her limits. She had no idea why the Ermoori felt the need to wear such heavy armour; it barely stopped their own guns, and did nothing to stop the *Kaizuun* or Shadow Magic. All it did was make them slow.

Most of the people at the dock were either workers or sailors; overseeing the transfer of goods on or off the ships, or preparing for another trip at sea. They wore all different clothing, and there were Omati workers as well as the occasional Tarsi supervisor. Even the Ermoori here wore different clothing; these were the lower class, the working class, who couldn't afford to wear the extravagant clothing worn in the city proper, nor cared to if they could.

Elana strode as casually as she could into the docks. She knew the guards had no idea what she looked like; in Dreadhold and Ivorstorm she'd been spotted wearing the red and orange armour, and she'd managed to go unseen other than that. But she was still a Shenza warrior, and would be captured on sight regardless of whether she was recognised.

In that moment, she hated that her tunic was sleeveless. Shadow Magic was much more effective when the spell tattoos weren't covered, but at the moment they were useless anyway. She'd never once feared to have her tattoos on display; until now.

Wandering down one of the piers, she came to a Tarsi supervisor. As diplomatic as they were, it was no secret that Tarsium held little love for Ermoor. She just hoped this particular Tarsi felt the same.

"Hello, supervisor," she said, keeping her voice low, "how goes business?"

"Business goes, child," the Tarsi said evenly, "day and night, it goes."

The Tarsi's eyes flitted over Elana's body, no doubt taking in every little detail; the tattoos, the wounds, the *Kaizuun*. Her massive eyes didn't blink, and the barest hint of a wry smile pointed at the end of her small mouth.

"Does it go to Tarsium? Tonight?"

"Business goes where it must. When it must."

Elana was running out of time, and patience. Her mind was slipping as exhaustion and pain took hold. She couldn't remember when she'd last slept, or eaten. The dock spun in front of her, and she was losing grip.

"Please," she said, "I need to get away. They're going to kill me if they see me."

"Ah," the Tarsi woman said, then focused her attention on the manifest in her hand.

"We are transporting silks and power reserves to Tarsium tonight. When we arrived, it was with a very large shipment of fish and other food. I believe two barrels were seen to be defective, somehow coming undone during the journey. They are not fit to eat, but Ermoor does not allow the dumping of unusable foreign stock in their oceans or even in their bins. Those barrels, unfortunately for me, must stay aboard until our return to Tarsium, and then will be emptied."

Elana smiled. *Finally, some good luck.* She thanked the Tarsi and moved towards the ship.

"Of course," the supervisor called after her, "all stock requires payment. Even defective stock must be paid for."

Riffolk

Riffolk screamed, and the servant who brought him the news of Mathys and Mara's escape exploded into white ashes. *She's gone?* He'd been prepared to attack again, prepared to destroy her once and for all, and she interrupted his plans yet again. Shaking with rage, he launched bolt after bolt at the wall, smashing huge chunks out of it each time.

However long it takes, he thought, *wherever I have to go to find you, I will hunt you down and kill you.* He focused the words into a shout, and pushed them with his mind, visualising Mara and her terrified little face.

She will not hear you.

"Then tell her for me."

I serve no mortal.

"Yet I held you in a cage and used your energy. You served me whether you wanted to or not."

Taranos didn't answer, and Riffolk smiled, his breath calming again. Knowing he'd taken a God and bent it to his will worked wonders to sate his rage. But Mara was still out there, somewhere. He couldn't feel her presence any more, which worried him; his research had revealed that magic interacted with its own kind no matter the distance between wielders. Theoretically, even if she was on the other side of Pandeia, he should have been able to feel her energy.

Launching one more bolt of lightning at the wall, he went back to focusing on his work; if magic couldn't help locate Mara, a global invasion certainly would. It would take far longer without Taranos, but either way, Ermoor was going to rule all of Pandeia, with Riffolk as its leader.

Arthor

In the weeks following the order for Mathys' death, Arthor got almost no sleep. His only solace was knowing the Twelve no longer wanted him dead too. That, and knowing Ellie was safe somewhere in Tarsium. He was on edge constantly, ready for Mathys to appear from the shadows. Ready for the Spectre of Ermoor.

Production was beginning on the weapons and vehicles required for the invasion. Without the creature powering fully automated factories as Riffolk originally planned, they were stuck with the manned factories and more limited operating hours. The time frame was long, but the Twelve had accepted that, and left him to oversee the operations.

He had soldiers with him every hour of the day, and the Twelve promised him they would stop any attack. Arthor wasn't so certain; he'd seen what the Spectre could do. He moved like a shadow, silent and faster than blinking. He could go from being on the ground to the top of a nearby building in seconds. Smoke appeared around him at will, and he seemed to have the strength of ten men.

He wore invincible armour made of black metal, and wore a dark cloak that folded in on itself, billowing, hiding his countless tools and weapons. The original Spectre was said to have wielded a sword made of lightning, but that was myth; Arthor had never seen anything like that.

He spent most nights in his office, with one hand on his gun and the other nursing a glass of Darkfire. Made in Ermoor, the dark red liquor was inspired by an ancient Thearan myth; the Darkfire was supposedly a prophesied warrior who could wield both Shadow Magic and Fire Magic. He was said to be capable of destroying all of Pandeia. It was sweet with a unique bitter twist, what he thought might be aniseed, and served with crushed ice. The deep red made him think of a pool of blood, but it got the job done. The building that contained his office had a kitchen, and as Lord Commander he could order whatever he wanted. Darkfire wasn't on their menu, but they made it every night for him. And every night, as he waited for death or victory, the voice whispered to him.

He is coming.

He will try to kill you.

He must be stopped.

You must kill him.

He'd given up arguing. He'd given up everything. Ellie remained in his mind, the sole beam of sunlight shining through thick black clouds. If she survived, it would all be worth it.

Not to mention the power you will possess once Ermoor controls all of Pandeia.

Arthor sipped his drink, staring into the shadows in his office. Every now and then he could have sworn he saw a twitch of movement in the darkness. His gun sat on the desk in front of him, pointing at the door, his hand resting on the grip. He'd seen many battles in his career, and the gun in his hand was his companion in all of them. It was as familiar to him as the faces of his Commanders and Generals, and just as valuable.

Mathys had an identical weapon. They'd both been carrying the same guns, ever since they had first been made. Of course, back then they were simple designs; manually loaded with gunpowder stamped into the barrel and a lead shot dropped on top. Difficult, time consuming, and not particularly accurate. Still, Arthor had made do, practising constantly next to Mathys, competing and laughing as they destroyed man-shaped targets in one of the training yards in Dreadhold.

Once Riffolk began inventing things, it didn't take the young man long to design a new type of gun and ammunition. They worked very efficiently, and had a wide target range, meaning accuracy wasn't as problematic. Arthor and Mathys had requested their existing weapons be fitted with the necessary upgrades so they could keep the original grip and muzzle; mostly for nostalgia's sake, but they'd also practised so much with the old guns that the fit and weight were easier to use than the lighter, smaller new designs. All the other soldiers took the brand new guns.

Sipping more of the Darkfire, Arthor wondered if Mathys would feel sadness whenever he looked at his old gun, after he'd killed his Lord Commander.

Did you ever feel sadness after killing your enemies?

"I didn't train every day for decades next to the enemies I've killed. They weren't my friends."

That did it. He was left again in silence, brooding and trying to keep his courage up. Waiting for death was a harrowing experience. If it wasn't for the drink, he knew his hands would be shaking.

The door handle gently squealed, disturbing the silence as suddenly as if someone had shouted at him. He brought his hand up, his gun levelled straight at the door, and fired without hesitation. The door was thick, but made of wood, and Riffolk's designs were potent. A wide pattern of holes slammed into the wood, and Arthor heard a muted grunt from the other side, followed by a heavy thud.

He reloaded as he rose from his chair, then palmed another round in his left hand as he circled around his desk. The Spectre had been known for using deception as one of his tools.

"Come in, Mathys, I know it's you. There's no need to play these games with me. Not any more."

A groan floated through from the corridor, followed by a couple of ragged breaths. If it was fake, it was incredibly believable. The door opened inwards, and the latch had been pulled before Arthor fired, so the door was slightly ajar. He approached from the side so he could see out through the small gap. A body lay on the floor; a body dressed in servant's clothes.

He scanned the corridor in both directions quickly, then rushed to the body, dropping to his knees. It definitely wasn't Mathys, and the corridor was empty. The man was still alive, choking and coughing, several ragged holes torn into his body. Arthor held the man's head gently.

"Damn it, what were you doing here?"

"I ha-" another cough stopped him, blood spattering out of his mouth, "message for... you."

The servant tried to take a breath, coughed up more blood, then tried again. A horrible bubbling sound gurgled from his lips as he fought for breath. Arthor had heard it before, on the battlefield; the man's lungs had been punctured, and were filling with blood.

"Is it written down?"

He managed a weak shake of his head, his mouth working soundlessly for a moment.

"Math... fled. Gone."

He died still trying to speak. Arthor understood the message, but didn't quite believe it; the news was too good to be true. *Mathys fled Ermoor? That's totally unlike him.* Mathys had never once retreated from battle, in the years they'd fought together.

There were two possibilities Arthor could think of. Either Mathys was simply disappearing to bide his time and strike later on; or, much worse and hopefully much less likely, he was going to strike where Arthor was weakest. Cursing, he ran to his desk, pressed the button underneath, and ran from the office.

One Crown. Again. He knew the situation was difficult, but he was fed up with being disregarded like this; not being worth the time or attention of more than one Crown. It was an insult.

"Is it true? Mathys fled the city?"

"Yes," the Crown said, "we don't know why, but our information suggests he has taken the girl with him."

The girl. Riffolk's wife. Mathys seemed to think she was far more involved than she appeared.

She is. She has been touched by the Gods.

"What?"

"Mara Hayne. Mathys took her with him."

"Yes, I heard, I was talking to... Why would he take her?"

"Maybe he knows more about us than we realised."

The Crown stood, tall and slim, and Arthor couldn't help but tense up for combat, his hand moving automatically to his gun. *It's a trap!* he thought, not quite ready to fight, not quite ready to die.

"Calm yourself, Arthor," the Crown said, raising his hands slowly.

His palms were out, his hands splayed wide; no threat. Arthor left his hand on the grip of his gun, though he settled into a more relaxed stance.

"I'm trusting you, Lord Commander. You need to trust me too. Put the gun on the floor."

Arthor felt an almost overwhelming urge to shoot the Crown just for suggesting such a thing.

"How do I know you're not Mathys?"

Laughter rang through the dark chamber, bouncing off the stone walls and receding into messy, inhuman echoes.

"Oh Arthor, you are entertaining. I'm not Mathys, though I can see why you would assume as much. No, I'm someone you'd probably prefer to see even less than the Spectre of Ermoor. Put the gun on the floor; I won't ask again."

His heart hammering, Arthor pulled the gun slowly from its holster. The trigger rested against his finger, beckoning with its slight resistance. First the Twelve, then Mathys, now possibly both at once; he was beyond trust.

Suddenly the fact that he'd only seen one Crown at a time, and received only written instructions, struck a chord within his mind. He should have seen it before. It *was* Mathys. The whole thing was a trap. He'd assassinated the Twelve and was now trying to kill Arthor.

He aimed at the Crown and fired. The chamber lit up suddenly, bright but pale yellow light burning his eyes and a crackling buzz exploding in his ears. He was thrown backwards, and his hand flared with a sudden and burning pain he'd never felt before. He hit the back wall of the chamber and crumpled to the ground, dazed and blind.

"I didn't want to do that, Arthor. I need you. I won't hurt you again, but you need to trust me."

Do as he says. You can trust him.

"How do I know that?" Arthor said as he struggled to rise.

His hand was destroyed; the gun had exploded while he held it. His pinky finger was still there, barely, but the rest of it was a mangled mess of flesh and bone. A white fog rolled over his sight, into his mind, and the ground beneath him felt suddenly soft, unsteady.

"We have the same goal, as difficult as it may be for you to believe. We always have. You may not have agreed with my methods, but we were always aiming for the same result."

"Wait..." Arthor grunted as he finally stood, swaying and delirious.

"*Riffolk?*"

The Crown lifted the hood off his head, and Riffolk's pale, smug face smiled at Arthor.

"Ermoor is mine, Arthor. I want you as my Lord Commander, but you're not necessary to my success any more. Join me, or die."

Mathys

Behind the Copper Dragon, tied to a tiny pier hidden amongst the rocks on the water's edge, a tiny row boat floated, waiting. With their belongings safely stored in the Copper Dragon's cellar, Mathys, Isobel and Mara snuck through the dead of night to the tiny boat. Mathys hadn't wanted Isobel to come with them, thinking he'd put her in enough danger already, but they wouldn't be able to find the Cubby-house without her.

Mara had never seen a boat, much less been in one. Her discomfort was apparent from the moment she saw it bobbing slowly up and down in the black water; even in the low light of the muted lamp Mathys carried, her face turned as white as bone.

It took a while to get her into the boat; but once she'd finally stepped into it and sat down, she grabbed hold of the edges of the boat and stayed completely still. It suited him just fine. The less she moved about, the safer they'd be on the water. Isobel laughed seeing Mara's utter terror sitting on a boat, but otherwise remained thankfully silent.

The ride itself was easy, but slow. They skimmed down the coastline to the west, Isobel and Mathys taking turns rowing. The weather was still, clear and cold. Mathys would have preferred fog to cover them, but no one would be looking in the poor districts for him anyway, let alone off the coast towards the swamplands.

Silence followed them along the pitch black coast; only the sound of water gently lapping at their boat broke the utter stillness. After several hours, Isobel turned back in towards land. Mara hadn't relaxed for the entire trip, and despite himself, Mathys let out a low chuckle as they finally neared the shore.

Another tiny pier stood waiting for them, hidden much better than the one outside the Copper Dragon; this one was made out of fire-treated driftwood, fashioned to look like washed up debris. After another ordeal getting Mara out of the boat and back onto solid land, they set out into the swamps. After maybe two dozen metres of slogging through gripping mud and twisting tree roots, a series of metal grates appeared, leading an easy path through the otherwise almost impossible terrain.

From there, though the walk itself was easier, they marched for several hours. Every few minutes they would come to a fork where the grating split into two or three separate paths. At each one, Isobel picked a path without hesitation, strolling on without even looking at the other paths.

"How do you know which to choose?" Mara said.

Isobel smiled. "There's a trick to it, I'll teach you when we get to the Cubbyhouse."

An hour later, Isobel stopped walking. In front of them, a group of strange vertical protrusions rose up from the swamp.

"What are those?" Mara asked. She looked almost as terrified as she had on the boat.

Isobel laughed again. "Those are dragon's nests. Very appropriate, don't you think?"

Mara almost fainted. She looked at Mathys as though she wanted him to confirm that Isobel was insane.

"Swamp Dragons are a kind of amphibious reptile, they build these odd nests that start with these towers above ground and spread all through the swamp as interconnected tunnels."

"Why are we here?" Mara's voice was just a squeak.

"One of these is a fake."

With that, Isobel walked up to one of the towers and pulled at it with both arms. A section of it came away, swinging out on a hinge. There was enough space for a person to climb in. A deep growl suddenly rolled from somewhere nearby, clicking and echoing in the dark. Mara screamed, and Isobel waved them over.

"Come on, the dragons are waking up."

They stayed in the Cubby-house for two months. Despite being built out of a lizard's nest underneath a swamp, it was surprisingly cosy. Mathys had stayed before, of course, but to Mara the entire experience never really seemed to settle into her mind.

The Cubby-house was mostly used to hide fugitives and anyone who needed to lay low for a while until the Ermoori guards stopped actively looking for them. Isobel also used it to hide smuggled goods and some valuables; though she had a second Cubby-house specifically to store goods, the location of which was unknown even to Mathys.

Two small candles lit the space, which was cramped but comfortable. Isobel had given them two bedrolls and two tiny pillows, and they slept on the floor next to each other. The Cubby-house consisted of just the one room, so they had no privacy or space from each other. With no bathroom, they had to go in the swamp itself, which wasn't comfortable at the best of times. Mathys dealt with it, having lived in much worse conditions on the battlefield at Shanaken; Mara was mortified.

Whenever they could, they continued training. Their tiny safe-house didn't allow for full sparring, but he continued to teach her techniques; focusing on close quarters and any moves which only used hands, fists or elbows. These they could do sitting down facing each other.

They talked about everything, and Mathys, who'd never had a daughter, felt himself growing more and more protective of Mara. There was a strange mix of feelings; he wanted to train her to be as tough and as strong as possible, but he also wanted to keep her completely out of danger. For now, he resolved to focus on the training, as there was nothing else to do while they hid from Ermoor.

Isobel visited every week or two with food and supplies, but only stayed long enough to hand over what she'd brought them; the journey to and from the Cubby-house took far too much of her time already, and she had plenty of other responsibilities. Mathys didn't blame her for the brief visits, but he did wish she could stay longer.

Two months after they arrived, Isobel showed up with good news. Mara's belly had grown, their training had stopped, and they were both restless to leave Ermoor. Isobel was ecstatic, relaying the situation and that the manhunt for Mathys and Mara was beginning to quiet down.

"Most of their search efforts seem to be focused in Tarsium now, but even then they're starting to give up. The posters in the city are disappearing. They still have a huge price on your head, mind you, but the actual search is winding down."

Mathys nodded. Riffolk wouldn't waste resources finding someone who'd fled. Arthor knew him better, and probably surmised he'd be back eventually.

"What's it like in Tarsium?"

"They've got soldiers there, and they've tried to put posters up, but they keep getting torn down." She winked when she said that, and Mathys laughed.

"So, what's the plan, Isobel?"

"I'll get your belongings onto a trading ship, then after it's left the docks they'll turn up the coast and drop anchor nearby, and I'll row over and pick you up. Two days from now, at midnight. Make sure you're at the hidden pier and ready. The ship will only wait so long."

Travel by sea was never easy. Mathys had gotten used to it, after countless campaigns and journeys in his duties as Commander. Mara, on the other hand, took to ships about as well as a fish takes to walking. Added on top of the pregnancy sickness, she looked ragged and drained after only a couple of days.

Through the trip, Mathys found himself taking on a parental role, taking care of Mara and making sure she ate enough for herself and the baby. It was strange, and terrifying, and wonderful. She filled a part of him that had been empty without him even realising it; before meeting Mara, he'd had absolutely no desire to settle into marriage or have children, despite constant mockery from his colleagues and friends.

Still, a weight settled onto him, like a thick storm cloud looming overhead. One empty space within him had been filled, but a new one was growing at the same time. As Mathys stood on the creaking ship, hands on the rails, the familiar shape of Ermoor's south coast filled the horizon.

He'd devoted his entire life to protecting that great city, and had been forced out in return. He vowed to himself then, staring at the country that had taken everything from him, that he would return.

Elana

Most of the trip back to Tarsium was a dark blur of delirious semi-consciousness. Someone, the Tarsi supervisor presumably, visited her several times to feed her and give her water. Occasionally she tried one of the regenerative spells to gain some energy, but her magic was still depleted. Her wounds were healing slowly without magic or potions to help. Every day was spent rocking, moving with the ship as she lay helpless on the floor of the dank storage room.

After three weeks that felt like a year, she finally felt well enough to stand, though she wasn't stable on her feet. Not caring about manifests or repercussions, she looted one of the barrels mentioned by the Tarsi overseer, taking out some dried, salted luduk meat. It tasted horrible; luduk was only ever eaten fresh in Shanaken and she'd never eaten salted meat before. But she needed food and it was all she had.

Almost a week after she could stand upright, the ship arrived in Tarsium. They arrived in daylight, and the combination of sunlight, solid ground, and the green grass and trees further inland brought her to tears. She rushed to the trees, limping, and threw herself to the grass, laying on her back. Shadow Magic, although deriving most of its power from darkness, was actually linked to life itself. So despite the dazzling sunlight and almost complete lack of shadow in the small field where she lay, she felt the life around her slowly filling her with magic.

Eventually, soft footsteps approached, and she glanced up to see the Tarsi supervisor sit next to her. They sat in silence for a little while, both enjoying the peace.

"You were quite injured, when I allowed you onto the ship," she said, "and exhausted, and starving."

"I had an... interesting time, in Ermoor." Elana didn't know what else to say.

"Do you remember our conversation before you boarded?"

"Yes. You want payment for allowing me safe passage?"

"But of course. Why else would I have helped you?"

The words were harsh, but an amused twinkle filled the woman's huge eyes, and her expression was soft.

"I have no money."

"Oh, I never wanted money from you, child; money is easy to come by. We need your help."

An intense discomfort filled her chest, bringing goose pimples over her skin. What would a Tarsi supervisor want with a *Kaizeluun*? They had their own magic, their own secrets. She wouldn't have been surprised if the Tarsi knew how to use Shadow Magic as well; they were notorious for their secrets. They were able to use magic, she knew that, but almost nothing else was known about them, despite Tarsium being the cultural and trading hub of Pandeia.

Shanaken maintained a mysterious reputation by utterly closing itself off to outsiders other than trade with Tarsium; the Tarsi maintained complete secrecy despite thousands of Shenza, Omati, Thearans and even Ermoori living on their land. Nobody knew what they did behind closed doors, nobody knew how they managed to enforce their strict no violence laws, and nobody knew anything about their history except for records kept about older communication between the countries.

So knowing her help was required by the Tarsi made her spine tingle in a slow, cold wave. Knowing she couldn't refuse was even more terrifying. There were too many questions, and she wasn't sure she'd even get any answers.

"What do you need from me?"

Elana had fought in countless battles. She had defeated every enemy who fought her. She'd fought against beasts and monsters, guns, armour and technology. She'd even been made to kill a shadow viper as part of her initiation into the ranks of *Kaizeluun*; her final test. The fastest striking predator in the world had been bested by the speed of her blade. And yet, when she asked her question of the Tarsi woman, her voice was small and weak, full of fear.

The Tarsi was gentle, quiet, almost loving as she laid a hand on Elana's forearm. Her tattoos tingled slightly. They stared into each other's eyes, the Tarsi unmoving and immensely confident, Elana nervous and growing fearful.

"There is something awful on the horizon," the Tarsi said, "a war, the likes of which this world has not seen for thousands of years. Our enemies will destroy Pandeia if we do not stop them."

"I know about the Ermoori's planned invasion," Elana said, "I believe I've slowed them down, and with some resources I know how we could stop them compl-" the Tarsi waved her hand, then shook her head.

"The Ermoori are but pawns, child. Pawns who've lost the hand of their leader and now unknowingly follow another into certain doom. That is not the battle we need to win."

Pawns? Elana frowned, thinking about everything she'd seen in Ermoor. If there was some more powerful person or people controlling them, she'd seen nothing of them. The scientist and the Lord Commander seemed to have all of Pandeia under their feet, between the two of them. They'd both mentioned something called the Twelve Crowns, but Hayne had spoken of them as though they were useless and the Lord Commander seemed to outrank them. She had no idea what the woman was talking about.

"What other battle could there be? The Ermoori are invading every country, I witnessed their plans!"

"You will know soon enough. Go to your *Duulshen*, tell them the Circle of Shadows is rising again."

Hearing the name *Duulshen* come from the mouth of an outsider struck a cold bolt of terror straight through her heart. No one outside of Shanaken knew about the *Duulshen*. She'd never heard of the Circle of Shadows, but suddenly she was more scared than she'd ever been in her life. *What have I gotten myself into?* She thought.

"What does that mean?" She said, but the Tarsi woman stood, a tiny figure silhouetted against the brilliant sky. She walked away without another word, leaving Elana to dwell on her words.

Getting back to Shanaken was much easier than escaping Ermoor, and even that had been relatively easy thanks to her luck in meeting the Tarsi supervisor. But the more she thought about that meeting, and the conversation that followed, the less she was convinced luck had anything to do with it. The supervisor had been far too confident, far too controlled, for the conversation to be happenstance.

Now, back in the forests of her home, her magic flowed through her again. Taking a couple of days to heal and regroup, she waited until she felt completely herself again before approaching the *Duulshen*. Despite the fear and confusion, she'd never felt better by the time she descended into the elder's chamber to report.

Shadow Magic pooled in the chambers of the *Duulshen*; they were places of immense shadow and ancient life, combining to create perhaps the strongest concentration of Magic anywhere in Pandeia. Every time she spoke with them, the chamber left her head spinning, her entire body trembling with strength and magic.

"Welcome back," one of the *Duulshen* said. The others nodded.

"Thank you, great *Duulshenza*," she replied, "I have much to report."

She described her time in Ermoor, leaving nothing out. The *Duulshen* listened without asking questions or interrupting. When she was done, they glanced at each other with some meaning she didn't grasp. She hadn't told them of the Tarsi overseer yet, or her cryptic message. Scared of what their reaction might be, she had to push herself into addressing them again.

"Great *Duulshenza*, something happened after the completion of my mission that I believe may be of great importance to you, though I don't fully understand it myself. I was saved and helped to escape

Ermoor by a Tarsi woman. When we reached Tarsium, she told me that something horrible is on the horizon, and told me to tell you that the Circle of Shadows is rising."

Just as she feared, the reaction of the *Duulshen* was immediate and intense. There was uproar, visible distress, and worst of all, anger. When they quietened again, one of them spoke up.

"She told you to speak to us, this Tarsi?" Elana nodded.

"And she said the words *the Circle of Shadows is rising*? Those exact words?"

She nodded again. They murmured amongst themselves, their words falling short of her ears. After a few moments, they turned their attention back to her.

"Very well. A successful mission. The *Duulshen* thank you for your service. We will discuss this matter with you when you return from your next mission."

A new mission already? The *Duulshen* never assigned missions so close together. Something terrible must have happened. Scenarios raced through her mind, each worse than the last; a predator had started attacking the fishers, or Ermoor had some weapon she hadn't learned about in time, or the Tarsi were moving against Shanaken... But when they spoke, she froze. The words sounded wrong. Sure that she'd misheard, she asked again.

"Forgive me, great *Duulshenza*, but what did you say?"

"The warrior who failed the Shadow Trials, Dakesh Zakiil, has stolen a *Kaizuun* and fled Shanaken."

No. It just didn't make sense. Dakesh was one of her closest friends. She knew he was smitten by her, of course, but she'd never given him false hope, and they shared a deep and genuine connection. All the time she'd known him, he never once acted like that. He had a fiery spirit, anyone could see that, but stealing the blade of a *Kaizeluun*? It couldn't be. She realised the implications of their words, slowly waking to the full horror of the situation.

The *Kaizeluun* were the elite, the absolute best in a culture that strove for perfection. They were tried, trained, and worked harder than any warriors in Pandeia. So when they passed their Trials and named *Kaizeluun*, they became closer than family. For a Shadow Blade to be stolen, its wielder would need to be dead. The situation still didn't feel quite real, but she pushed herself into asking anyway.

"Which *Kaizeluun* fell?"

"Kailen Deshai."

She was sleeping. That was the only answer; she was asleep, and this was a nightmare. One of her only best friends had been killed, and the other stole his blade and fled the country as a fugitive. It was pure insanity. An overwhelming wave of sickness crashed over her, and she felt suddenly certain she was back on the dank ship leaving Ermoor, delirious and hallucinating. But the *Duulshen* didn't joke, and never lied.

Before they said it, she knew the specifics of her new mission; there was only one thing they would send the best of the *Kaizeluun* to do. Desperately hoping the words wouldn't be spoken, but knowing they would, she could only stand in silent terror and mourning as the *Duulshen* assigned the mission.

"You must find the traitor. Bring him and the Kaizuun back to Shanaken. If he will not come, kill him and bring the Kaizuun back to Shanaken where it belongs."

Epilogue

Lord Commander Arthor Symond stood tall, his hands clasped imperiously behind his back as he stared at the army before him. Prime Overseer Hayne stood nearby, smug and self-assured as ever. Arthor's right hand man, Commander Eli Barton, stood next to him, eyes scanning the soldiers. Twenty years of work stood before him, twenty years of honest work, with no creature involved.

Arthor's forearm pulsed painfully. Every now and then it ached, deep and sharp, and nothing could take his mind off it. From the wrist up, it was artificial, a new invention that allowed him almost the same movement as a real hand. It was the least Riffolk could have done after destroying his hand.

To the public, Riffolk had been kidnapped by Mathys, who was masquerading as the fictional "Spectre" and in league with Shenza savages in order to carry out a treasonous plot against Ermoor and the Twelve Crowns. He'd been miraculously saved by the Lord Commander himself, before Mathys escaped and fled the city.

The story left a sour taste in Arthor's mouth when he first told it, but he told it anyway, and the public listened. They always listened. He wondered how many things they'd been told that weren't true; how many secrets the Twelve had kept even from him.

That had been just over twenty years ago, and Mathys still hadn't been seen. Ellie never returned from Tarsium, and no longer wrote back to him. He was a different man now anyway; she would be better off with whatever new life she'd chosen. He hoped she was happy and safe.

But everything he'd done, the lies he'd told, the people who died, all of it, led to this moment. The army before him was finally ready. Thousands upon thousands of soldiers, outfitted with the latest technology in armour, weaponry and communications, stood ready to fight.

Vehicles stood behind the soldiers, war machines the likes of which the world had never seen. Riffolk called them tanks, and they would lay waste to anything in their path. He'd watched Riffolk's demonstrations a few years ago, and was deeply disturbed by their destructive power.

Building the weapons, armour and vehicles had taken a long time. Without Riffolk's creature, which remained unfound, they were forced to use the factories that relied on power gleaned from Tyra and had to be manned by workers from the poor districts.

The voice was speaking to him less now, but he wasn't sure if his thoughts were completely his own any more either. He still occasionally felt doubt about what Ermoor was doing; but even if he'd wanted to, he couldn't go against Prime Overseer Hayne. Not any more. He had nothing to fight with, nothing but his life; and Riffolk held that in his hands.

As conflicted as Arthor felt sometimes, he was at least relieved to be on the right side of things; he was the right hand of the leader of Ermoor. With his fortune returned after his wife fled the country, Riffolk was the most powerful man in the world. Ten years later, he'd been named Prime Overseer, and the 'Twelve Crowns' had stepped down; he was the first public ruler in Ermoor's history since the actual Twelve Kings of old. And the first sole ruler ever. Ermoor was his. Arthor was his. And after his armies set sail, Pandeia itself would be his.

He stared out at the vast army before him, their shining black armour gleaming in the morning sun. Even knowing they served him, they were terrifying. None would stand against them for long. The giant ships they'd built were waiting at Onyxport, ready to take soldiers and tanks across the sea. Arthor glanced at Riffolk again.

"Give the order, Lord Commander," he said without making eye contact.

The soldiers stared at him, unmoving; disciplined, lethal, and ready. Their weapons, glowing from the power that fed them, were held steady in well trained hands. An unstoppable army, with a brutal and bloodthirsty goal; total control, total domination.

"Soldiers," he said into the amplifier, "to Onyxport. Board the warships, prepare for battle. For the good of all!"

The synchronised reply of the soldiers was deafening; and even to Arthor himself, it was terrifying.

"FOR THE GOOD OF ALL!"

THE END

If you loved this book (or even if you didn't), please leave a review on Amazon, Goodreads, or anywhere else that hosts reviews.

It really makes a huge difference to me being able to share my books with the world.

www.ingramcontent.com/pod-product-compliance
Lightning Source LLC
Chambersburg PA
CBHW020717310726
48979CB00004B/948

* 9 7 8 0 6 4 8 4 2 9 4 9 4 *